DON'T LOOK NOW

Richard Montanari is the Top Ten *Sunday Times* bestselling author of *The Echo Man*, *The Devil's Garden*, *Play Dead*, *The Rosary Girls*, *The Skin Gods* and *Broken Angels*, as well as the internationally acclaimed thrillers *Kiss of Evil*, *The Violet Hour* and *Don't Look Now* (previously published as *Deviant Way*). He lives in Cleveland, Ohio.

Praise for Richard Montanari

'Told at breakneck pace, with more than one truly frightening villain, and a protagonist whose tenacity in the face of evil makes him a hero for our times, you turn the pages as if your very life depends on it.'
Daily Mail

'A specialist in serial killer tales . . . a wonderfully evocative writer.'
Publishers Weekly

'A relentlessly suspenseful, soul-chilling thriller that hooks you instantly.'
Tess Gerritsen

'A no-holds-barred thriller that thrusts the reader into the black soul of the killer . . . those with a taste for Thomas Harris will look forward to the sure-to-follow sequel.' *Library Journal*

'Montanari's superior thriller . . . [is] a welcome change from the gore typical of the serial killer subgenre. Likewise, Byrne and Balzano possess a psychological depth all too rare in such fiction.' *Publishers Weekly*

'One of the most terrifyingly evil stories I have read. Yet, with all its violence, it is balanced by much compassion and beauty. I just couldn't put it down. This could be the book of the year.'
Norman Goldman, Barnes & Noble

Also available by Richard Montanari

The Violet Hour
Kiss of Evil
The Rosary Girls
The Skin Gods
Broken Angels
Play Dead
The Devil's Garden
The Echo Man

DON'T LOOK NOW

Richard Montanari

arrow books

Published by Arrow Books 2011

8 10 9

First published in 1995 by Simon & Schuster Inc (as *Deviant Way*)
First published in Great Britain in 1996 by Penguin Books Ltd (as *Deviant Ways*)

Arrow Books
Random House, 20 Vauxhall Bridge Road,
London SW1V 2SA

www.randomhouse.co.uk

Addresses for companies within The Random House Group Limited can be found at:
www.randomhouse.co.uk/offices.htm

The Random House Group Limited Reg. No. 954009

A CIP catalogue record for this book
is available from the British Library

ISBN 9780099524830
ISBN 9780099538721 (export)

The Random House Group Limited supports The Forest Stewardship Council (FSC®), the leading
international forest certification organisation. Our books carrying the FSC label are printed on
FSC® certified paper. FSC is the only forest certification scheme endorsed by the leading environmental
organisations, including Greenpeace. Our paper procurement policy can be found at
www.randomhouse.co.uk/environment

Typeset in Perpetua by Palimpsest Book Production Limited,
Falkirk, Stirlingshire
Printed and bound in Great Britain by Clays Ltd, St Ives plc

For Dominic and Darla, who said I *could*

I feel so good I'm gonna break somebody's heart tonight,
I feel so good I'm gonna take someone apart tonight,
They put me in jail for my deviant ways,
Two years, seven months and sixteen days,
Now I'm back on the street in a purple haze,
I feel so good, I feel so good,
I feel so good I'm gonna break somebody's heart tonight.

– Richard Thompson, 'I Feel So Good'

One
Delirium

She was a redhead, tall and slender, a libertine in training if I ever saw one: Calvin Klein suit, twenty-three, Prius owner, loved her job, hated her boyfriend, never been properly fucked. Regard the redhead, she said from across the room. Regard the regal redhead who doesn't just give it away.

Eyes like a cat.

We had watched her for the better part of an hour as she fielded the advances of the happy-hour boys, dancing the occasional dance with the ones who looked well-heeled, her expression alternating between the bored-and-too-beautiful-for-you look that women like her worked hard at in such a setting, and the working-girl ennui that inevitably made its way to the top.

There were thousands like her across the city that night, this night, every night. Budget microwave meals for dinner, a quick shower and meet the girls for a drink. To wear the good lingerie or not, that was the question. She was strangling her twenties and she wasn't married and she had no children and she read a lot and she masturbated a lot and wondered what was wrong with the world that she didn't yet have the American dream.

She was bored and beleaguered.

She was ready for the beast.

*　*　*

Saila leaned forward. 'She wears a rose,' she said, a hint of lace peeking around the bodice of her dress. 'What do you think?'

'I think I can smell her,' I said. 'It's bohemian sex she's wanting. Mr Goodbar. *Very* exciting.'

'She looks so young. Like a child.'

The redhead glanced at me. Or did she? She gazed in my direction, then quickly looked away. She was talking to one of her suited throng, laughing at all the funny parts, trying to fill in the multitude of lulls. Sip, sip, sip. A chardonnay now. She looked at her watch until the suit got the message. The music changed into a slow song.

'Do you think her legs are strong?' Saila asked.

I really didn't know the answer, but I knew my cue when I heard it. I turned my drink in its napkin, straightened my tie.

Saila put her finger into the middle of my back, stiffly, like a gun. 'Bang-bang, kitty-cat,' she said. 'I want to know every detail when you get back.'

'Bang-bang, dirty mother,' I said.

And took my leave.

I made my way across the crowded bar, drawing admiring looks from the women, along with a medley of sneers from the men. I was used to it, though. This *envy*.

As I neared the redhead I noticed that her teeth were perfect, her breasts were small and firm, her legs shapely. She regarded me with a half-smile in the moment before I spoke to her.

'Hello,' I said.

'You've been watching me.'

'I have.'

She regarded me further. 'And why *is* that?'

Chit-chat-chit-chat.

'It's purely physical, I assure you,' I said.

She smiled. 'I mean, let's face it, you could have any woman in here. Why me?'

She was going to press me on this. I would break her with her own mindless cocktail chatter. I leaned very close and said: 'Does the rose question the advance of the honey-bee?' It was bad Broadway and the redhead lapped it, like the cat she was.

'Who *are* you?' she asked, looking me up and down.

'I'll show you.' I extended my hands as another slow song began. 'Dance with me.'

She looked into my eyes, then at my lips, then back into my eyes. She smiled fully and I knew then that I had her. Without a word she took my hand and led me to the dance-floor. I glanced at Saila. She was stirring her drink, looking at the floor, smiling.

We began to slow-dance, the redhead and I.

'Are you with her?' she asked, nodding in Saila's direction.

I pulled back and looked into her eyes. She was beautiful. Her face was delicately featured, absolutely symmetrical. Her eyes were an emerald green. 'Now, do you think I'd be up here dancing with you if I was on a date?'

Another smile.

'You never know,' she said. 'There's all kinds of people.'

She really had no idea. 'Well, if she *was* my girlfriend and she saw me up here dancing with a beautiful woman such as yourself, I think she'd be rather upset, don't you?'

The redhead blushed. I loved it when they blushed, it meant there was still some girl left. She pulled me closer and I started to get hard, the warmth of her body and the tease of her perfume running roughshod over my senses.

'I think you're full of shit,' she said. 'But don't stop, okay?'

A few moments later this woman – this beautiful young woman who had not laid eyes on me one hour earlier – put her head on my shoulder and kissed me on the side of my neck.

Softly, like a lover.

And thus she was ours.

I fucked her in the back seat of my car, in a dark corner of the parking-lot, while Saila drove to the motel and waited. I pushed her skirt up around her waist and brought her to just this side of orgasm, promising her the rest and more if she'd only come to the motel with me for an hour. Just an hour.

She came with me. They always did when they let me inside their minds, even for a few moments.

By the time I got the redhead to the motel, Saila was ready for her: wet and flushed and violent, her eyes blazing with the thrill of the game.

Out came the cameras, the make-up, the steel.

Out came the animal.

And the redhead – she of the pale complexion and wild auburn mane, she of the promising career and Nordstrom charge-card – died screaming.

And coming.

Just like the others.

'And so you chased him?' the woman asked.

'Yep,' Paris replied.

'And you were . . .' She waved her hand in front of his face as if saying the word out loud might cause him to lose control and sexually assault her right there in the bar.

'Naked,' he said.

The woman covered her mouth with her heavily jeweled hand. 'You're *kidding*.'

'Nope,' Paris said. 'Buck-shriveled-naked, running down the middle of Carnegie Avenue at two in the morning.'

The woman threw her head back and laughed. For the moment it erased a few of the hard years she'd spent holding down bar-stools. Jack Paris had seen her up and down the avenues for at least a decade – on the job, off the job, sometimes doing the job. She had this style that was right out of the eighties: leg-warmers, stirrup pants, oversized tops, Ocean Pacific T-shirts. Paris was sure that over the years she'd slept with a lot of cops, been abused by a lot of cops. She was sweet, but she was used up in a way that only the corner-tavern life could impose upon a woman. It was a shame.

But she still hung out where the cops hung out. Because sometimes they drank free and, if the lighting was right, so did she.

Her name was Nedra.

'So, did you get him?' she asked, posing with an unlit cigarette.

Paris grabbed a pack of matches off the bar, struck one and lit her cigarette. He took one for himself, hesitated, put it in his mouth, then returned it to the pack. 'No,' he said, blowing out the match. 'But I got three offers of marriage.'

Nedra laughed again.

The Caprice Lounge was starting to fill up with second-shift cops from the Third District. They all looked tired to Paris, browned around the cuffs. Cleveland had been averaging a homicide every five days for three years, and although it was only mid-March, it looked like they were going to beat the quarterly stats by a half-dozen. At least, that's the way it looked from Paris's perch at the Homicide Unit. Drive-bys were up, robbery homicides too. The Brick City Lords — a drug gang that Paris had battled for almost five years in a zone car — had recently declared war on a Jamaican posse, part of Cleveland's Caribbean crimewave. And then there was the other shit: the car-jackings in broad daylight, the stabbings over who spilled what drink on whose fucking pant-leg, people getting shot because they looked at somebody wrong or because somebody bitch-slapped somebody else five years ago. Lucasville and Mansfield were busting at the seams and there seemed to be a never-ending train that kept dropping the new criminals on Public Square.

But even though the Caprice was located at Fifty-fifth and Superior, ground zero in the combat zone, it remained a virtually crimeless area. No cars were ever stolen from its unprotected, poorly lit parking-lot. There were no drug sales for at least three blocks in every direction. At times, it was even considered to be a rap-free zone, with boom boxes and car stereos being dutifully dimmed out of respect for the aesthetic sensibilities of the dozen or two law enforcement types who seemed to be permanently rooted inside.

In the thirty or so years the Caprice Lounge had been a cop bar, it had only been robbed once. Needless to say, that incident didn't end well for the guy with the mask and the gun.

Danny Lawrence, a patrolman from the Fourth District, stopped by and shook Paris's hand. Paris motioned to Victor to set them up again.

'What's doin', Danny?' Paris asked.

Lawrence was knee-walking drunk. 'Fuckin' McGuinn, man,' he said. He tried to light a cigarette, but it fell out of his mouth, on to the floor. He kept talking anyway. 'Upstairs is up my ass about these smash-and-grab punks at the Galleria. Three *months* they're in my face. If I see 'em I'm gonna fucking *cap* 'em. Swear to God.' Danny turned to Nedra, tried to focus his eyes, unsuccessfully, and slurred, 'If you'll 'scuse my French, ma'am.' Danny Lawrence was twenty-six and fair, ocean-blue eyes, lean and handsome. Nedra blushed like a schoolgirl.

'Certainly,' she said.

Paris steadied Lawrence, guiding him to a bar-stool. 'Don't worry about it, Danny. How long can McGuinn have? Another fifteen, twenty years, tops.' Carl McGuinn was a captain at the Fourth District. Hardass lifer. Nobody trusted him because he didn't drink, which was hard to believe about a man named Mc-Anything. 'Doesn't matter anyway. Eighteen months, you're gonna make detective.'

Danny sat down hard and zeroed in on the glass that Vic

Ianelli had placed on the bar in front of him. After a few moments, he knocked it back in one gulp. 'So tell me, Jack,' Danny said. 'How'd you know when it was time?'

'Time? Time for what?'

'You know. Time to give it up. Time to get married.'

'Me? You're asking *me* that question?'

'You were married, right?'

'Twelve years.'

'You had to be happy for a while, no?' Danny tried a second cigarette, but that one fell out of his mouth too. 'Weren't you?'

'Yeah, we were,' Paris said. 'But things change. People change. And it takes a certain kind of woman to be a cop's wife.'

'Yeah? What kind of woman?'

'I'm not really sure. All I know is *I* didn't find her,' Paris said. 'Why? Are you in love, Danny? Is that what this is all about?'

'Head over high heels, Jack.' He clutched his heart with what looked like real pain.

'Live with her first,' Paris said. 'That's my advice to you. Live with her. Spend a couple of years in the same bathroom, the same kitchen, the same car, the same bed. See how enchanting she is when she snores and farts and makes noises when she eats and uses your razor to shave her legs. If you still think that's cute after a couple of years, go for it.'

'But I know now, Jack.'

'No, you *think* you know now.'

'I do too know,' Danny slurred, trailing off, sounding unconvinced. He looked balefully at Nedra, who reached out and smoothed the hair across his forehead.

'Sure you do,' Paris said, catching Victor's eye.

The barman nodded. He would start watering Danny's drinks.

Paris left the lovesick Danny Lawrence in Nedra's more than capable hands and made his way to the men's room. As he washed his hands he caught his reflection in the barely silvered mirror, or what passed for a mirror at the Caprice. At least a dozen times Paris had told Vic and Marie Ianelli, the owners, that cops were probably the vainest people on the planet, they needed a better mirror. There was even loose talk about a fund to improve the lighting in the Caprice's johns, in the hope that Vic would get the message. Regardless, a bare bulb on a bare wire remained, and looking into the mirror at the Caprice was like looking into a flattened-out saucepan.

Paris noticed with a spike of dismay that some of the silver that was missing from the mirror was starting to show up in his hair. He brought himself close to his reflection; a droopy, fun-house face stared back. Bleary eyes, heavy lids, midnight shadow. He poked at his hair.

He knew that all men, regardless of race, color, religion or country of origin, have one thing that they rely upon to get them laid throughout their lives. For some guys it's an athletic ability or a talent of some sort. Rock stars and jocks who are ugly enough to clog a drain get laid all the time. For some guys it's their intellect. For others it could be their shoulders, their cars, their dicks, their apartments, their eyes, their attitudes – who the hell knows with women?

The point was, if you're a man, and you get laid more than once in your lifetime, there's a reason. And for Jack Paris, it was his hair. He had great hair. And a quick sense of humor. He could always make a woman laugh.

Except, of course, a woman named Beth Shefler-Paris.

The day he lost the ability to make her laugh was the day she walked.

On his way back to the bar Paris saw Angelo Tucci, an old-time player from Murray Hill. They shook hands, embraced. Paris also spotted a pair of new recruits, female rookies, hovering around the video games. One of them, a pixieish but solid-looking little blonde in her early twenties, smiled at Paris when he walked by.

Before he could spin around his cell phone rang.

He looked at the number in the light thrown by one of the neon beer signs. At first he didn't recognize it, but two and two added up in short order. Paris answered.

'Tommy, what's up?'

'Hey, Jack, how ya doin'?'

Paris could hear Tommy's signature hump music in the background.

'From two hours ago? I'm fine, Tommy. What's up?' He knew very well what was up.

'Good, good.'

'I'm not doing it.'

'I didn't say a fuckin' thing.'

'Like I don't know what's coming? Jack, I'd like to introduce you to Tommy. Tommy, this is Jack. What, we just met over here?'

Pause. 'Just this once.'

'No.'

'Jack, please. Be the primary on this one and it's pastry for a month.'

'No.'

'Two months,' Tommy said, his voice dropping to a whisper. 'Jack, she's wearing a garter belt.'

Paris was quiet for a while, working him. 'Two months?'

'My mother's eyes, Jack.'

'Pastry from where?'

'Is Stone Oven okay?'

'Casa Dolce,' Paris said. He loved doing this. Casa Dolce was all the way up in Mayfield Heights.

Silence.

'Well, gotta run,' Paris said.

'All right, suck my blood, Jack.'

'I think you're the one getting something sucked here, pal. Tough duty, is it? Putting in for hazard pay, are you? Because if you can't handle it, I'd be glad to relieve you. Code three and I'm there in six minutes.'

Tommy laughed.

'I want bear claws, starting tomorrow,' Paris said. 'I want them fresh, I want them wrapped in one sheet of that wax paper with the serrated edge and I want them delivered with a smile.'

'You're a prince, Jack.'

'Prince of the city,' Paris said. 'Where and who?'

'See the man. Red Valley Inn on Superior. Coroner's already rolled.'

'Bear claws, Tommy,' Paris said as he scribbled down the information and the time of the call.

'I love you, Jack,' Tommy said. 'And I'm not just talking a summer thing. I love you for the man you are, the man you've helped me become. I *will* call you in the city.'

'Go fuck yourself, Tommy.'

Paris felt his bacon cheeseburger about to travel north.

'*Could* be skin,' Ocasio said. He held the translucent, pinkish strip high into the air, suspended from his large forceps. He turned it around and around. The flap of skin – which measured two inches across and four or five inches in length – slapped together wetly as Ocasio taunted Paris, whipping the pelt from side to side. 'On the other hand, it could be beef jerky.'

Morrison and Dolch, the two hyenas from the Special Investigation Unit, let out a snort and a barrage of adolescent cackling. They always thought whatever Ocasio said was hysterical as hell, especially if it caused Jack Paris to grab his ever-rumbling stomach.

'What the hell's the matter with you, Reuben?' Paris said. 'How many times are we going to do this?'

'I don't know, Jacquito. Maybe as long as you keep throwing up at scenes. You're too easy, *padrone*.'

'Jesus, man,' Paris said, breathing deeply. 'It's amazing we have any kind of solve rate at all.'

Reuben Ocasio smiled and, for Paris, it ruined what little there was to like about his face in the first place. Yellow teeth, bits of tobacco on grayish-brown gums. Paris shook his head and walked out of the oppressive motel room, the late-winter chill helping to calm the mixture of pickles, ketchup and Maalox churning at the base of his throat.

Ocasio had joined the coroner's office four years earlier, and from day one he had played with Paris's better nature, especially during the days, weeks and months following Paris's full-contact divorce. The two men had nearly come to blows one night at the Black Mountain Tavern, a cop bar on Payne, over something stupid like a crack Reuben had made about Paris's ex-wife and a small-time doper named Grady Pike. Then, two weeks later, Reuben Ocasio put in twenty hours of overtime to close one of Jack's cases. Paris found it difficult to hate the man completely.

But the sick shit – the leaving of spleens in lockers, the intestine-on-a-roll sandwiches wrapped up in Subway sandwich paper – made Paris want to shoot the asshole.

Hadn't he known the moment he walked into the room? Hadn't he known as soon as he rounded the corner and saw her face? That agonized mime face: perfect, beautiful, silent. Paris had seen Emily Reinhardt up close. It was his case and, in almost six months, he hadn't turned up a single lead. He knew that whoever did that was an artist, a journeyman in the techniques of sexual torture, and wouldn't strike just once. Paris knew that one day he was going to walk into another crime scene and see that death mask staring up at him again from an ever-widening pool of red.

And then there was Maryann Milius. Greg Ebersole's case.

Three women now. Bodies torn, faces made up like cat-walk models. Eyeshadow, blush, mascara, powder, lipstick.

Conclusion, Inspector Paris?

Cleveland had a serial on its hands.

And who was going to put it together? Tommy Raposo? Too busy with his tailor and his stockbroker and his harem. Greg Ebersole? Maybe. Except Greg had been shutting down the Caprice quite a bit himself these days and he was getting sloppy.

Paris lit his last cigarette.

Reuben already knew. Or he would soon. Then, of course, the *Plain Dealer* would have it. Then Channel 5 and their Crime Watch or Cop Watch or whatever the hell it was.

But in the end, and probably within the next forty-eight hours, the task of setting a trap for this psycho was going to fall to one man: Jack Paris.

The woman's face, like the others, was free of blood: white

and wooden against the navy-blue carpeting. Her lipstick was fresh, deep red, glistening in response to the flashbulbs exploding around the room. All she wore was the remains of a black-lace camisole which had been cut clean away at the shoulder blades, and a pair of high heels, now flecked with red. The patch of skin had come from the woman's right calf. It bore a tattoo.

A pair of roses.

The comforter lay on the floor to the right of the bed, unstained and folded, as if set carefully aside. It looked incongruously pristine, as if it were on sale at JCPenney's amidst a display of blood and flesh. The sheets were gathered at the foot of the bed as witness to a session of violent sex. Bloody sex. The killer was either monstrously large or had used an object on the woman. The blood from the wound that had most likely caused her death – the deep razor cut to the top of her spine – had spread to a diameter of four or five feet and looked black against the dark blue of the carpet. Paris noted that the death blow could have easily been dealt from behind in the throes of passion.

He slipped on a rubber glove and began to look through the woman's purse as the forensic activity in the room died down and the lab boys and the team from the coroner's office wrapped up, taking the body with them. Paris pulled out a small, red leather wallet, bulging with plastic, the snap all but torn off. He looked at the driver's license and was once again taken aback by the woman's face. She was striking, even in the blurry little picture laminated in clear plastic.

The dead woman was Karen Schallert, twenty-three, five six, one-twenty. Lived in Lakewood on Bunts Road. Paris pulled out a small stack of business cards. All belonged to men. Andy Sipari, attorney-at-law. Robert Hammer, theatrical management. Joe Najfach, Prestidigitator Deluxe! Marty Jevnikar, Lakeside Lexus.

Paris searched her purse further. A half-finished bag of peanut M&Ms, a pair of matching combs, different widths. There were a few cosmetic basics like lipstick and a perfume atomizer. Paris found no mascara, no blush, no powder.

Because, he thought, *the killer carries his own, doesn't he? And he is putting it on these women after he cuts them.*

Paris made a note about funeral parlors, and drove back to the Caprice.

Drunk. Staring at the side of the Red Valley Inn. Had to be four, four-thirty. Long after the crime scene techs had left, long after the yellow tape had secured the crime scene until morning. This one, it appeared, even rated a cop at the door, stationed there to protect all the juicy evidence that wasn't going to add up to shit. Paris parked his car alongside the motel, cut the engine, dimmed the lights, unscrewed the cap on his fresh pint of Windsor. He flashed his badge to the uniform, who nodded in deference to Paris's gold shield, his seniority.

Paris stared at the door to 127 and tried to imagine the scene from earlier in the night. According to the desk clerk, a tall white man had rented the room. Thirtyish, mustache, tinted glasses. He wore an Irish tweed walking-hat that covered most of the upper part of his face. There was, of course, no register to sign at a place like the Red Valley Inn. The Valley was strictly pay and play, no questions, no paper. The night clerk had gone to the room after receiving a number of complaints about the TV being on full blast. He knocked on the door and found the body a few minutes later.

Paris sipped from the bottle. The liquor warmed him. He

closed his eyes, imagined the man opening the door, all charm and compliments and cologne, letting Karen Schallert, twenty-three, late of Lakewood, Ohio, into the room. His abattoir. Paris imagined them making love, Karen Schallert a bit nervous at first, but soon becoming aroused.

Had she enjoyed it? Did she think she had made the right decision, making it with this guy who was, most likely, a total stranger?

What did she think when she saw the blade?

Paris hit the bottle lightly, replaced the cap and stepped out of the car. The night was clear and still, the traffic had diminished to a procession of only the most desperately addicted – food, cigarettes, dope, sex, booze. He walked to the back of the motel parking-lot and ran his flashlight around the base of the two giant Dumpsters parked there. Beer bottles, a few candy wrappers, fast food detritus.

He directed his light along the crumbling concrete retainer wall at the rear of the motel's property. Nothing. Nothing *moving*. A few fifty-gallon drums, a couple of chained-down picnic tables, the remains of an old cast-iron barbecue.

If I had a brain, Paris thought, I'd pack this in until morning.

He glanced at his watch. It *was* morning. He clicked off his flashlight and—

The sound came from directly behind him. The sound of heavy boots on broken glass. Paris turned quickly, but the tall man in the Irish walking-hat was already upon him. He grabbed Paris by the hair and ran his straight razor across his throat.

'You wanted to fuck her too, didn't you?' the man said, his voice gravelly and wet. 'Admit it, Jack.'

At first, Paris thought the man had pinched him – the contact seemed so light, so *minor* – but a scant moment later the blurt of bright red blood that slapped against the side of the rusted Dumpster told him all he needed to know.

The man had severed his jugular vein.

Paris fell to his knees and screamed.

The man came at him again, swinging the razor in broad, muscular arcs, striking Paris's face and chest, chopping away the flesh in burger-sized chunks. For Paris, the pain soon coalesced into an excruciating red knife in the center of his brain.

He screamed again.

Soon, in his mind, his scream became a brain-rattling bell and the bell became the telephone and it was the phone, not the sunlight or his pounding skull or his fear, that brought him raging back to consciousness.

It rang again. *Screamed* again.

Paris looked around, terrified and disoriented, clutching at his neck. He was in his apartment and it was at least noon. He sat up, grabbed the receiver – his heart still racing furiously, his head a violent echo chamber – and brought it to his ear.

'Daddy,' the young voice said. 'I *knew* you'd still be there.'

Paris tried to speak, but his mouth was thick with wool.

'Dad-eeeeeeeee!'

It was Melissa, his daughter. And *man* did she sound pissed. 'What's the matter, sweetie?' Paris sat up, assaulted by the noonday sun streaming through the high jalousie windows. He had to get some fucking *drapes*.

'You were supposed to be here already,' she said, clearly on the verge of tears.

'Wait, sweetie,' Paris said. 'Wait for Daddy one second. I'll be right back. Don't hang up, okay?'

Not a word.

'Missy?'

'All right.' Her voice sounded so small, so betrayed, that Paris's heart clogged with shame. He ran to the bathroom, barking his shin on the coffee table en route, and doused his entire head with ice-cold, rusty water. He caught a glimpse of himself in the mirror on the way out and was nearly frightened by the look of the jowly, red-eyed man staring back.

And then he remembered.

Today was his birthday.

He glanced into the kitchen and tried to determine if he could at least get the water on the heat before his daughter disowned him right there on the phone. But he decided that the instant coffee would have to wait. He stumbled back to the couch, the quarter-bottle of Windsor staring up at him in mockery.

'Sweetie?'

'Yes, Daddy.' This was a very, very solemn Melissa Adelaide Paris.

'Where was Daddy supposed to be, honey?'

'*The Olive Garden*,' they said in unison.

And then everything came flooding back at once. Melissa had saved her money for six months to take her father out to lunch on his birthday at the Olive Garden restaurant on Chagrin Boulevard. Beth had even called to remind him about it three days earlier. The plan was for Beth to drop Melissa off at the restaurant, and for Paris to take her home.

Paris was going to try and explain everything to Melissa, but the woes of an overworked, boozy Cleveland homicide detective didn't carry much weight these days, especially with slightly cynical eleven-year-old girls. 'What time is it now, sweetie?'

'It's, like, twelve-oh-five already.'

'Daddy's on his way, okay?' Paris said, scrambling for his

pants, hoping they weren't too creased. 'You just wait right there, okay punkin?'

More silence. Big, cold, Beth-silence.

'Okay, sweetie?'

'Where am I going to *go*?' Melissa said softly. 'It's not like I have a car or anything.'

Eleven going on thirty, Paris thought. She knew how to work him. Just like her mother. 'Love you. On my way.'

Manfred, who was every bit the cur Paris felt – and probably the man's one true friend and over-burdened confidant of late, this being the duty of Jack Russell terriers worldwide – rolled over with an indifferent woof and went back to sleep.

'Andie's on line one,' came Jennifer's voice over the intercom.

Matt Heller took a deep breath, loosened his tie, held his finger over the blinking, clear-plastic button. He closed his eyes for a moment, imagining an outcome, visualizing, hoping. Will she? *Would* she? He picked up the receiver and hit the button with all the authority he could muster. 'Hi babe, what's up?'

'Are you sitting down?' When Andrea Heller started off with that rhetorical question, it was usually good news. When she started with 'You're gonna kill me', it usually meant a fender bender, a jammed computer printer, or that she had set the entire deck ablaze with the Charmglow. But he knew his wife's moods as he knew his own, and that underlying fizz of Andie-ebullience in her voice was a good sign for Matt Heller and his naughty little plan for the evening.

It was serendipity.

'You got L'Etoile,' he said, heading her off at the giant, career-move pass. L'Etoile was a chain of upscale fragrance mini-boutiques that Andie had been stalking for six months. The account probably meant another $25,000 gross to the Heller annual household coffers.

'I got L'Etoile,' she echoed.

'*Unbelievable!*' Matt's shout was loud enough to draw a glance and a smile from Jennifer in the outer office.

'Excuse me?'

'I mean, I *knew* you could do it, babe.' They laughed at their routine. All through Andie's meteoric rise to regional sales representative for cosmetic giant Cinq, Limited, they'd run that by each other. Often for the mini-plateaus in Matt's career, as well.

Couldn't have been luck, they'd say. *Had to be you.*

While Andie's job kept her on the road four or five days per month, the two had often thought, although never sharing it with each other, that it was just that time apart – and not some magic formula that their divorced friends kept bugging them for – that kept their marriage alive and electric.

'So, Primo at seven-thirty? Braciole and some ridiculously expensive amarone?' Matt asked.

'What about somewhere a little more private?' Her voice dropped a sexy half-octave and sent a ripple of excitement down Matt's spine.

'We're feeling private, are we?'

'Ummmmmaybe.' Andrea sing-songed the word, a girlish ploy she knew her husband found absolutely maddening. Like when she wore her plaid skirts and knee socks. Or a hair ribbon. Or barrettes. Or the strappy shoes, his favorite.

'I see,' Matt replied. 'Then how about the Terrace Room? Nobody goes there much anymore. It's dark and private.'

'That'd be great. Haven't been there in years.'

'Not too déclassé for a woman of your international reputation?'

'Screw you,' she whispered.

'You know, if you whisper it, it's not a curse anymore. If you whisper, it's more like an invitation.'

'I know.'

'Let's make it six-thirty then.'

'You are *so* bad,' she said. 'I'll see you at seven-thirty. I've got a few things to wrap up here and I want to stop at Beachwood Place.'

'What if we . . .' He was pushing it. He was going to blow it.

'What?'

'Nothing.'

She knows, Matt thought. But it sounded as if she might be up for anything.

'We'll see,' Andie said.

'Can't wait.'

'And honey?'

'What?'

'We're going to have fun.'

She *was* teasing him. 'See you tonight.'

The knock broke his concentration. He was an engineer, a mathematician. He couldn't afford to lose concentration.

'Yeah?'

'I'm going to lunch.' It was Jennifer. 'Do you want something?'

'No thanks,' Matt said, trying to sound normal. Not easy to do when you've been interrupted while masturbating in the executive washroom in the middle of the day. He felt like a bigger pervert than usual.

'Are you okay?'

'Yes Jenny, I'm fine.'

He watched the shadow beneath the door hesitate for a moment, then disappear. He waited until he heard the office door close before he went back to the business at hand.

This time Andie and he were on vacation somewhere. It was summer, the middle of the night, and they were staying at a two-story motor lodge that wasn't more than one-quarter full. There were fewer than a dozen cars scattered around the parking-lot.

Andie had told him to go out to the parking-lot and sit beneath their sliding glass door. She said she wanted him to see something. Matt had grabbed a pair of beers off the dresser and hurried down to the car like a hormonal teenager.

After fifteen minutes or so, after sitting in their sensible rental car, sipping his Bud Light, and watching Andie walk around the room, teasing him in her working-girl suit and high-heeled pumps, Matt noticed a man sitting in a car to the left and in front of him.

The man, it seemed, had been watching Andie too.

Matt thought about getting out of the car and going back to the room, hoping he could get there before his wife started actually stripping, but the idea of this stranger watching Andie excited him. He wasn't sure why. Maybe it was because he just wasn't sure how far Andie would go.

Was this fair to Andie? he wondered.

He didn't know, but he didn't move.

For the next twenty minutes the two men watched Matt Heller's wife take off her clothes, slowly, piece by piece, drawing out the part where she walked about the room in her pink lace camisole – a present from her husband. Andie then slipped out of the lingerie in front of the mirror and brushed her hair, her breasts rising and falling with the movement. She stood briefly in front of the sliding glass door, totally nude, her hourglass figure silhouetted against the white walls of the motel bedroom, then closed the curtain.

And although none of this had ever happened – nor had

any other of Matt Heller's bulging Rolodex of voyeur's fantasies about his wife – the prospect that it might someday never failed to arouse him.

Even at the office.

Maybe tonight, he thought as he closed his eyes.

Maybe tonight.

She was big and she was small in the doorway to the restaurant. Big because she was getting so tall. She would be a woman before Jack Paris knew it. Small because here she was on her own – no Beth, no Jack, no mom or dad. Just a dressed-up little girl with a purse full of hard-earned money, waiting for her father. Her juicehead father who can't even keep a date with an eleven-year-old.

As Paris walked across the lot he made a solemn vow. He would never let her down again.

Melissa Paris screwed up her mouth, tapped her foot and stared as her father opened the door. She looked like a pint-sized Beth. Her hair, a deep mahogany in color, seemed to have grown considerably since Paris had seen her last, even though it had been just a few weeks. It fell to her shoulders now, luminous in the midday sun.

'Hi sweetie,' Paris said, planting a wet kiss on the top of her head. 'Sorry I'm late.'

'Twenty-one minutes late,' she said, trying to hold onto the mad-look for all it was worth, but rapidly losing ground to a smile. Paris hadn't been able to get that smile out of Beth in years, but his daughter still loved him, still trusted him. 'Did you forget?'

Paris cleared his throat. 'Forget? Are you kidding? What kind of guy forgets his own birthday?'

'A cop.'

Paris smiled. 'You know, you can still be arrested for being a wise guy. Just because you're a detective's daughter doesn't mean you get any special privileges.'

Melissa gave him a big hug. 'Sure it does, Daddy.' she said. 'Besides, they don't arrest *angels*.'

The hostess approached them. 'I see your gentleman caller has finally arrived,' she said, grabbing two menus, saving Paris from any further scrutiny. The woman exchanged a wink with Melissa. 'Right this way.'

Paris scanned the *Plain Dealer* but found nothing on Karen Schallert's murder. These days murders were relegated to page one of the Metro section and, unless they were spectacular or involved someone of celebrity, warranted no more than a few column inches. Paris had gotten to the scene at around one-thirty, far too late to make even the late-morning edition. He took out his notebook and scribbled a note about calling Mike Cicero, the best of the *PD*'s crime reporters.

'Daddy!'

Paris looked up. 'Yeah, honey?'

'You're *working*.'

Paris had gone easy on his daughter's budget, ordering just a sandwich and coffee, even though she had encouraged him to order whatever he wanted. He took a bite. 'So how's school?' He wiped his lips with his napkin.

Melissa rolled her eyes. 'You already asked me that.'

'I did?'

'Yes.'

'Oh. And what did you say?'

Another glance at the ceiling. 'I said it was fine and that I was going to be in a play and that we went on a field-trip to Hillside Dairy and we had to watch them make cottage cheese.' She wrinkled her nose.

'That sounds great.'

'And I told you that I took my third karate class.'

'*Karate* class?'

'*Heee-yah!*' Melissa shouted, then smiled, drawing her hands into a defensive position.

Paris was dumbfounded. 'Since when are you taking karate lessons?'

'Since, like, three weeks ago.'

'Man, nobody tells me *anything* around here.' Paris shook his head.

'So tell me,' Melissa asked in her strange, formal tone, now that she seemed to have her father's undivided attention, 'how is Manfred?'

'Manny's fine, honey.'

'Do you take him out for runs?'

'Of course.'

'*Daddy.*'

'What?'

'I don't mean walks. I mean *runs*.'

'Well, occasionally we break into a trot-like sort of rhythm.' He could see she wasn't buying it. 'Okay, I'll take him out for a *run* tomorrow. I promise.'

'Dogs have to run.'

'I promise.' Paris held up his hand and rested the other one on the place-mat, in lieu of a Bible. 'Cross my heart.'

'Pinkie swear?'

'Pinkie swear,' Paris said. Observing the solemnity of such

an oath, as was their custom, they dutifully locked fingers across the table. Melissa then reached into her book bag and pulled out a long, white envelope.

'Here, Daddy.'

Paris's heart fluttered as he took the birthday card from his daughter. She really was remarkable, he thought. Most kids would not have been able to sit all through lunch without giving away the fact that they had a birthday card on them. Most kids would have boiled over. But Missy was cool and methodical. Her cop half.

Paris opened the envelope. On the front of the card was a cartoon of a man, at least ninety years old, leaning on a pair of crutches. Beneath the cartoon it read: 'Two, four, six, eight . . .' Paris opened the card. The sentiment continued: '. . . boy, did you depreciate!' Melissa had started giggling the moment Paris lifted the flap on the envelope. By the time he read the card, she was all but collapsed with laughter.

'Oh you think it's *so* funny, don't you?'

'Yes,' Melissa said, full of false composure, 'I do.' She then reached into her bag and produced the big surprise of the afternoon. A brightly wrapped package that was the size and shape of – although almost certainly not – a pint bottle of booze.

'Melissa *Paris*.'

'It's from both of us,' Missy said. 'Maybe you won't be late for appointments now. Maybe you can make notes for yourself.'

Paris opened the package and was not all that surprised to find a Panasonic digital recorder inside, secured firmly in a huge blister package. Paris had casually mentioned it to Melissa six months earlier, and his daughter never forgot a good gift idea.

'Thanks, honey,' Paris said, leaning over and placing a kiss on his daughter's forehead. 'Tell Mommy thanks too.'

'There are batteries in the box. It's ready to go.'

'I'm not the least bit surprised.' Paris opened the card once again, this time finding a little more humor in the sentiment. 'And who taught you what "depreciate" means?'

Melissa's slight hesitation answered the question. Because she never lied to him, she just raised her shoulders and stared at the table.

'Did you buy the card with Mommy?' Paris asked, somehow thinking he was changing the subject.

'You really just want to know about William, don't you?'

'Huh?'

'Oh, *please*.'

He had never been able to fool her. Not with 'Peekaboo'. Not with 'Which hand has the gum?' Not even with 'Find Daddy in the leaf pile'. Paris avoided her eyes. 'Is it that obvious?'

'Um-hmm.'

'And he never calls himself Bill?'

'Nope, William. Always.'

'Never Billy or Will or Willy?'

'Nope.'

'And he really has a—'

'Jaguar.'

Paris thought about his own car for a moment. He stopped. 'And he's a pharmacist, right?'

'Daddy. You know he's a doctor. A pediatrician. And Mom doesn't love him,' Melissa toyed with her napkin. 'He stays over sometimes, but mostly they go out to dinner. Or rent movies and kiss on the couch. But Mom doesn't love him.'

Paris wiped his lips, ricocheting between 'stays over' and

'doesn't love him'. Which to hold on to? 'I see,' he said. 'And does he take you places and buy you things?'

'Oh, Daddy,' Melissa said. 'You are *so* jealous.' She stopped, tilted her head to one side and called for the check. Then she smiled at him – a huge, confident, grown-up, career-girl smile – and Jack Paris's heart flew into a thousand pieces.

She would be a woman any minute.

Then she would leave.

Before Paris could make it to the office he had a two-thirty appearance before the grand jury, an obligation he surely would have missed had Melissa not called. It was a case involving the mother of a young Hispanic kid who had been killed in a King-Kennedy Estates drug dispute that had nothing to do with him. According to the investigation, about nine months earlier, a few days after the shooting, the dead kid's mother conned one of the gang members responsible onto the roof of her building and threw him off. Seven stories, on to a jungle gym.

Witnesses had contacted Paris a few weeks earlier – people who had just remembered that they had seen somebody throw a human being off a roof around that time – and Paris had reluctantly passed the information along to the prosecutor's office. Reluctantly, because he was not looking forward to building a case against the poor woman. The little fucker she tossed had it coming.

But he *was* looking forward to meeting Diana Bennett, the new assistant prosecutor for Cuyahoga County.

Tommy Raposo, Paris knew, had hit on Diana Bennett a few times, with no evidence of success. Then again Tommy hit on everybody. Word was that Diana Bennett did her home-work, always came prepared, but was no immediate threat to Chief Prosecutor Ardella Patterson-Jones for the top spot. She was not the overly ambitious type, if Paris could believe his ears, and that's probably what made her even more appealing.

He couldn't wait to see what all the fuss was about.

It was for that reason alone that Paris stopped home, showered, shaved, and did his very best to wrest the wrinkles from the only suit he had that wasn't at the cleaners.

The waiting room for the Cuyahoga County Grand Jury was virtually deserted when Paris arrived. He imagined the jurors were already in session and that the couple who had decided to come forward – Lucius and Azalea Quarles – were already on the stand or in the witness room.

Paris saw Rocky Dobson, one of the oldest bailiffs in the entire American justice system, cut quickly across the reception area. Rocky was seventy-five if he was a day. Paris found him in the small lunchroom reserved for county employees.

'Hey Rocky,' Paris said, perhaps louder than he needed to.

'Jack Paris,' Rocky said. 'How the hell are ya, buddy?'

Rocky was of an age where words like 'buddy', 'pal', 'mac', 'chum', 'champ', 'chief', 'jocko' and the like were automatically attached to the end of every sentence.

'How's everything?' Paris asked.

'Oh, let me tell *you*, bucko,' Rocky began, lowering his voice. 'The world's going to hell in a sidecar faster'n Jack got nimble.' He smiled and knocked on the worn Formica conference table twice. 'You can take that to the bank, my friend. And smoke it.'

Paris laughed and drew a cup of coffee from the urn as Rocky continued his diatribe on societal ills and their proper solutions, a monologue that was years running when Jack Paris became a cop and was bound to continue long after he retired.

Paris leaned against the doorjamb and blew on the hot coffee. When he looked up, over the rim of his Styrofoam cup, he saw Diana Bennett at the opposite end of the long hallway. Tommy had described her perfectly.

Paris watched her walk the entire length of the corridor, desperately trying to find a sense of symmetry and balance for her files, folders, attaché case, and oversized purse. As she got closer Paris could see that she was around thirty years old and very fit; five-eight in her sensible heels, she wore a charcoal blazer and white blouse, a dove gray skirt cut just above her knees. Her dark brown hair fell just past her shoulders. She had ice-blue eyes.

Paris was tongue-tied.

'Diana Bennett, prosecutor's office,' she said.

From somewhere amid her cargo of paper, cardboard and leather, she extended her hand. Paris took it as if it were bone china.

He waited a few beats, composing himself. 'Jack Paris. Pleasure.'

She certainly was as striking as he had heard, and he knew she was unmarried, but he had reached a point in his life where he was certain there was absolutely no point in chasing after women as pretty as Diana Bennett. He was getting old and the last thing he wanted to hear was: 'No thanks, *pop*. I'm busy Friday.'

Paris watched her, feet leaden, as she deposited her parcels on the table and exchanged a quick pleasantry with Rocky Dobson.

'We'll try not to keep you too long this afternoon,' she

said to Paris as she drew a half-cup of coffee from the huge urn. 'You'll be first, in fact.'

'No hurry.'

'Great,' she said. She extended her hand once more. 'Nice to have met you, Detective Paris.' They shook. 'See you inside.'

Paris exchanged a quick look with Rocky, who gave him a wink as if to say 'hubba hubba' or whatever guys Rocky's age say when they meet a bona fide babe. Rocky, it seemed, was still looking.

'You got that right,' Paris said as he clapped the old-timer gently on the back and walked around the corner to the witness room.

'And how long have you been a police officer?'

Paris told her. It sounded like forever.

'And how long have you been a homicide detective?'

'Four years.'

'And how many homicides would you say you've investigated in that time?' she continued. 'Approximately.'

He knew that she was merely trying to establish his competence, validate his instincts, because all the evidence against Marcella Lorca-Vasquez was purely circumstantial. 'Maybe a hundred.'

'And what percentage of those were closed? Once again, approximately.'

Paris knew exactly. He was at 81 per cent. He wasn't sure how to say it out loud without sounding like some pompous asshole who would actually get that specific about it. 'About 80 per cent, I believe.'

Diana Bennett walked forward, stopping a few feet from Paris's chair. 'That's a rather remarkable record, Detective Paris.'

Paris knew it was courtroom histrionics, but he was still flattered. 'Not for me to say,' he said, trying to sound humble. Diana Bennett walked over to her table, reached into her briefcase.

'But thank you for saying so,' Paris added. 'Counselor.'

At that moment Paris noticed the slightest smile forming at the corners of Diana's mouth. She continued. 'Please tell us what occurred after you arrived at the King-Kennedy Estates on the evening of June eighth of last year.'

After taking a moment to organize the chronology in his mind, Paris related how, when he arrived at the scene, the body of Dennell 'Too Bad' Breland, sixteen, was enmeshed in the jungle gym directly below the fire escapes at number 1728. He told how witnesses said that someone definitely threw Too Bad off the roof, but nobody could say just who it was. The fact that Too Bad was a Crip, Paris was assured at the time, had absolutely nothing to do with the mass amnesia that seemed to have descended over King-Kennedy that night.

When Paris made it to the top floor of 1728, the door to Marcella Lorca-Vasquez's stifling apartment was wide open. Lorca-Vasquez was sitting at the table, handkerchief in hand, weeping. Paris knew that she was the mother of eight-year-old Rodolfo Insana, a boy who had been killed in a recent gang related shoot-out, a homicide for which Too Bad Breland had been a person of interest. These circumstances led investigators to suspect that Lorca-Vasquez may have been the one who gave Breland the ride of his life.

The fact that she stood five nine and weighed in at about two-sixty told Paris that she was, indeed, capable.

'Detective Paris,' Diana Bennett said from just a few feet away, her perfume taunting him, 'we thank you for your time.'

*   *   *

The Homicide Unit occupied the sixth floor of the Justice Center on Ontario Street, six floors below the grand jury room. It was well after four o'clock that afternoon before Paris walked through its doors. The pile of pink and yellow while-you-were-out notes nearly obliterated the blotter.

'You ever going to clean this desk, Jack?' Tommy Raposo asked, setting down one of the two Styrofoam cups of coffee, along with a fat bear claw, wrapped in a single sheet of bakery wax paper from Casa Dolce. 'I think this might be a little stale, though. I got it, like, this *morning*.' Tommy knew how to grind it in. 'You look like shit too.'

Paris glanced up. 'Anything else?'

Tommy lifted his hands in surrender. 'I'm done.'

'Good, then take it around the corner. No mood.'

Tommy Raposo was the precinct fashion plate, always dressed to the nines. He had been Paris's partner for only a few months, having transferred from the Akron PD when Paris's partner of three years, the legendary Dom Tomei, had taken his twenty and headed to Florida. Tommy's style, to Paris's taste, was a little too slick, but he seemed to be a damn good detective.

This day Tommy wore a navy, double-breasted suit, blinding white shirt and maroon jacquard tie. 'Let me know when you want to hit the street.' Tommy knocked twice on the desk, left the office. Paris suddenly felt like an asshole for snapping at him.

'Hey G,' Paris yelled. They called Tommy Raposo 'G' for *GQ.*

Tommy poked his head around the doorjamb. He hadn't moved.

'Thanks for the coffee.'

'And?'

'The bear claw you owed me, *paesan*. The first of many. The coffee was, I'm sure, out of the kindness of your heart.'

'Of course.' Tommy stepped back into Paris's office and picked at a microscopic piece of lint on his forearm. 'So how'd it go at the grand jury?'

'Grand jury's a pain in the ass sometimes,' Paris said. 'But they should give the woman who threw that little shit off the roof a fucking medal.'

'You get Diana?'

'Jesus, Tommy. You ever zip that thing away?'

'Never.'

'It's gonna get you in trouble.'

'You think it hasn't?'

Paris shook his head.

'What was she wearing?' Tommy asked.

'She was wearing a bright orange Danskin and black hot pants,' Paris said, dumping a spoonful of sugar into his cup. 'She also had on these spike black patent-leather heels and an ankle bracelet made out of puka shells.'

'No hat?'

'Didn't I mention her hat? She had a silver derby on, too.'

'C'mon, Jack,' Tommy pleaded. 'How'd she look?'

Eventually, Paris caved in and told him, which resulted in Tommy saying that he had to take another serious run at Assistant Prosecutor Diana Bennett. As if bedding half the available women in the department and half the working court reporters in town wasn't enough, Tommy now wanted to work his way through the prosecutor's office. Paris felt a needle of jealousy – or was it rivalry? – when Tommy mentioned Diana Bennett in those terms. It was as if he had shared something with her already.

Tommy walked over to the file cabinets and thumbed

through the files in the top drawer. 'I read the report from last night,' he finally said. 'Was it as bad as you wrote it up?'

'Worse,' Paris said. 'You know I'm no good with the gory details.'

'Same MO as . . .'

So he *had* put the cases together. 'Reinhardt?'

'Yeah,' Tommy said. 'And Mills?'

'Milius.'

'Who caught that case again?'

'Greg.'

'Yeah. I remember the photographs.'

'Let me make a few calls,' Paris said. 'Then we'll go terrorize some citizens, okay?'

'Fuckin' A.'

Tommy winked at Paris, straightened his tie, spun in place and strutted down the hall in an exaggerated homeboy roll.

The man who stepped between Tommy and Paris's door was built like a Maytag – five eight, thick-waisted, oak-necked. He looked to be in his early sixties but he still held on to a full head of unruly, cloud-white hair. The man stared at Tommy's back for a few moments, watching him walk down the corridor. Then he said, 'You keep usin' that language and I'm gonna kick your ass.'

Tommy stopped and slowly turned around, a broad smile on his face.

The two men embraced, talked for a few moments, then turned toward Paris's office. Paris got up and walked around his desk, sensing an introduction.

'Jack. This is my father, Nick.' The two men stepped into the office. 'Pa, Jack Paris. Best nose in the unit.'

Nick Raposo held out his hand.

'Nice to meet you,' Paris said.

'Likewise,' Nick answered. 'Heard a lot about you.'

'You haven't heard my side of things yet.'

Nick Raposo laughed.

'So what are you doing downtown?' Tommy asked Nick.

'Taking Uncle Sal to the VA. Everything's fucked up with him, all the time. He can't eat, he can't piss, he can't fart, he can't get it up. You know how he is.'

Tommy and Paris exchanged a glance.

'So I tell him, "Sal, you're ninety years old. You're not *supposed* to get it up."' Nick shook his head. 'And what the hell is he gettin' it up for anyway? The guy's a mess. All the time.'

'Pa,' Tommy said. 'Jack doesn't need to know *every* detail, you know?'

'You're right. Anyway, I gotta go,' Nick said. 'Sal's down in the car and he's probably blowing the horn by now.'

'I'll walk you down,' Tommy said. 'C'mon,'

'Okay,' Nick said, holding out his hand for a second time. 'Good to meet you, Jack.'

'Same here.'

'I'll be back in ten and we'll roll,' Tommy said to Paris.

Nick and Tommy turned and headed down the hall. By the time they got to the end of the hallway, they ran into Greg Ebersole, and the three of them shared something that resulted in Greg stamping his feet and laughing his high-pitched goat-laugh.

Paris dialed the coroner's office, hoping Reuben was still home sleeping and that sweet blond lab tech would pick up. No such luck.

'This is Reuben Ocasio,' said Reuben's voice mail. 'I'm

either away from my desk now, on the phone with one of Cleveland's finest or up to my elbows in somebody's innards. Leave your message when you hear the beep. Adios.'

'Reuben, Jack Paris. Call me the minute you have the Schallert preliminary.' He moved to hang up, stopped. 'Oh yeah, *adios*.' He hoped the sarcasm dripped through.

Paris pulled out the rubber-banded stack of business cards that were in Karen Schallert's wallet out of a clear-plastic evidence bag. He looked at the top card. Arthur Banks, Investment Counselor. If only it said *Arthur Banks, Psycho Fucker*, my job would be a lot easier, Paris thought. He flipped the card over. Blank. He flipped it back.

Did you do it, Artie? Huh? Are you tall and partial to Irish walking-hats? Got a mustache? Were you dumb enough to give her your card, wine her and dine her and screw her, then carve her up like an Easter ham?

Are you hung like a Shetland pony, Artie?

Paris got up, pulled the files on Reinhardt and Milius.

It had been five months since the murder of Emily Reinhardt; three since Maryann Milius. Both were career women. Maryann Milius was twenty-two, a short, trim brunette with a three-year-old daughter, Desiree, who was now living with grandparents. Maryann worked as a teller at the Key Bank branch at Eightieth and Superior, which was located only a mile or so from the Red Valley Inn. Her body was found in an abandoned building on East Fifty-seventh Street, slashed and beaten, a patch of skin removed from her left calf.

Emily Reinhardt was much taller, blond and willowy. She had worked for an accounting firm at Ninth and Euclid, and as Paris stared at her picture, he wondered how many times she had been part of that rushing herd: flirtatiously coy, handing out her phone number with cautious optimism, swimming her part in the frenzy that is the downtown happy-hour life, never suspecting that one night someone would feed upon *her*.

Emily was twenty-four when she was murdered. She was found in a room at the Quality Inn on Euclid Avenue and East Fortieth, her throat cut. She also had a piece of skin missing, this time from her right shoulder blade.

And now Karen Schallert.

Hers was the first patch of skin that had been recovered. *A rose tattoo.*

Side by side, it was obvious. Maryann, Emily, Karen. Six eyes so full of life, so full of promise. The tableau looked not unlike a page out of a yearbook. And that is what made the first domino tumble. It *could* have been out of a yearbook. A high-school yearbook. Because if there was one thing that leapt out at Paris when the photos sat in a row it was how *young* the three women looked. Reinhardt was twenty-four but she could have passed for eighteen. Maryann Milius looked sixteen, maybe younger. Karen Schallert might have been a varsity cheerleader.

Paris made a note to roust the pedophiles, the teen-baiters.

He also made a note to compile a list of all the tattoo parlors between Toledo and Erie, Pennsylvania.

Paris was just about to pick up the phone, when it rang.

'Homicide, Paris.'

'Hey Jacquito.'

'Talk to me, Reuben,' Paris said. 'Gimme something good.'

'Well, I don't have much yet. Karen Schallert was drunk. One-five.'

'Cause of death?'

'Cause of death? Shit, Jack. She stopped breathing and her fucking brain shut down. It's been twelve hours. You think you got the only stiff in town?'

'I thought—'

'I got a drive-by lying here from Central this morning. No face. Legs, arms, chest, shoulders, dick, balls, everything else is there. No fucking face. And Medavoy's up my ass for cause of death. Can you believe that? How about "no face"? The victim died because he no longer had a face. That's my ruling. Death by lack of face.'

Reuben was cooking. Paris tried to jump in. 'Okay, just give me—'

'To top it off, I got a stack of messages from QB on this Choo Choo asshole.'

Choo Choo Green was a homeless black man who had died while in police custody three weeks earlier. White police custody. QB stood for Queen Bitch: Ardella Patterson-Jones, Cleveland's chief prosecutor. Reuben had deposed that the man had choked on his own vomit, but the perennial cop-haters were out in force on this one and wouldn't let up on the case surrounding the beloved Choo Choo Green, who nobody seemed to give a shit about until he ended up in the newspaper. Patterson-Jones kept whacking the ball back into the coroner's office. Somehow, somebody was supposed to craft the evidence into something that would support a charge of excessive force at the very least, but there was simply nothing there this time.

'So, you want cause?' Ocasio continued. 'How about death? She died. Next case.'

'Jesus, Reuben,' Paris said. 'Ease up on the NyQuil there, pal.' He tried to shift gears. 'Whenever you get the chance – and there's no *huge* rush on this – I'd like to know about

her make-up, too. Especially her lipstick. I want to know if
it was applied after she was killed.'

'Why does this sound so familiar? You got something, Jack?'

'Maybe,' Paris said. 'Check it out and get back to me.' He
paused, then added, 'And I want to know what she ate and
when.'

'Anything *else*?'

'*Where* she ate would be nice. Who *with* would help.'

'Reinhardt,' Ocasio said. 'And there was another one.'

'Milius,' Paris said. 'Maryann Milius.'

'Yeah, yeah. Pretty girl. Young.' He paused, formulating.
'We have a *serial*, Jack?'

'Not sure. But try and keep it quiet for the moment, okay?'

'Shit.'

'What?'

'Now I'm interested. Fuck you, Paris.'

'Maybe later, Reuben. But I want dinner and dancing first.'

'*Gringa*.'

'Call me.'

He clicked on line three and dialed the number.

The man who answered was Gunther Reinhardt, Emily's father.

'Mr Reinhardt, this is Detective John Paris with the
Cleveland Police Homicide Unit. I'm the investigator—'

'I remember you quite well, detective,' the man said. 'How
are you?'

'I'm just fine, sir.'

'Have you caught him?'

Paris had heard the question a thousand times before, but
never, he thought at that moment, quite so clinically put.
Reinhardt was a colonel in the Austrian army, long retired.
He was not a man who wasted time.

'No, I'm afraid not, Mr Reinhardt. I do have a few more questions for you, though. And I'm afraid they're kind of delicate. You'll forgive me.'

'Of course.'

'Do you know if your daughter had any tattoos?'

'Tattoos?'

'Yes.'

'You're talking about the skin that was missing from my Emily's shoulder, aren't you?'

'Yes, sir.'

'Is that why my daughter was murdered, detective? Is that what you're telling me? Because she had a tattoo?'

'I don't think it's quite that simple.'

'I disapproved of it, of course. Such things. But you see, when Emily's mother died, I had to raise her myself. Emily was only six. What a job for a soldier to do on his own! She was ordinarily so shy, but sometimes she could be so *willful*. Tattoos.'

Paris waited for the man to continue. When he didn't, Paris moved on. 'It's just that we believe the party responsible may be singling out women who—'

'It was roses,' Reinhardt said softly.

The word seemed to echo on the phone line. 'Sir?'

'The tattoo on her shoulder,' Reinhardt said. 'It was roses.'

When *had* his voyeurism begun? Watching Judy Minnissale change at the Essex Heights pool? Sixth-grade camp when he spied on the girls' cabin and saw Darcy Adelman taking a shower? Maybe it was the time he happened upon the couple having sex in the MetroPark, the two thrashing around in the leaves, so fully consumed by their passions that they didn't hear the twelve-year-old Matty Heller nearly fall off his bike and scramble behind the boulders that surrounded Squire's Castle?

As he pulled on to I-90 he concluded that the whole thing had been decided for him long before he realized that anyone else had anything different in their diapers than he did.

The fact that he liked to watch strangers was one thing. But when had it begun with Andie? When had he started to think about his wife in those terms? They had been married for two years before it had even crossed his mind, and even then he hadn't dared discuss any of it with her.

Because Andrea Della Croce hád been raised a 'good-a Catholic-a girl', as her grandmother would often remind them when they were dating. Which meant, of course, that every chance that Andie got she would screw Matt Heller's eyes out. Over the years they had tried every position, had played around with a 'marital aid' or two, had even made love in their semi-private backyard in Shaker Heights on a few warm summer nights. But for the most part, the kinky things were relegated to the back of Matt Heller's mind.

Yet Andie *did* have her moments.

Twice they had gone grocery shopping, in a manner of speaking, by driving to a west side Heinen's. Andrea wore a short skirt and a very thin tank top, while Matt took a separate cart and walked the store behind her, fielding the looks Andie's perfect legs and soft, pendulous breasts would fetch. Both times, the escapades had heated their sex life for weeks afterward.

Matt was certain that there wasn't one of his male friends – single, married, divorced or otherwise – who didn't envy him, didn't want to do the Sealy samba with his sexy wife.

Andrea Heller was a shade over five four and very well proportioned. She had a tiny waist, a Pilates-toned body. Although her hands were petite and young-looking, she rarely painted her nails. This was a cause of great concern for a woman who made her living in the cosmetics business. Her skin was an alabaster white, her hair a rich brunette that complemented the natural red of her lips.

Of the few times they had gone out to play – mostly when they were out of town, usually nothing more than a casual flirtation in a bar while Matt watched – Andrea's outfits were planned down to the smallest detail. Like what kind of shoes she wore. How short her skirt should be. Would she wear a slip, hoop earrings, nylons, a bra, jewelry.

Matt Heller was a pro. A voyeur's voyeur. In his six years as a civil engineer he had helped design huge multimillion-dollar municipal projects with less attention to detail than a single Andie Heller outfit. But he wanted more. It was time.

He wanted . . . *what?*

When he rounded the corner and saw his wife standing in the lobby of the Terrace Room Restaurant, wearing a blond wig, he knew.

For Matt, of course, the fantasy began the moment he saw his wife in the lobby.

For Andrea, this first time she walked the edge of her *own* fantasies, it began midway through dinner.

Their waiter, an Italian-looking kid about twenty-five, couldn't seem to keep his eyes off Andie. Lots of extra butter for their table. Lots of extra rolls. Gallons of water. Much repartee. Matt could see that the attention was not lost on his wife. Andie seemed to arch her back a little more often when the waiter was around.

Matt waited for him to leave. 'Are you flirting to turn me on?' he asked.

'What do *you* think?' Andie raised her wine-glass to her lips.

'I'm not sure. I've never had a blond wife before.'

'Do you really like it?'

'Are you kidding?' Matt whispered. 'Of *course* I like it. I'm just a little . . .'

'Shocked?'

'Yeah.'

'Me too.' Andie laughed and threw her head back, knowing that every man in the restaurant wanted to take her to bed; every woman wanted to be like her.

While Andie looked around the room, Matt considered his wife. She looked like a different woman. A total stranger. He could have her, even in the car if he wanted to, and he wouldn't be cheating on Andrea.

No guilt!

'You know, I'd *die* if we ran into someone we know,' she said.

Matt spoke quickly. No negative thoughts, please. 'So, what possessed you to do this?'

'I thought you'd like it.'

'Oh, I do.'

'And besides, I know I've been a real bitch lately.'

'Nah,' Matt said, hoping she wasn't losing the mood.

She slid around the booth, closer to him. 'And I wanted to make it up to you.'

'It's working, believe me.'

The waiter returned and poured the rest of their wine into their glasses. Andie leaned forward in front of him, her breasts shifting noticeably beneath her blouse.

'Will there be anything else?' the waiter asked, trying not to gawk.

'No,' Andie said. She stared at her husband, slowly uncrossing her legs and slipping her hands under the table. 'That will be all.'

The kid placed the check on the table, smiled, and took his leave.

'You're a real piece of work, Della Croce,' Matt said, moving closer to her.

'Want me to flirt some more?'

'Well, let's see. Are you going home with me?'

'*Always.*' She drained her glass, set it on the table. 'But that doesn't mean we can't have a little fun while we're out.' It was her third glass of wine and Matt knew that that was prime Andie buzz-level for sex. She ran her finger up and down his leg. 'Let's go play,' she said.

'Andrea *Heller*. Now who's the naughty one?' He felt himself start to harden. Something was definitely happening here.

'Me.'

'Where would you like to go?'

'Oh,' she began, running her hand over his thickening erection, 'let's go someplace where nobody knows us.' She squeezed him. 'I've got this idea.' She stuck her tongue in his ear. 'Tell me what you think.'

He sat at the bar, scanned the room. Forty or fifty people. Mostly men. Mostly business types.

They had driven to a hotel bar they had never gone to, just to avoid any possible run-ins with anybody they knew. Between their two jobs, their circle ran rather wide, and Andie Heller in a blond wig on the opposite side of a bar from her husband would warrant some pretty good tap-dancing to explain.

Matt's erection had reached furious proportions before he even made it inside the bar, so he had ducked into the men's room first and hidden out in a stall until it was manageable. All that Andie had said – that is, the new Andie, as Matt was beginning to think of her – was to go in, sit at the bar and she'd be there in ten minutes or so. That was it. Matt had no idea what she was up to, but he was absolutely delirious with the possibilities. How far would she take this?

Was she going to pick someone up?

Would she actually *do* that?

And if she did, how would he really feel? He had no idea, but the very notion filled him with an intoxicating mix of arousal, jealousy and a physical euphoria.

After a few minutes, Andie walked into the bar and sat three empty stools to Matt's left. She crossed her legs and ordered a White Russian, another first.

Before long, one of the business types stepped between them. Dark hair, medium build, gray suit, thirtyish. Matt heard the man say something about buying her a drink. Andie said something about having one on the way. They chatted for a bit, but Matt could only pick up bits and pieces over the music. Ten minutes later the guy left.

Matt found that his heart had been racing the whole time, and for the first time in his life he was beginning to wonder if he was cut out for the actual fulfilment of his fantasies.

Andie looked over at him and smiled. Matt was just about to slide over and suggest they leave, when another of the business types slipped between them. Taller, much better dressed, much better looking. He paid for Andie's drink and said something that made her laugh.

Somehow, for Matt Heller, that wasn't part of the fantasy.

6

Paris stared at the bottle. Manfred stared at him. He had walked the dog twice, smoked a pack and a half of Marlboro Lights, eaten an entire package of turkey hot-dogs without benefit or comfort of mustard and drunk a six-pack of Diet Pepsi. Everything but clean the tiny apartment. What was left? He looked at his watch. Eleven-o-five.

Let's see, there was news, more food, another cigarette, another walk. *Fuck it.*

He grabbed the pint of Windsor, as he had a dozen times already, then put it back. He patted the sofa twice and Manfred leapt to his side. 'Are we going for another walk, Manny?' The word put a motor in the terrier's abbreviated tail. 'You're gonna be the best-conditioned mutt in Cleveland.'

Paris clicked the remote, turning on Channel 5. Hank Theodore, the never-aging cyborg who anchored the six and eleven o'clock news, was chatting with a citizen in Collinwood who was carrying a picket sign. Paris shook his head. All he ever heard was people bitching all week about the drug problems in their neighborhood and how nobody gives a shit, but come Saturday night when some dealer with a 9-mm pistol in his hand gets capped on somebody's front lawn, you can bet they'll be on the streets Sunday carrying signs about how the cops are killing their children. Paris reached for the remote.

Before he could change the channel the words cut across the screen in eye-popping red, superimposed over the silhouette of a man brandishing a butcher knife. Then came a huge black question mark. 'Serial Killer?' Paris's heart sank. He turned up the volume.

' . . . have a serial killer on our hands? Well, our very own Triple F-Fact Finder Five-has been sniffing out the details. TV Five's Paul Coaklin has more. Paul?'

The camera cut to a medium shot of the Red Valley Inn. The reporter stood in front of room 127 and began to speak as the camera zoomed slowly in.

'Hank, she was twenty-three years old, single, active in the community, a woman who, according to friends, didn't date much, due to her extraordinarily high standards. A graduate of Cleveland State University, a career woman just trying to make it in the big city.

'So how did Karen Schallert end up here, in a cheap motel, savagely murdered by someone who, in all likelihood, was someone she trusted. Someone to whom she had reached out in love or friendship. Someone who—'

Paris shut it off. He couldn't handle the soap opera bullshit. Next they'd have his boss, Captain Elliott, commenting on how it was too early to tell if there was a connection between the three murders and yes, it was safe for women to go out of their houses and yes, the investigation was continuing and yak, yak, yak.

When Paris stood up, Manfred dove off the couch and all but slid to the door on the wood flooring. 'All walked out, Manny,' Paris said. 'Going to hit the showers.'

Manfred, banking on the outside chance of an after-shower jog, staked his place by the door.

*   *   *

Taking a shower at the Candace Apartments, a twenty-suite Gothic nightmare at the corner of East Eighty-fifth and Carnegie, was a science. Early in the cleansing experience, when the water was hottest, it was also rusty as hell. As the water got clearer it also got cooler, so there was this window of opportunity no more than two or three minutes long when the water was warm enough and clear enough to take a shower.

When Paris stepped in, the water was still pretty hot. He soaped himself quickly, feeling better by the second. Better about not stopping at the Caprice after his tour. Better about not touching the Windsor. Better about Missy.

He knew that there was a good chance that Elliott would call him in the morning and give him the job of organizing the task-force to catch this psycho. His solve rate was one of the highest in the department and it had been two years since there had been any real movement in his career.

Was he up for it? He knew it would mean less time off, less time with Melissa. Less time at the bars, too, he thought with a curious mixture of emotions. It would also mean that the media would be in his face until it was over. Unless he was going undercover, something he had not done in years.

He thought about Karen Schallert and what a shame it was. She was so pretty. So *fresh*. He thought about her body, the contrast of the black-lace camisole against her fair skin, the curve of her hips as she lay, naked and violated, on the carpeting. He closed his eyes and saw Karen Schallert's beguiling face before him. But it wasn't the face so mechanically rendered on her driver's license or even the twisted death mask in the police photographs that would haunt his desk by morning. Paris instead imagined a more impassioned

Karen Schallert: expressive and very alive, moving, smiling, laughing and—

Sweating.

Beneath him.

You wanted to fuck her too.

7

'Pharaoh knows.'

The blond woman rolled over, on to her stomach, and bit her lower lip. Like a child. 'Pharaoh *doesn't* know,' she said, pouting.

I ran the feather along her spine, over her hips, around to the side, up along her torso. Her skin was porcelain white, smooth and supple. She had a few imperfections, a blemish or two on her back, but overall her skin was soft and fragrant. One of the current-rage perfumes. When I met her at the bar the scent had been a little weaker. She had put on more for me, and I appreciated it.

I reached her breasts, which were ample and pressed tightly against the sheet, and drew the feather up and over on to her back. The blonde shivered. 'Pharaoh will show you.' I climbed on top of her and reached toward the headboard, turning up the volume on the stereo. It was a Bill Evans recording. *For Lovers.*

I grabbed a condom.

'Pharaoh has something he knows you're going to like.' I reached down between her legs and touched her. She was very wet, very warm. 'Pharaoh wants to please you.' When I inserted my fingers she let out a little gasp, as if she had not been touched in quite some time. She tried to turn over and face me, but I gently resisted her.

'You have something for me?' she said.

I raised my fingers to my lips and tasted her. '*Oh*, yes.' I slipped the condom on and flattened myself against her back for a moment. We locked fingers and I drew her hands toward the headboard. I nibbled on her ear.

'Fuck me,' she whispered.

'No.'

'*Fuck* me.'

'No.'

She writhed beneath me. 'Please. Fuck me *now*.'

'I said, no.' I ran a fingernail down the center of her back, raising a thin welt. The blonde shuddered with delight. She liked a little pain, it seemed. But how much? When would she bid me to stop?

'Let me turn over,' she said. 'I want to watch you fuck me.'

'In time.' I pulled the handcuffs from beneath the left pillow as I gently spread her thighs.

In my periphery I saw the door to the closet open slightly.

I brought the handcuffs around to the right and began to run them up and down the slicked planes of her back, her shoulder blades, the tops of her arms, all the while toying with her, probing her, drawing her deeper into the game.

I gave her an inch, then took it back. She emitted a sigh.

The closet door opened a little more.

'And what do you want, little kitty?'

'You,' she said softly.

'You want me?' I leaned over and kissed the back of her neck, tugging lightly at a wisp of baby-fine hair.

'Mmmmm . . .'

'Why do you want me?'

'Because you're so big.'

I teased her as she said the word, moving my whole body forward.

'I knew when we were dancing,' she said. 'I could feel you. I *knew*.'

'And you want all of me?' I let slide another inch or so.

'Yes.'

'You can't handle all of me.'

'Try me.'

Another inch, then back.

The blonde moaned. I got the cuff over to her right wrist as I thrust myself halfway inside her, moving her body up toward the headboard, up where I could secure the shackle to the post. The blonde screamed once and tried to get up on all fours, trying to buck me deeper. She was strong. When we eased back down to the bed, the handcuffs swung into her face and fell between the headboard and the wall. I reached for them but, in that instant, the blonde made the game. She began to fight me off.

'What the hell are you *doing*?' she screamed, struggling to turn over.

I grabbed her arm, trying to get it near the headboard. 'It's just a game,' I said, but I knew that I had lost her. She was *very* strong.

'I'm not going to let you handcuff me!' She wrestled herself free of my grip and rolled onto her back, then off the bed. 'Are you fucking *crazy*?'

'It's okay,' I said, trying to calm her. 'We don't have to if you don't want to.'

But the blonde already had her skirt in her hand and was

backing toward the bathroom and the rest of her things. She was nearly hysterical with rage.

'Look, I'm sorry,' I said, stepping off the bed, slipping the small Taser unit out from between the mattresses. I just needed to touch her once. 'I got a little carried away. We'll forget the kinky stuff, okay?'

'I don't even *know you*.'

I stepped closer to her, naked, led not by my desire now but rather by my obligation. 'If you'd just—'

'Don't come near me.' She wiggled into her skirt, pulled her blouse over her head. She gathered her shoes, held her hands out in front of her. 'Just stay away.'

She looked so incredibly beautiful, still flushed with her nearness to orgasm, her hair matted with the sweat of our lovemaking. As she turned to leave the closet door closed completely and I knew then that the blonde would get away. It was a first.

'No hard feelings?' I dropped the Taser into the pile of sheets at the foot of the bed.

'You turned me on, you bastard,' she said. 'I can't believe I . . . *shit!*' She threw open the motel door and the light from a nearby streetlamp washed the room.

And then she was gone.

I walked over to the door and closed it. I smelled my hands: perfume, sweat, the woman's musk. I touched myself with what was left of it. As I walked back to the bed I noticed that the blonde had left her bra and panties. They looked very expensive, but something told me she wouldn't be coming back for them.

I slipped into her panties and pulled the make-up kit from underneath the bed. I set it on the nightstand next to the bottle of Absolut. I lay down on the bed, cuffed myself to

the headboard and waited. After a few moments, the closet
door swung wide.

I closed my eyes.

And took my punishment.

8

Above the fold yet, Paris thought. This was going to be a long one. The *Plain Dealer* had run the three pictures side by side – Maryann Milius, Emily Reinhardt and Karen Schallert. It had been just a few hours since the Schallert investigation began and already the newspaper had more information than the police. The *PD* had managed to fit all three pictures under the headline: *Are these women victims of a serial killer?* The article beneath carried no answers of its own:

Michael A. Cicero
Plain Dealer Reporter

As Karen Schallert stepped through the door of room 127 at the Red Valley Inn on Superior Avenue, she probably had every intention of leaving in just a few hours. According to Donna Ballou, the woman's sister, Karen Schallert taught a morning reading group at Mayfield Regional Library and this Saturday they were going to read from Oh the Places You'll Go *by Dr Seuss.*

Her partner had no intention of letting Karen Schallert go anywhere.

Because according to police reports, sometime early Saturday morning Karen Schallert, 23, a personnel assistant with the United Way organization, was brutally murdered in room 127 at the Red Valley Inn.

A random killing? There are indications that it was not.

On 21 October of last year, the body of Emily Reinhardt, 24, was discovered in a second-floor room at the Quality Inn on Euclid Avenue. On 23 December, police say, the body of Maryann Milius, 22, a bank teller living in Bedford Heights, was found in an abandoned warehouse on the city's near east side. Her body had been severely battered, her throat cut.

Although Cleveland police have not yet confirmed that they are treating these three murders as the work of a serial killer, according to Captain Randall B. Elliott of the Homicide Unit, the similarities are growing as the investigation continues. Capt. Elliott said that a taskforce — to be led by Detective John S. Paris — was being formed to catch the killer or killers. The details surrounding the [see serial/3b]

And all of it above the fold.

Paris had found out that he was to lead the task-force at five-thirty that morning, when Elliott had awakened him and briefed him over the phone, prior to the *Plain Dealer* hitting the stands. It was nice to see it confirmed in print, though, Paris thought — right there on the front page, right over a double order of blueberry pancakes in the back room at Eddie's on Coventry. It seemed his appetite had returned with a vengeance after only one night of not drinking himself into a coma.

He returned to the front page and began to reread the article. He looked at his name in print and wondered if Beth was reading about him at that moment. If she was proud of him. If she was pointing it out to Melissa.

He also wondered if someone else had had the chance to read it. He wondered if the tall man in the Irish walking-hat was sitting somewhere at that moment — perhaps in a little

Italian bakery on Murray Hill, or in a booth at the Detroiter, or maybe even at the other end of the back room at Eddie's – and perusing the article over his scrambled and sausage.

The *Plain Dealer* was on the story full press, with three writers contributing to the lead story, and a pair of sidebars. There was even a graphic of the city with each of the three crime scenes depicted with a star.

'You're gonna get fat eating that shit.'

The voice came from behind him. Paris spun around. It was Tim Murdock, one of the best detectives in Beachwood, ex of the Third District, and Paris's senior by one year at the academy. 'Timmy,' Paris said. 'What's doin', big man? How goes the rat race?'

Murdock had taken a .38-caliber slug in his shoulder three years earlier – a drug shoot-out at the Carver Estates. He had arms the size of a football player's thigh and a complexion like a Maine shrimper, but his grip was weak because of his torn-up shoulder. Paris could never remember if he was supposed to squeeze his hand hard or go easy on it when they shook. He usually opted for both, always waiting for Timmy to double over in pain, clutching his shoulder.

'Fucking rats are still winning, Jackie.' Murdock slipped into the booth and tried, unsuccessfully, to get the waitress's attention. 'Congratulations on getting lead dog,' Murdock said. 'Is Dietricht gonna shit a potato or what?'

Bobby Dietricht was the Homicide Unit comer. He had his gold shield before he was thirty and had designs on captain by forty. It was just this kind of task-force that would have saved Bobby Dietricht a year or two on the ladder. But Captain Elliott didn't care too much for Bobby Dietricht, and Paris got the call.

'Thanks, Timmy.'

'Play this smart, Jack.'

Paris smiled. 'I got two till my twenty, man,' he said. 'After that, I'm out.'

Murdock laughed and called for the waitress again. 'What the hell are you gonna do off the force, Jack? Go security? Go PI? I don't think so, buddy. You're too much like me. Blue all through. Just another lifer.' The waitress finally came over, took Murdock's order, grabbed his menu and walked back to the kitchen. Murdock lowered his voice. 'So what do you have?'

Paris matched his volume. 'I have shit,' he said. 'Not a print, not a partial, no blood from the killer, no semen. Not a fucking thing. Except three bodies.'

'DNA?'

'All three samples are out to the feds.'

'What do you have on the asshole?'

'I got a tall white male, thirties, glasses, mustache and a tweed hat. *Maybe*. And *that's* probably a disguise. Could be you, even. If you had a mustache.'

Murdock smiled. 'And if I was tall and still in my thirties.'

'We don't even have this guy anywhere near the Milius murder. She leaves work one day, she shows up dead. Could have been someone else. Except—'

'Except what?'

'It doesn't leave this booth?'

'Hand to God, Jackie.'

Paris took a moment, debating. 'All three had patches of skin removed.' He kept the information about the bodies being made up after they were killed to himself. He trusted Tim Murdock as much as any other cop, but some things were better kept inside the investigation for as long as possible.

Murdock didn't press Paris on any other details for the time being. He knew the routine.

'How's the hot shot?'

'Tommy's fine,' Paris said. 'He's really going to be the lead sniffer on this one, though. Great instincts for a guy his age. He's the real sleeper at the Unit. Everybody's talking Bobby Dietricht, but Tommy might just smoke him.'

'Kid's that good?'

'That good,' Paris said. 'I don't know too much about him personally yet. Never been asked to his place.'

The two caught up quickly on each other's ex-wives and children and Paris rose to leave just as Murdock's breakfast arrived. Paris, whose stomach was legendarily susceptible to any and all sick jokes, knew that Tim Murdock was just as bad, if not worse. As Reuben Ocasio couldn't resist taunting *him*, Paris found that he couldn't resist taunting Murdock. For the first time, Paris thought he understood Reuben.

'I'm telling you, Timmy,' Paris began, laying down a tip, 'this guy sliced the skin off in a wide strip. And when you look at it like that, it's almost transparent, you know?'

Murdock — whose face was beginning to drain of color — looked down at his two pieces of slightly undercooked bacon and called for the waitress.

Paris drove south on Coventry, noting that the dogwood trees that lined Fairmount Boulevard were straining at their buds once again. He had told Beth that he would stop by on his way to the office, knowing that she and Melissa would prob-ably be going to ten o'clock mass. He needed a built-in excuse for leaving, in case his emotions got the best of him, as they seemed to be doing with unnerving regularity of late.

He found a space right in front of Beth's building, got out of the car, raised his collar against the wind.

It may have been Easter Sunday, but it was still March in Cleveland.

Beth wore a pale apricot dress and matching heels. Her hair was much shorter than Paris had ever seen it. Lighter too. She seemed to have taken on the look of a woman who was content to move among her new circle of friends: the movers and shakers of Cleveland society. Paris always scanned the society column in the *Plain Dealer* to see if Beth Shefler-Paris attended this society function or that hospital benefit. He saw her name once in a column about a recent chichi gourmet function called the Five Star Sensation, and it made him feel like shit for a week.

Beth kissed him on the cheek, looking much younger than her thirty-six years. She took the dozen lilies Paris had grossly overpaid for at the last minute, knowing well enough to let him hand Melissa the huge Easter basket himself. 'How are you, Jack?' she asked, walking him into the kitchen. 'You look good.'

'Overpaid, underworked, overstaffed,' he said. 'The usual.'

Beth found a vase for the lilies, cut them, filled the vase with water and arranged the flowers on the dining room table. 'Read about you in the paper,' she said as she poured him a cup of coffee. Just like old times. 'Does one say "congratulations" at a moment like this?'

Paris thought she would have known that. 'Yeah,' he said. 'It's a good move.'

'Congratulations.'

'Thanks.'

She brought his coffee over to him, sat down. 'Melissa said lunch was a lot of fun. She said you hardly ate a thing.'

'I've never been a big lunch eater.'

'I know. It hasn't been *that* long.'

Paris sipped his coffee, put his cup back into the saucer, realizing that he had never seen this china pattern before. Like half the things in the apartment, it looked brand new. And expensive. 'Not for you, maybe,' he said, then instantly regretted it.

Shit.

Beth reached forward, placed her hand on his. 'Jack . . .'

Melissa came racing around the corner. She wore a white dress, white shoes and a white ribbon in her hair. But, because she was Jack Paris's daughter, her purse was a shocking lime green. 'Happy Easter, Daddy!' She flew across the kitchen and into his arms. Out of the corner of his eye, Paris saw his wife look away.

'Hi punkin,' Paris said. 'Let me look at you.'

Since she was five or six that had been her cue to walk around the room like a cat-walk model, spinning, hand on hip, flipping her hair. 'Don't *we* look pretty,' Paris added.

'Thanks, Daddy.'

Paris retrieved the basket from behind the island.

'Easter bunny left this for you at my . . . house.' Paris felt strange, in the company of his wife and daughter, talking about *his* house. It had been a long time since they had all lived under one roof as a family, but he was still wrestling with geographic demons; those real, and those whose boundaries were etched only on the map of his heart. He was still madly in love with his wife.

'Wow!' Melissa exclaimed, looking through the purple cellophane for her favorite Easter candy, knowing, of course, it would be in there. She spotted them. 'Cadbury Creme Eggs!'

As anxious as she was to get at all that sugar, she slowly, methodically removed the cellophane and bows, folded them and stacked them on the kitchen counter. A cop's kid at work.

Melissa walked over to the dinette table and plucked a hard-boiled egg from the centerpiece: a two-foot-high bunny made out of accordion paper and surrounded by green cellulose and what looked like two dozen brightly painted eggs. She removed a strand of hay and handed Paris the egg. 'Easter bunny left this for *you*,' she said. The egg was light blue with dark-blue speckles. It had a bright red 'Daddy' across one side, and a decal of a duck with a policeman's cap on the other.

'It's beautiful, sweetie,' Paris said, 'Thanks.' He kissed her on the top of her head in the instant before she grabbed her basket and raced into the living room, leaving a trail of a dozen or so Jelly Bellies in her wake.

'She worked really hard on that egg,' Beth said, crossing the kitchen with the coffeepot. She topped off Paris's cup. 'All I got was a plain white egg with a "Mom" sticker on it.'

Paris crouched down and began to pick up the jelly beans. 'She's getting so big. I nearly walked right by her at the Olive Garden.'

'Junior high next year.'

The words filled Paris with disquiet. Junior high. His little angel. Paris stood up and dropped the jelly beans into his pocket. 'Wasn't it just a few weeks ago she went running up to the glass wall at Sea World yelling "Samoo, Samoo" and got splashed and screamed her brains out?'

Beth smiled. 'Or, remember the time – I think she was about two, maybe two and a half – when you told her that airplanes were exactly the same size as they looked in the sky, and that they could fly really low and get tangled up in her hair. And then she heard the plane that one day and—'

'She ran out of the house with a saucepan on her head.'

'I could've killed you for that,' Beth said, laughing. 'I think she got over that one about a week ago.'

They went quiet for a few moments, Paris turning the handle of his coffee cup around and around. It had been so long since they'd laughed together the sound was foreign to him. Finally, he asked. 'So how is she, Beth?'

Beth shrugged. 'She's still adjusting. She doesn't cry every day anymore and she's doing better in school. Her friends are coming around more now. But she still talks about you all the time. Her daddy, the cop. Even *with* the karate lessons, it's still her most effective playground threat.'

'She isn't . . . she doesn't have a boyfriend or anything, does she? Like some kid who walks her home or something? Or some kid she goes to the library with or somewhere?'

'Jack, she's *eleven*. You think she's dating?'

'Well,' Paris began, feeling a little stupid, 'she's going to be twelve and that's one year away from being thirteen and that's a teenager. And teenagers *date*.'

'You are too much, John Paris. I'll try to keep the little Lotharios in line for a few more weeks. Keep those raging hormones in check.'

Paris tried to keep a straight face, but it was hopeless. They both laughed.

It didn't last long, though, and soon they were back to their awkward postures. Paris stood up. 'Gotta run. Thanks for the coffee.'

'You don't have to . . .'

They stood face to face for a few moments, clumsily out of love. 'Happy Easter,' Paris said. He leaned forward to kiss

her. On the other side of the huge apartment a key turned
noisily in the lock.

'Bethy?' It was a man's voice.

Paris made Dr Bill to be about forty, trim and tanned,
collegiately handsome, perhaps an inch or two taller than
himself. He wore a navy-blue suit with some kind of club tie,
and the standard wing tips that befitted a man of his standing.

'You must be Jack,' William said, his hand leading him the
entire twenty or so feet between the front door and the
entrance to the kitchen. Paris waited until the man's hand
was in the same zip code as his own before reacting.

'Someone has to be,' Paris said with a smile. 'I must have
lost the coin toss.' They shook hands. 'And you have to be
William, right?'

'Yes . . . yes . . .' He looked at Paris, at Beth, back again,
not really sure how to react to this rumpled ex-husband-cop-
daddy stranger. 'Hi hon,' he said to Beth, but didn't dare lean
across and kiss her.

'Hate to just run off like this but duty calls, I'm afraid,'
Paris said, immediately thinking that he was starting to sound
like a TV cop. 'Nice to have met you, *Bill*,' he added. 'Take
good care of my girls.'

'I'll do my best,' William said. His frozen grin remained
in place and unthawed.

'Or I'll arrest you,' Paris added with a wink. He kissed
Beth on the cheek, and once again shook the rather limp right
hand of Dr William Abramson, pediatrician, surrogate daddy
and brand-new boyfriend.

Paris stopped at Arabica on the Square and picked up a pair
of mega-muffins and two large coffees for Tommy and himself.
The coffee at the Justice Center on Sundays was generally a

lot worse than during the week, due to the fact that one of the detectives was responsible for brewing it. In line he heard two women discussing the morning's *Plain Dealer* cover story about the killings. They seemed to think that the killer was a mother-hater, sadly deprived of affection when he was weaned, someone from whom the legal and psychiatric communities could learn a great deal if they would only see the poor man as a victim, not some sort of devil.

Deprivation? The only thing Paris wanted to deprive this sick asshole of was air.

He drove up Fairhill, cut across University Circle and got on Chester Avenue just as the churches let out their nine o'clock Easter masses. Paris noticed the families dressed in their finery: snug little units that sauntered up the avenue, renewed and renewing. They all looked so happy, so together, so cohesive.

He pulled into the lot at the Justice Center just as Tommy was getting out of his car, a year old Camaro. Word had it that somehow Tommy had managed to buy a new Chevy every two years since high school and each one of them had been some combination of white, black and gray. It was only one of Tommy Raposo's quirks, pulled from his bottomless bag of superstitions. 'Hey Jack,' Tommy said. He was dressed casually, much the same as Paris – jeans, polo shirt and deck shoes – but somehow it looked a lot better on him. 'See the *Plain Dealer* yet?'

Paris shut off the engine of his car and listened to the post-ignition do its drum solo for about twenty seconds. 'You believe it?' he finally said, stepping out of the car.

'You earned it.'

'I need you big-time on this one, *paesan.*'

'You own me, Jack,' Tommy said. 'I don't eat, I don't sleep.

I'm yours twenty-four, seven, three-sixty-five till this fucker's in jail or dead or both.'

'Let's hope it ain't three-sixty-five.'

The two men stepped inside the Justice Center and were met with total chaos.

Sunday morning is the time of the week, especially in law enforcement and emergency-room care, when the brilliant ideas of the previous Saturday night cash in their vouchers. Drunk tanks are always full, assault and drug charges always lead the way among complaints. Everybody is bitchy and sleepy and strung out and hung over and not about to recover anytime soon.

'Hey *Serpico* . . .' someone yelled in Paris's direction. 'When's the movie coming out?' Paris heard some greasy laughter from the other side of the room. The noise had come from a junkie named Scotty Delfs, whom Paris had used as an informant while working Narcotics.

Paris just nodded his head at Delfs as he and Tommy quickly wound their way through the crowded booking area, holding their coffee cups high.

On the way up, Paris caught a glimpse of something even more ominous than the milling dregs of Cleveland's underworld. Even though the press conference wasn't scheduled for another six hours, Paris could see the media already setting up.

The sixth floor was a lot quieter, with only two secretaries on duty and a handful of detectives. Paris looked into the common room and saw Greg Ebersole and Bobby Dietricht talking animatedly about something. It was probably Dietricht bitching about the politics of interdepartmental cocksucking that resulted in him – King Collar – not getting this cherry

DON'T LOOK NOW   73

of an assignment. Paris was going to enjoy running Dietricht ragged.

Paris checked the messages on his desk. Nothing pressing. He started to gather the files when Miriam Bostwick, the secretary whose services he shared with Tommy and Greg Ebersole, poked her head into his office.

'Congratulations,' she said in a loud whisper. She made a fist and shook it in the direction of Bobby Dietricht's office. 'Go *get* him.'

'Thanks, Miriam.'

Miriam Bostwick, an old navy pilot's wife, gave him a quick thumbs-up. 'I've made five sets of copies of the important files,' she said, pointing toward the copier table. 'They're ready whenever you are.' She winked, walked down the hall.

'I think she digs you, Jack,' Tommy said.

'I'm too old for older women, Tommy. You add up the numbers, it's frightening.' He put the files under his arm, grabbed his coffee and exchanged a woeful glance with his partner.

'This is it, boss,' Tommy said. 'Start of something big, eh?'

'Start of something.'

The commanding officer of the Homicide Unit was Captain Randall Elliott, but everyone in the department referred to him as Oscar Meyer. Behind his back, that is. It seems that one night Elliott, in the throes of passion with his wife, *in flagrante delicto*, heard a noise in the kitchen, threw on a pair of pants, surprised the perpetrator and chased him out the back door. After some hand-to-hand combat Elliott collared the man and took him into custody as three patrol cars arrived at the scene.

Elliott, fired up from the chase, emboldened by the act of

besting the intruder, had no idea that a certain part of his anatomy was swinging in the breeze as he dragged the suspect to the patrol car – in plain view of at least thirty neighbors and six cops – his little back-up unit dangling freely from his unzipped station door.

The nickname never went away.

But you never said it to his face. Especially on a day like today. This day, Captain Randall Elliott had the look of a man with a ten-ton mayor on his back.

The task-force was made up of five detectives, including Paris and Tommy Raposo. There was also Greg Ebersole and Cynthia Taggart, on loan from the Fourth. Last, last but not least – certainly not in his own opinion – there was Robert Dietricht, who seemed to be taking the news with a surprising amount of tact and team spirit. Paris wondered what he was up to.

Five big-city detectives, combining their respective Rolodexes of informants, stool pigeons, crackheads, their networks of fringe players, cast a rather wide net, reaching far beyond the city or even the county's borders. In all, it amounted to a few thousand people who, when push came to shove, could be pressed into action.

In this case, push came to shove the moment the razor descended upon Karen Schallert.

'We think we have a psychopath on the loose, people,' Elliott said in his slaggy Midwest brogue, bringing the group to order. 'Three women, nearly six months, no leads. And we've been averaging a half-dozen calls an hour since the *Plain Dealer* broke the story this morning. How do we tell them it's okay to leave the house? Or that it's okay to stop at the corner tavern for a drink?' He turned and looked at Paris. It was Elliott's awkward way of passing the baton.

Paris rose, opened his portfolio. 'Let me first brief you on what we have so far. All three women were white and in their twenties but, as you'll see, they all looked much younger.' He placed the crime-scene photos on the easel at the foot of the table. 'Karen Schallert was twenty-three, Emily Reinhardt was twenty-four, Maryann Milius was twenty-two. They were all working women, no criminal records. No drugs, no gang affiliations, no intrigue.' Paris placed the last of the photos on the easel and stepped to the side. 'Neither Milius nor Reinhardt were seeing anyone special at the time of their deaths. Maryann Milius had an ex-boyfriend, but he has an airtighter in Phoenix the week of her murder. As far as Schallert goes, we haven't interviewed her family yet as to the woman's personal life.'

'What about murder weapons?' asked Cyndy Taggart.

'It looks like a straight razor,' Paris said. 'All three had patches of skin removed, but Karen Schallert's was the only one recovered at the scene. On it was a tattoo of a pair of roses. I spoke with Emily Reinhardt's father and he told me she had a rose tattoo on her shoulder, which is consistent with the patch of skin that was missing.'

'Were the other two patches of skin ever found?' Dietricht asked.

'No,' Paris said. 'What else appears to link these three murders is that the victims were all found with carefully applied make-up on their faces — powder, blush, lipstick, eye-shadow, the works. Reuben believes that in two of the cases the make-up was applied *after* the time of death. Lab's working on a comparison study which we should have by Tuesday or Wednesday morning. The crime scenes were covered in prints and hair and fiber, along with everything else secreted in a cheap motel room, so it will be a while until it is all sorted out, if ever.'

Paris leaned against the wall. 'All three women went out to a nightclub alone and were never seen alive again.'

'It sounds like we're going undercover,' Greg Ebersole said.

'I'm afraid it's the only way,' Paris said. 'This psycho is cruising the bars and that means we cruise with him.'

Paris placed the sketch of the suspect as described by the night clerk of the Quality Inn on to the easel. The oversized Irish walking-hat effectively hid the upper half of the man's face, and the rest was taken up by tinted glasses and a big mustache. The man's nose was straight, his jawline square.

'That's our boy?' Tommy asked.

'That's him,' Paris said. 'White male, thirty, over six feet. Checked into the rooms at both the Quality Inn and the Red Valley Inn. Paid cash for both, of course.' Paris distributed the files to each of the detectives. 'Looks like we're going to be spending some time at the meat-markets.'

'Could be worse,' Tommy said. 'I saw that movie *Cruising*, you know.' He was referencing the 1980 film where Al Pacino goes undercover into the gay leather culture.

'What, like heteros don't get vicious?' said the politically correct Bobby Dietricht.

Tommy turned slowly and glared at Dietricht. The feud between these two was three months running already, and everybody in the room rolled their eyes because they knew exactly what was coming next. 'I'm sorry. Did you take that *personally*, Bobby? Because if you did, I apologize. I didn't mean to offend you.'

'Fuck you, Raposo.'

'Right here?' Tommy said, sliding off the desk. 'You want me to bend over and drop my pants right here? Is that what you're asking me to do?'

Greg Ebersole placed a hand on Dietricht's arm. 'Guys.'

'You know,' Dietricht said. 'You people and your—'

'*What?*' Tommy yelled as he walked straight into the chest of Greg Ebersole, who stood about four inches shorter than Tommy's six-two frame. 'You *people?*'

'You're so goddamn typical, Raposo.'

'I'm so—'

'*Shut the fuck up!*'

The shout came from the back of the room. Tommy and Dietricht nearly jumped at the volume and force of the command. They turned, like two third-graders caught misbehaving on the playground, and looked at Cyndy Taggart.

'Gentlemen,' she said, stirring a cup of coffee with her pen. 'We have a job to do.' She sat down and crossed her legs. 'Let's play nice until we catch this motherfucker, okay?'

Because of the undercover assignments on the case, Randall Elliott conducted the news conference while the five detectives remained out of sight. Paris and Cyndy Taggart, they had determined, would be going undercover on the east side; Tommy, Ebersole and Dietricht would all team up with female vice-officers and cover the south side, the west side and downtown respectively.

Paris put his homework in his briefcase – including photographs of all three crime scenes and the autopsy protocols for the first two victims – and grabbed his coat. He was wrestling with whether or not to stop at the Caprice for a quick one before heading home, when his phone rang, deciding for him.

'Homicide, Paris.'

'Officer Paris?'

It was a woman, maybe in her mid-twenties by the sound

of her voice. And she was nervous. '*Detective* Paris,' he said, correcting her. 'What can I do for you?'

'I was calling about the story in the *Plain Dealer*?'

She made it sound like a question. They all did. Paris had spoken to hundreds of people like her in his years on the force, people who are afraid to get involved. They figured that if it all sounded like a question, the answer might be: No. No, you aren't going to die. No, you're not going to jail.

'This morning's *Plain Dealer*?'

'Yes. You see, I met this man.'

Paris waited a few beats, sat down, prompted her again. 'And?'

Deep breath. 'I think he might be the guy you're looking for.'

Paris sat up a little straighter. 'What makes you think so?'

'Well, I can't really talk about it on this phone. I'm at work.'

'Were you harmed in any way?'

'No,' she said. 'I'm fine. Nothing like that.'

Paris eased up. 'Would you like to come down to the station and talk? We're located at the corner of—'

'Could we meet somewhere else?'

'Sure,' Paris said. 'Where do you have in mind?'

'How about the lounge at the Radisson?'

'Which one?'

'The Radisson East,' she said. 'In Beachwood.'

'That's fine. What time?'

They made arrangements but, as they did, Paris sensed that he might be losing her, that she might be setting him up for a no-show.

'If you like,' Paris continued, 'I could bring a female officer along.' He caught Cyndy Taggart's eye and waved her into his office. She came in and sat on the edge of his desk. 'She's very nice and she's very good at her job. I could even send her alone if you'd like.'

The woman hesitated for a few moments, but then said, 'No, it's okay. I'll be there. I really will.'

'Sure?'

'Yes.'

'And how will I know you?' Paris asked.

'Oh, well, I'll be wearing . . .' She trailed off again, a career woman who didn't know she'd be planning an outfit this late in the day. 'I'll be wearing an oatmeal skirt and a beige cardigan.'

'Fine,' Paris said, jotting the information down in his note-book, knowing he would look at the word 'oatmeal' somewhere down the line and wonder what the hell it meant.

9

Andie hung up the bedroom phone and peeked around the corner, looking for Matt. But there was no sign of him. He was still eating dinner. She crossed the bedroom to the bathroom, letting her robe drop to the floor, turned the water on hot and stepped into the shower.

The water soon reached the perfect temperature and Andie turned into it fully, letting it cascade over her breasts, down her stomach, her legs. She followed the stream with a smooth bar of soap, rounding the curve of her hips, creating a lather slowly, rhythmically.

She knew she had crossed a line the previous night – she was willing to bet that she had crossed nearly all of them, from the look on Matt's face at the end of the evening – but there was something beneath the surface of the game, something that drove her to do what she did, as if she had little or no control of herself. She had wanted to flirt. She had wanted to be wanted. She had wanted . . . *what*?

She still wasn't sure. But she knew enough to know that it wasn't over.

When she stopped at Ava's at Fourth and Prospect at around four o'clock that afternoon, she had no idea what she would buy. She had never bought a wig in her life and, although she was bound and determined to finally live out at least the first phase of her fantasy, she wasn't about to drop $200 on something that, best-case scenario, she might wear a half-dozen times in her life.

'What can I do for *you*?' the saleswoman asked with that knowing smile that some women, women who are far freer about their sexuality than Andrea Della Croce-Heller on Wheels would ever hope to be, always seem to possess. This time the woman was black, mid-thirties. She smiled as she looked Andie up and down. She wore a deep red wig, cut into Prince Valiant bangs in the front and razored into an inverted V in the back. Her fingernails were bright turquoise and sported small opalesque stones in the center of each.

What *am* I up to? Andie thought. What was she doing in a wig store on a sooty downtown street, gearing up, literally, to do God knows what – with, near or in front of her husband? 'Well,' she said, 'what I'm up to is getting my husband up to—' She stopped, seized by the *double entendre* of what she had said, and burst into laughter. The saleswoman, whose name was Denisha, joined her.

'I know what *you* need, girlfriend,' Denisha said. 'It's what all us women of brunette shading must turn to at times.' She sashayed down the narrow area behind the counter. 'That is, if we want to keep our men up and running.' Denisha wore a tight red and black pin-dot dress, silver drop earrings in the shape of T squares.

Andie followed her, marveling at the array of wigs and hairpieces and color sprays. A person could walk out of this place another woman, she thought. Denisha reached into the window and pulled out a blond, shoulder-length, spiral-curled wig.

Andie tried it on.

At first she thought the wig made her look like a

streetwalker and, at first, that was a negative. Because Andie Heller always took the traditional road to fashion: Pringle sweaters, Burberry coats, Land's End polos and espadrilles. But when Denisha spun her around in the chair and held a mirror up behind her, and she saw the soft, golden curls splayed out against the black of her blazer, Andie Heller *was* another woman. Even her friends might not have known her from behind.

Even Matt.

There was something about it that seemed to transform her. Perhaps, she thought, as Denisha rang up the sale, it had something to do with the fact that although she spent most of her time at the high end of the cosmetics industry – lunching in the best restaurants, cocktailing with the international fashion crowd – there was something about *this* end that excited her. Something about the chalky scent of the cheap powders, the look of the outrageously colored eye-shadows and the low gloss of the waxy lipsticks.

Andie left the store wearing the wig, her collar up, her huge sunglasses snugly in place, standing guard between her and the daylight world.

All through dinner Matt had stared at her in something that approached wonderment. Like a kid at his own birthday party. She knew that, beneath that boyish fascination with her admittedly outrageous prank, Matt was very excited. She knew she was turning him on.

During dessert, when she reached over and felt the measure of Matt's erection beneath the table, she had her answer.

'I've got this idea,' she said. 'Tell me what you think.'

They drove to Painesville and she sent Matt into the bar first, alone. She waited in the car, and even though the alcohol was hammering at her to just do it, to take this all to the next level, she still had second thoughts.

But when she walked through the lobby of the Painesville Sheraton and drew the stare of every man in the room, she was energized again. And terribly aroused.

She sat a few stools to the left of her husband and ordered a White Russian. A hooker's drink, she thought. It didn't take long for the men to swoop.

The first man to hit on her was named Geoffrey Faragut, Jr. He said he was an attorney with Sanders and Zoldessy and that, no, he didn't come to the Painesville Sheraton all that often, but yes, he sure would like to buy her a drink.

There wasn't anything terribly wrong with Geoffrey Faragut, Jr, in Andie's eyes – he was pleasant-looking enough and he had a certain boyish *joie* – but she met a lot of Geoffreys in her line of work. Average-looking men. No spark, no flame. And none could hold a candle to Matt Heller, of course. Andie sighed a few times, and when the conversation lapsed into a coma, Geoffrey Faragut, Jr, got the hint and took off.

She had glanced over at Matt as the deejay spun out of a sequence of slow songs and into a heavy reggae tune. Matt's face was a mixture of lust and loss; like he wanted this to go on for ever and he wanted to leave. Andie saw him lean over just as another man stepped between them. He was taller and far better looking than the first.

The man didn't introduce himself right away, but instead made a comment about the extraordinary resemblance between the recently departed Mr Faragut, Jr, and one Opie Taylor of Mayberry. Andie laughed, partially because she saw it was true and partially because she was somewhat overwhelmed by the man's looks.

They chatted for a while, but Andie would later be

hard-pressed to say about what. The man asked her to dance as the deejay swung back into a slow number.

Andie said yes.

She slow-danced with the stranger as Matt moved to the edge of the dance-floor and sipped his beer, running his eyes over the two of them, watching her hands, his hands. Andie could not believe that she was in the arms of another man in front of her husband. The thought, as much as the alcohol, had an intoxicating effect.

She had no idea what to do next, or what Matt wanted her to do next.

So she did nothing.

She thanked the man for the dance, walked briskly past her husband, grabbed her blazer off her stool and walked out of the bar. She was spooked but she was also pretty damned proud of herself. And wet as hell.

They had come in separate cars and they took different routes home, both dallying along the way for their own reasons. After they got home they didn't speak much and, after undressing silently, they climbed into bed. Their love-making seemed a bit tentative at first, as if Matt wasn't quite sure how he felt about any of it, even though he had carefully planted the seed of an evening such as this years earlier. After a few minutes they began to pick up steam, as they always did.

Midway, Matt asked Andie to put the wig back on.

She did, and more than once wondered if Matt imagined he was having sex with another woman. If he thought she was—

The shadow nearly made her jump. The water had cooled considerably, and she wondered how long she had been in the shower. Matt's fleshy, distorted image on the other side of the frosted glass threw a bolt of excitement and fear down her back. In the instant before he pushed the glass door to the side, Andie looked down and was somewhat surprised to find her hand between her legs.

Her husband stepped into the shower. 'Hi,'

'Hi.'

Matt was already half-erect. He had been watching her. 'Need any help here?' He cupped her breasts in his hands.

'I might,' Andie said.

'So do we go out or stay in tonight?' Matt asked with the makings of that lascivious smile.

'I have an appointment tonight,' she said. 'I have to leave in a little bit.'

'Again?'

'Sorry, honey,' Andie said. 'But we'll go out and play soon, okay?'

'Soon?' Matt said softly as he closed his eyes, holding on to the top of the tub enclosure.

'Yes.' Andie dropped to her knees. 'Soon.'

10

Her name was Eleanor Burchfield and she was late.

She had called Paris back almost immediately, probably with the intention of cancelling, but Paris had talked her out of it. At least, he hoped he had. In an attempt to explain it all over the phone, she said that she had met the man, they had danced a few dances, tossed a few drinks back, then gone to his motel room in Solon, nearly twenty miles away. Paris asked her if she hadn't thought it strange for the man to have met her at a hotel bar and then to have taken her to a motel. Eleanor Burchfield replied that that was only one of the things she felt pretty damn stupid about regarding that night.

Paris posted himself at the end of the bar, near the entrance to the lounge at the Beachwood Radisson, hoping the woman hadn't been spooked.

'Can I get you another?' the barmaid asked. She was young, petite, athletic-looking, wearing a tight red vest over a white shirt, short black skirt.

'Sure,' Paris said.

According to her tag, her name was Rita. When she put Paris's beer down in front of him she knocked twice on the bar. 'On the house,' she said. 'Officer.'

They stared at each other for a few seconds, exchanging

resolve, until Paris broke away and sipped his beer. 'What makes you think I'm a cop?'

'Seriously?' Rita said, giving him the twice-over. 'It's the jacket. Definitely, the jacket.'

Paris had stopped at his apartment and thrown on a suit jacket over his polo shirt. He thought it made him look pretty hip – casual and elegant at the same time. He was about to hear differently. He was glad Tommy wasn't with him. He'd never have heard the end of this.

'What do you mean?'

'Well, only a cop would think a suit jacket is the same thing as a blazer,' she said. 'They're not interchangeable, you know. Suit jackets go with a specific pair of pants. For life. One pair of pants per jacket. That's it.' She lifted Paris's beer, wiped the bar beneath it, then set it down on a fresh cocktail napkin. 'Now a blazer,' she continued, 'a blazer goes with jeans, slacks, corduroys. Blazers are a lot more practical because you can wear them with anything. Blazers are the way to go. Especially for divorced men.' She winked at him and placed a small bowl of goldfish crackers on the bar.

'You could tell that, too?'

'Hey, what the hell do you think I do here all night?' She got a call from the other end of the bar. 'I watch people,' she said, walking away backward. 'I *know* people. I could be a *cop*.'

Maybe you could, Paris thought.

The hotel bar was starting to fill up, mostly with what looked like graduate students trying to get in that one last cruise before heading back to school after their Easter break. The men still outnumbered the women – at least that much had not changed since Paris had gone wolfing the first time around, nearly twenty years earlier – but he noticed that the young women were a lot more aggressive than he recalled. That was certainly different.

Yet it was the young Elizabeth Shefler that had asked *him* to slow-dance that sweltering July night so many years ago. 'Reunited' by Peaches and Herb, already a golden oldie by then. Paris still played the forty-five, in all its scratchy splendor, whenever the Windsor Canadian was on all-night duty.

He looked at his waitress, leaning over the opposite side of the bar, her perfect derrière high in the air, and was just about to concede that he had bunions older than Rita the Barmaid when the voice came over his left shoulder.

'Officer Paris?'

Paris turned on his bar-stool. The woman was in her mid-twenties, strawberry blond, medium build, very pretty. He decided not to correct her on his title again. 'Yes,' he said. 'Ms Burchfield?'

She extended her hand. 'Call me Ellie.'

'Sure,' Paris said. 'Jack Paris.'

'Sorry I'm late. Easter and all.'

'Not a problem. Can I get you something?'

'No thanks. I appreciate you meeting me here. Not making me come downtown.'

Paris noticed a slight waver in the young woman's voice. She was scared. He let her continue when she was ready.

'This is where I met him,' she said. 'I figured that if you and I met here I might stay angry enough to actually go through with this.'

Paris had heard it before. The scene keeps you mean. 'It's fine,' he said. 'If you're not pressing any charges, there was no real reason to come down to the Justice Center.' He hoped his point was getting across, but there was no evidence of that happening yet.

Paris showed Eleanor Burchfield the police sketch, but because most of the man's face was obscured, she could not say for sure if it was the same man. They fell silent for a few moments. Eleanor Burchfield took a deep breath, and told Paris how she came to meet the man who called himself Pharaoh.

'Do you know how he spells that?'

'No.'

'No business card or anything?'

'No. I just assumed it was "Farrow" as in Mia Farrow. He never gave me a first name. That might have actually *been* his first name. He said it as if he had just the one name. Like Cher or Madonna or something.'

Paris wrote 'Farrow' in his book and made a note to check alternative spellings.

Eleanor Burchfield went on to describe her life in brief sketches. She was twenty-five, a speech pathologist at Lake West, unmarried, not really the nightclub type. But when she did go out, she rarely went alone. The night in question had been an exception. She told Paris that she had seen the man from across the room and had been immediately taken with him – his looks, his confidence, his impeccable tailoring. Paris decided to wait until she was finished to get the full and detailed facial description of the man.

She described their slow-dance, how the man had seduced her, talking her into going to the Solon Motel with him. Every so often, as she trod lightly over the embarrassing parts, she would look skyward, perhaps for some sort of divine explanation as to why she did what she did.

As if sheer loneliness wasn't good enough, Paris thought. He'd been there many times.

'Could you ID this man if you saw him again?' Paris asked.

He knew it was a rhetorical question, having heard how inti-
mate the two had become, but he learned a long time ago to
just ask the rhetorical questions and get them over with.

'Oh yes,' Ellie said. 'I don't think I'll ever forget this guy.'

'What makes you think he had anything to do with these
murders? Did he strike you, threaten you?'

'Not really. I mean, he was charming as hell in the beginning. Actually, right up until I saw the handcuffs. But there
was just something about him. Something dangerous. Maybe
that was part of the attraction for me. Most of the men I
know are, I don't know, *boring*, I guess.' She looked at the
floor, perhaps unwilling to meet Paris's eyes. He knew that
this meant something revelatory was forthcoming. He
remained absolutely still. 'So when he tried to handcuff me
to the bed, I wasn't so much surprised as I was frightened. I
just got the hell out of there.' She sat down on a bar-stool as
if a great weight had been lifted. 'I feel so *stupid*.'

'Look,' Paris said, trying not to sound judgmental, 'we're all
allowed a few mistakes in life, aren't we? This guy, how were
you supposed to know?' He finished his beer and pushed the
empty glass across the bar. 'And on the stupid scale, believe me,
you're not even close to the top ten. Stupid is my business'

Eleanor Burchfield smiled. It lit up her face immeasurably.

'Would you like to get a booth?' Paris asked.

'Okay. But I'm going to out to my car and get a cigarette.
I know, I know. It's a filthy habit. Please, no lectures.'

'No lectures,' Paris said. 'Are you sure I can't get you
something?'

'I'm good.'

'Sure?'

Eleanor Burchfield thought about it. 'Okay. Diet Coke's
fine. Be right back.'

Paris signalled Rita and watched the woman walk out into the hotel lobby. He could see how what happened to her got started. Eleanor Burchfield was a very attractive woman, very stylish in a *Town & Country* way.

He had discreetly looked her over for tattoos, but he hadn't seen any. He would ask.

'Another one?' Rita asked.

'Coffee for me. Black, one sugar,' Paris said. 'And a Diet Coke.'

Rita grabbed a cup, poured the coffee, smiled.

'What?'

'Nothing.'

'Rita,' Paris said, sounding far more paternal than he would have liked. 'With all we've been through together.'

Rita laughed. 'It's just that she wasn't drinking Diet Coke last night. But that's none of my business, right?'

'You saw her last night?'

Rita put the mug of coffee in front of him, grabbed the nozzle for the Coke. '*Oh* yeah,' she said. 'She was with this fucking dreamboat.' She looked up quickly, a little embarrassed. 'Sorry.'

'I've heard the word once or twice,' Paris said. He retrieved the police sketch from the adjacent bar-stool. 'Could this be the guy?'

'This could be anybody. This could be a million different guys.'

Paris said nothing.

'Anyway, I noticed the guy right away, even though he was hanging around the corner over there,' she said, motioning to a dark corner of the bar, across from the entrance. 'Tall, dark suit, wavy hair. Like a movie star.'

Paris took out his notebook. 'What color hair?'

'Brown, I think. Like your. Maybe darker. There's not a lot of light in here, you know.'

'Of course,' Paris said. 'What's your full name?'

'Shit.'

'Can you spell that for me please?' Oldest cop joke on record.

'Am I allowed to ask what this is about or no?'

'Just routine,' Paris said. But he already knew Rita well enough to know that that wouldn't be the end of it.

'Routine about, like, *what*?' She made small circular motions with her hands, punctuating each word.

Paris told her. She straightened up immediately, as was befitting the gravity of the circumstance, and did her civic duty. She told him all that she remembered. Rita – full name, Rita Constance Weisinger – told him, no, she had not seen this man before and, yes, believe her, she would have remembered. She also said she thought he was drinking Absolut on the rocks but couldn't be sure. She didn't wait on him. She went on to say that he was in for about an hour, danced slow once or twice with Eleanor Burchfield, then left. And no, she hadn't seen them leave.

'Would you be willing to talk to a police artist?'

'Sure,' she said. 'You know, I'm starting to regret buying you that beer.'

Paris smiled and put his notebook in his pocket. 'Yeah, but think of how you'll swell with civic pride when we catch this maniac.'

Rita rolled her eyes.

'I'll talk to you when I'm done with this interview,' Paris said. He looked at his watch. The Burchfield woman had been gone ten minutes. He grabbed the drinks and pointed toward one of the booths. 'We'll be over here if you remember anything else.'

'Yeah, yeah,' Rita said, wiping down the bar, finding nothing surprising at all about the fact that the gorgeous ones were always the ones who turned out to be crazy.

Eleanor Burchfield had no matches or a lighter in the car. There was probably nowhere to smoke in the hotel anyway, but someone might have a light. She walked back into the hotel, crossed the lobby, headed for the small gift shop. No luck. When she turned to leave the tiny alcove, she ran straight into a woman carrying a plastic glass full of Cabernet Sauvignon. The deep burgundy liquid seemed to hover between them for a moment – apparently deciding who had the more expensive outfit – then proceeded to splash on Ellie's chest.

Let's see, Ellie thought in that instant, insult plus injury equals, exactly 325 dollars for the cardigan she would soon contribute to the landfill.

'Oh my *God!*' the woman said, covering her mouth in shock. 'I am so *sorry.*'

The woman was fiftyish, on the tall side, mousy, dressed in a rather ordinary cotton-print smock, carrying an overcoat and overnight bag in her other hand, the hand not engaged in spilling wine on Ellie Burchfield. She wore thick glasses, cheap perfume, and had a beauty mark on her cheek.

'Oh, it's all *right,*' Ellie said, meaning exactly the opposite. 'I am *so* clumsy.'

'Don't worry about it.'

'You know *what,*' the woman said, snapping her fingers. 'I have a bottle of club soda in my room. I'm just around the corner in one-eighteen.'

Ellie looked at her sweater. 'Well, if it's not too much trouble.'

'*Nah*. Not at all. Least I can do. Name's Earline Pender.' She stuck out her hand.

Ellie introduced herself.

They rounded the corner and the woman pushed open the door, which was slightly ajar already. She called out.

'Ben?'

No answer.

'Women on the poop deck, Ben,' she said with a chuckle. 'Stow your anchor.'

Ben Pender? Ellie thought. What a curse of a name.

'Oh well. In the bar'm sure.' She tossed her bag on the bed. 'Club soda's on the table, bathroom's over there,' she added, heading back out the door. 'Be right back. Was going for a couple of candy bars myself. Can't get enough of those damn Twix.'

She left the room.

Ellie grabbed the one-liter bottle of club soda, crossed the room to the bathroom, spread the sweater out on the vanity top, poured the carbonated water over the deep red stain.

She decided that she would go back out to the bar and apologize to Detective Paris for wasting his time. Then, of course, she realized that he'd never let her go without asking her a million other questions about Mr Handcuffs, so she decided to just leave.

Because the man from last night simply was not the killer he was looking for. Couldn't have been. He was just some dance-hall Romeo, a little kinky maybe, but just a gigolo nonetheless. Why would a guy like that have to kill women? He was beautiful. So he liked to tie girls up when he had sex. Big deal. We all have our deviant little ways, don't we?

Sure we do.

*   *   *

Although it was probably against the rules, Ellie found matches in the room, lit a Winston Light. The red wine stain on her sweater was permanent, and that seemed to be that. She had already given up on the notion of having a beige cardigan in her wardrobe so, unless the clumsy Mrs Earline Pender was really filthy rich and intended to flip her a trio of hundred-dollar bills for her trouble, the cardigan was heading for the Dumpster.

Without the ivory buttons, though, Ellie thought. No need to make it a total loss.

She drew on the cigarette once, then tossed it into the commode. As she flushed the toilet she thought she heard the door to the hotel room click shut.

Or did she?

'Mrs Pender?' Ellie looked out into the darkened bedroom, her eyes momentarily confronted by the sudden change of light. 'I don't think I'm going to get this stain out after all.'

Silence.

'*Mr* Pender?' Ellie tried again, but decided she was mistaken. The noise must have come from the hallway. She felt along the wall for a light switch.

Then came a glimmer from near the bed, just a few feet away. A brief sword of incandescence in the black room.

Ellie stepped forward. 'Earline?'

A hand shot out of the darkness. It closed quickly around Ellie's mouth, then slammed her head against the steel door-jamb, stunning her, her mind showing her stars. Ellie began to struggle but there was another hand immediately at her chest. The fingers were powerful, ironlike.

The petroleum smell of the latex glove filled her nostrils and Ellie saw in an instant that the reflection she had seen danced off the blade of a straight razor – long, highly polished, pearl-handled. Muscular arms dragged her back into the brightness of the bathroom and tossed her against the wall, pummeling the air from her lungs.

The woman who called herself Earline Pender held Ellie tightly against the cool blue tile. Her breath was hot and sweet with cinnamon mouthwash.

Ellie glanced down and saw that the woman had changed her shoes. She now wore white stiletto heels. Through the opening in her coat, Ellie also saw that the woman was nude.

'I know who you're talking to out there,' the woman said. She lifted a finger from Ellie's mouth, daring her to make a sound.

Ellie remained silent.

The woman increased the pressure, the razor now lying up against the fleshy well at the base of Ellie's throat.

'Don't *fuck* with me, kitty-cat,' the woman said. She tapped the razor once with her forefinger, drawing a trickle of blood. 'I know who he is. He's a cop.'

Ellie could see that the woman was younger than she had originally thought. The lines on her face seemed to have been drawn in, the gray streaks in her hair sprayed on. The beauty mark was real. 'Yes.'

The woman looked at the floor for a moment, thinking. She brought herself to within an inch or two of Ellie's face. 'Where does he think you are right now?'

'Having a cigarette.'

'And what were you going to tell him when you got back?'

Eleanor Burchfield said nothing.

'Were you going to tell him all about last night?'

The tears began to flow freely now.

'Were you going to tell him about how you're a fucking whore?' The woman ran her hand around the back of Ellie's neck, grabbing a fistful of hair, pulling her down to her knees. The woman threw her leg over Ellie's head and sat down on the toilet behind her in one perfect, fluid motion.

'I saw you, you know,' the woman said. 'I saw what you did with him.' She extended her legs and gathered Ellie closer to her, locking her ankles around Ellie's chest. 'Just tell me that you realize you made a mistake, and I won't hurt you.' The woman eased the pressure on the razor. 'Tell me you're sorry.'

'I—' Ellie began, fully prepared to say anything that this woman wanted. But the woman interrupted.

'Because, you know what we do to scheming little cunts?' She brought the razor to rest at a ninety-degree angle to Ellie's throat and reached into her overnight bag. She pulled out a digital camera, turned the screen to face them, began flipping through the pictures. She stopped at a medium shot of the man Ellie had gone to the Solon Motel with. He was standing in the very same motel room, near the foot of the bed. Even considering the horror of her situation, Ellie was still taken with the man's physical beauty: the marble hardness of his chest and abdomen, the aristocratic line of his jaw.

He was naked and fully erect.

'Look familiar?' the woman asked. Playful now. *Girlfriends*. She flipped to another picture of the man, this one a side view. 'Rather impressive, isn't it?'

The woman then flipped through three more photographs. The first picture was a close-up of a woman with a thin red scarf draped loosely around her shoulders. The woman was nude from the waist up and was lying across a bed, staring vacantly at the ceiling. 'How about these?' the woman asked. 'You recognize these gals, don't you? Sure you do. You read the papers.'

The picture of Maryann Milius that Ellie had seen in the

Plain Dealer had been cropped from what might have been an Olan Mills type portrait. Ellie had thought the young woman pretty at the time.

But the image of Maryann Milius in front of her now – the likeness that soon told Ellie it was not a scarf at all but rather a broad swirl of blood from the gaping wound in her neck – was hideous beyond belief. She opened her mouth to scream, but the sound that came forth instead was small and thin.

A doll's scream.

Earline Pender wrapped one leg around the base of the toilet for leverage and bore down with all her strength.

At the moment the steel slid silently across Ellie's throat, exposing her trachea to the cornflower-blue bathroom in room 118 at the Radisson East, Eleanor Burchfield looked at her shoes and thought about the day she had bought them.

Funny, Ellie thought, to think such a thing at such a moment as this.

Soon she thought nothing at all.

Saila got back into the car and I knew immediately that she had been bad. Her lips were slicked with saliva, her breast heaved, her eyes were rimmed with red and full of fire. Before I could shift into reverse and pull out of the space, she placed her hand on my forearm, and from the strength of her grip, I could tell she was wired. She pulled the release on the side of her seat and slid back, falling into a reclining position, unbuttoning her coat, spreading her legs. Her thighs were perfect in the light that drifted in from the parking-lot. I shut off the engine as Saila ran her left index finger slowly down her thigh, back up.

She told me the details of what she had done.

When she was finished, I moved closer. Saila placed her right foot on the dashboard and, with the draining hull of a woman she had cut with a razor lying no more than a hundred feet from where we sat, she took my head in her hands and directed it down between her legs.

She stroked my hair as I did her bidding.

Hers. Again.

Within moments she began to hum a tune, one to which she had been a slave all evening.

An old song by Peaches and Herb.

Paris asked the first person he saw. Black woman, well dressed, early fifties.

'Excuse me,' he said. 'I was wondering if you could help me. My cousin Eleanor left the bar about a half-hour ago, and I thought perhaps you could pop into the ladies' room here and see if she might be in there, see if she's all right.'

'Sure,' the woman said, pushing open the door. 'You say her name's Eleanor?'

'Yes. Ellie, actually. About this tall, blondish, wearing a light brown cardigan.'

'Hang on,' the woman said, and disappeared into the ladies' room.

Paris leaned up against the wall and looked both ways down the hallway. Empty. The front-desk clerk had told him that Eleanor Burchfield had walked across the lobby, and around the corner toward the ballrooms and convenience lobby. The small alcove, which contained a Coke machine, an ice machine, and a candy machine, along with a tiny gift shop, was empty when Paris glanced in. Whoever had worked behind the counter had closed and shuttered the shop for the evening. His heart had leapt when he saw the deep-red stain on the carpeting, but when he knelt down, he saw that someone had spilled some wine. No bogeyman, no razors, no blood.

But no Eleanor Burchfield either.

The door to the ladies' room opened and the woman came out, shrugging her shoulders. 'Sorry,' she said. 'It's empty. I even looked in the stalls.'

'Okay. Thanks very much.'

'You're quite welcome,' the woman said, and walked toward the lobby.

Paris made a once-around the first floor, listening at the doors of some of the guest rooms, looking into the pool room and the arcade. She was gone.

She had seen a real-life cop with a badge and a gun and a notebook and realized that the whole thing just wasn't worth it.

Fuck the next victim, right?

Right, Paris thought as he sauntered back into the lounge, which was now reduced to a handful of only the most desperate of holdouts. There were two women in their forties sitting in one of the booths by the dance-floor. One of them kept looking over at Paris every time she used her hands to make a point to her girlfriend.

Rita waved Paris over to the bar.

'I remembered something else,' Rita said.

Paris said nothing, retrieving his notebook.

'I seem to recall this guy talking to another woman. Over there.' She gestured to a darkened corner to the right of the dance-floor. 'Not for long, but I'm pretty sure it was before he and your friend got together.'

'Did they look like they were a couple?'

'I don't know. Maybe.'

'Can you describe her?'

'Young and pretty. Like everyone else. Kind of on the tall side, I think. Although, when you're five two, everyone's on the tall side.' Rita curled a fingerful of hair. 'But that's about all I remember. It's dark in here. Couldn't even tell you her hair color, which for me is pretty rare.' She poured coffee into Paris's cup. 'Let me think about it. I don't know why, but I seem to think he may have even come in with this woman.'

'Okay,' Paris answered, absently tapping his index finger on the edge of the cup. Rita grabbed a bottle of Crown Royal, slid a California shot in the side door of his coffee.

'You know,' Paris said, tilting the coffee cup to his lips, 'you are damn good at what you do, you know that?'

'Of course,' she said. 'Tips don't always show it though.'

Paris dropped a twenty and his card on the bar. 'If you think of anything, give me a call. Or just stop down at the station when you have time and we'll hook you up with the police artist.'

'Okay, captain,' Rita said, saluting. 'Be careful out there.'

Paris pulled out onto the boulevard, functioning on autopilot. All he wanted was a good night's sleep and a big, fat lead.

When he turned right, onto Lee Road, he didn't notice the white BMW that made the turn behind him.

Paris got to the office at just after eight am. He dialed Eleanor Burchfield's number at eight forty-five, but there was no answer. Nor was there voicemail.

The storefront window at 1190 East 185th Street held an intricate web of neon lighting which, from the other side of the street, could be deciphered as the slogan for the Ultimate Line Tattoo Company, Inc. 'From Roses to Dragons!' it exclaimed in pink and blue tubing.

Inside, the counter area was small, crammed even tighter with wobbly plastic chairs and charity gumball machines.

The man who stepped through the soiled red curtains separating the reception area from the parlors was forty, bearded, wearing a sleeveless denim jacket and well-travelled Levi's.

'My name is Detective Raposo. This is Detective Paris. We're with the Cleveland Police Homicide Unit,' Tommy said, flashing his shield.

'Homicide,' the man said. 'What can I do for you?'

'And *your* name?' Tommy asked.

'Chuck Vasko.'

'Mr Vasko,' Tommy continued, 'we'd like to ask you a few questions in regard to a homicide we're investigating.' He placed the suspect sketch on the counter-top. 'Do you recognize this man?'

Vasko looked at the sketch. 'That's the guy from the newspaper,' he said. 'This is the guy who's killing those women, right?'

Paris saw a thin, paste-white woman peer out from between the curtains. She was mid-twenties, holding an infant in her arms.

'Do you *recognize* him, Mr Vasko?'

'Only from the newspaper. I mean, he's not a customer, if that's what you're asking. Does he have a tattoo?'

Paris stepped forward. 'If you don't mind, could you let Detective Raposo ask the questions for the time being?'

'No problem, boss man.'

He's done some time, Paris thought. 'Thank you.'

'Do you do a lot of rose tattooing, Mr Vasko?' Tommy asked.

'Oh yeah. Very popular,' Vasko said. 'In fact, our motto is—'

'Yeah, we caught it on the way in,' Tommy said. 'Mr Vasko, what kind of people get rose tattoos?'

'Well, women, of course.'

'Young women?'

'Absolutely. Teenagers too. Then of course, there's your occasional, you know, *freak*.'

'Freak?'

'Yeah, you know, guy comes in, a little pervy-lookin', wants a tattoo of a rose on his dick, his ass, his balls. I do 'em. Can't say I enjoy 'em, but I do 'em. On the other hand, I sure as hell ain't gonna let my wife handle it.' Chuck Vasko let out a loud snort of laughter and uncovered a thick row of uneven yellow teeth.

'Do you keep records of everyone who gets a tattoo here?' Tommy asked, once the man had composed himself.

'Some,' Vasko said. 'But this is mostly a cash business, as you might imagine. Tattoos are a strange thing, gentlemen. People get 'em, but then they don't want anyone to know they have 'em.'

'Who has access to your customer list?'

'Just me and my wife,' Vasko said. 'Me 'n' Dottie.'

Paris looked at the skinny woman and the fat baby in the doorway and tugged once on Tommy's coatsleeve.

They were wasting their time with the Vaskos.

The two detectives spent the remainder of the morning talking to Karen Schallert's mother, Delores, in the woman's two-bedroom ranch in Parma Heights. They learned that Karen had had a long relationship with a man named Joseph Turek, an airline mechanic, but the affair had ended nearly two years earlier over a slight difference of opinion regarding Mr Turek's avocation of hydroponic pot growing. A quick check revealed that Joseph Turek had died in an automobile crash in January.

Karen, Delores Schallert told them, had been a lot more involved in community work in recent days than she had been with men. But Delores also said that once in a while, maybe four or five times a year, Karen would let her hair down and go out to bars with one of her girlfriends. Or sometimes, over the strenuous objections of her widowed mother, on her own.

Delores Schallert gave them a recent photograph of Karen, the same one that had run in the *Plain Dealer,* and as they rose to leave, Paris scanned the collage of framed pictures on the wall over the couch. There, above the cream and brown afghan, were photographs of the toothless baby Karen Schallert, the high-school Karen, the college Karen, the career-girl Karen, all grown up now, handing an oversized check to a grayhaired man in front of the United Way building.

As he stepped into the bright sunlight and raised his sunglasses to the assault, Paris thought of the pictures over his own couch.

They grabbed a coffee at The Cup on Brookpark, and Paris tried once again to contact Eleanor Burchfield, with no success. He also had her paged at Lake West Hospital, but was told she wasn't answering. Thanks to the thousands of orange barrels that made four lanes magically turn into one on I-480, Paris didn't arrive at his desk until noon.

As soon as he sat down – a pile of message slips on his desk, the coffee starting its march uphill – the phone rang. He debated on whether or not to let his voice mail get it, but he remembered that he was in demand now. He was management. He picked it up on the third ring.

'Homicide.'

'Detective Paris?'

He couldn't believe it. It sounded like Diana Bennett. 'As charged,' he said, wincing, instantly regretting it.

'This is Diana Bennett. How are you?'

Paris felt like he had a water balloon between his neck and his collar. 'I'm just fine, thanks.'

'I just wanted to let you know that the grand jury voted not to indict Marcella Lorca-Vasquez.'

'No kidding? Something I said?'

Diana laughed. 'Maybe. You were *awfully* persuasive.'

'Yeah, but I was the one supposedly bringing evidence against her.'

'Albeit reluctantly.'

She had him pegged. 'That obvious, huh?'

'I can always spot a softie. Especially when I get him on the stand.'

Was she flirting with him? Amazing! And Rita the Barmaid from last night too? Maybe this side of forty wasn't so bad after all. 'She probably did it, you know,' Paris said.

'I'd hate to think so, detective. That would mean that neither of us did our job properly. And *that* would mean that we're taking our money under false pretenses.'

'Speaking of false pretenses,' Paris said, feeling a little of the old Paris charm returning. 'Would it be terribly out of line if I asked you to have lunch with me today?' He closed his eyes and waited for the bullet.

'Lunch would be lovely.'

He opened his eyes. 'Really?'

'Really,' she echoed.

'Okay. Am I supposed to pick the restaurant?'

'Let's see,' Diana began. 'I have that handbook right here.' Paris heard the sound of rustling paper. He smiled. 'Yep, here it is, you pick the restaurant and I pay. For dinner it's exactly the opposite. Of course, if one of us cooks, it complicates matters geometrically. Wine, flowers, dessert – stuff like that.'

'Okay, how about Fat Fish Blue?'

'That will be fine,' Diana said. 'One o'clock?'

'Who says you get to be in charge of the time?'

Diana laughed. 'See you at one, Detective Paris.'

She hung up.

Diana Bennett, Paris thought. Tommy was going to fucking *kill* him.

And he would love every minute of it.

She was already at the table and cruising a menu when Paris arrived. He was ten minutes late.

'Ms Bennett,' he said awkwardly, extending his hand. 'Nice to see you again.' They shook and Paris immediately noticed how smooth her hands were. 'Sorry I'm late.'

Diana Bennett wore a conservative navy-blue belted dress. Her hair was pulled back. She wore no jewelry. 'I'm on the same clock, Detective Paris. I know how it goes.'

'Okay then,' Paris began, seating himself opposite her and placing the napkin on his lap, 'should I say it or do you want to?'

'You.'

'Okay.' He cleared his throat and sat up straight. 'Please, call me Jack.'

'Diana.'

'Good,' Paris said. 'I'm glad we got that out of the way.' He opened his menu. 'And in the words of Woody Allen—'

'"Now we can digest our food,"' Diana said, offering the rest of the line from *Annie Hall*, one of Paris's favorite movies of all time. In fact, the film was in his DVD player at home. He was impressed.

Their waiter brought water and rolls, took their orders.

They sat in awkward silence for a few minutes, buttering their bread, sipping water, straightening themselves in their chairs, sensing each other's sexual presence. Finally, Paris spoke. 'So you think I soft-pedaled my testimony?' he asked, not really knowing what else to talk about.

'Let me put it this way,' Diana said. 'No one's going to accuse you of trying to railroad Mrs Lorca-Vasquez.'

'That's the last thing I wanted to do, believe me.'

Diana leaned forward and fixed Paris with a slight arch of an eyebrow. He noticed that her eyes were no longer the ice blue of the other day, but now a deep forest-green. The magic of contact lenses.

'Can you keep a secret?' Diana asked, almost whispering.

'I'm a cop,' Paris said. 'So I guess the answer would be no.'

'I didn't press too hard on this one myself.'

Paris smiled. 'And you think that's a secret?'

'That obvious, huh?' She leaned back as the waiter brought their plates. When he left, Diana added, 'I just don't know how deeply the world is supposed to mourn the loss of one more gang-banger, you know?'

'Amen,' Paris replied.

The conversation flowed easily as they ate their lunch. Caesar salad for her, burger with blue cheese for him. By the time they were served their coffee, Paris had learned Diana's story: thirty-two, never married, no children, born in Norwalk, Ohio, where her mother still lived. An only child. She had been with the prosecutor's office for six months; before that, three years with the Summit County office. There was no current boyfriend because she had had her fill of lawyers, and that's about all she ever met anymore. Except for criminals.

And, she confessed, the line was getting increasingly blurred between the two. So she had decided to drop out for a while.

'And what about you?' Diana asked.

'Not much to tell, I'm afraid.'

'Tell me anyway,' she said, smiling. 'I'm a prosecutor. We need all the evidence we can get.'

Paris gave Diana the *Cliff's Notes* version of his life. Born and raised on the near west side of Cleveland, graduated St Ed's, four years at John Carroll University. Father passed away when he was sixteen. Cop, married, divorced, one incredible daughter: his life.

Diana seemed genuinely interested. 'Do you have a picture?'

'You want to see a picture of my ex-wife?'

'Smartass,' she said. '*Melissa.*'

'You kidding?' Paris said, producing Melissa's sixth-grade school picture in less than three seconds.

'She's beautiful, Jack.' She studied the photograph intently before handing it back.

'Thanks.' It sounded like she really meant it, and Paris liked that. 'So,' he said, replacing Missy's picture in his wallet, wondering if he was about to blow it, 'what made you say yes to lunch with an old flatfoot like me?'

'Oh,' Diana said, 'I figured you were going to ask me out the day of the grand jury. But no such luck.' She smiled again. 'So a girl's gotta do what a girl's gotta do, right? Besides, you're going to be famous when you catch this psycho.' She sipped her coffee. 'I wanted to be able to say, "I knew you when."'

Paris ran his hands through his hair like he always did when a woman gave him a compliment. 'Well, it's going to be a team effort, I assure you.'

'Wouldn't mind making the team myself.'

'Beg your pardon?'

'I mean I would *love* to prosecute this guy. Everybody in the office is drooling over it. It's all that anybody's talked about for the last three days.'

'We have to catch him first.'

'I have no doubt that you will.' She looked at Paris with, what? Admiration? *Adoration?* 'The man who put Cyrus Webber on death row can catch a little old serial killer.'

Paris was surprised for a moment. The Webber killings nearly four years old. 'How do you know about Cyrus Webber? You weren't even in Cleveland then, were you?'

'I have my ways.' She finished her coffee, her blue-turned-green eyes rimming the cup. 'Okay. I googled you. There. I said it.'

Paris laughed, mainly because he had considered doing the same thing. He tried to shift the conversation back to Diana. He was always a little uncomfortable talking about his accomplishments. Especially with pretty women. 'So what's so appealing about a case like this? The chance to put a big-time wacko away?'

'That, and the chance to smash the insanity defense we all know will come when you catch him. It's what we prosecutors live for, you know. Taking on some sociopath who thinks he can go around doing what he wants.' She crossed her legs beneath the table, accidentally brushing up against Paris's leg. He nearly jumped. 'But personally, I'm not all that interested in the fame. I *am* interested in clout, however. Clout trades higher.'

She was a little more ambitious than Paris had thought, but it was sexy-ambitious. It was a kind of single-mindedness that Paris liked to see in himself, in his fellow cops. Goal without greed. Or, at least, *obvious* greed. He was enchanted.

The waiter approached their table. 'Are you Detective Paris?'

'Yes.'

'There's a phone call for you, sir.'

'Thanks,' Paris said, silently berating himself for turning off his phone. He was on duty, so he had signed out at Fat Fish Blue. He hoped this wasn't an emergency 'Excuse me.'

'Certainly,' Diana said.

Paris followed the waiter to the front of the restaurant. He picked up the phone.

'This is Jack Paris.'

'Jack, it's Tim Murdock.'

'*Timmy*. Twice in twenty-four hours. You must need some serious bailing. Lay it on me, babe.'

'Got a stiff at the Radisson East you might be interested in.'

Paris's heart plummeted. For a moment, his skin broke out in stiff gooseflesh.

'*What?*'

'Female, white, twenties,' Murdock said.

Paris felt the bile start to rise. 'Pretty blonde?'

Murdock exhaled quickly and Paris had his answer. 'Not anymore.' Paris heard some rustling papers. 'Victim's name is, let's see here, Eleanor Catherine Burchfield, age twenty-five. Weapon was probably a knife. Razor maybe. It's a pretty bad scene though, Jack. Hacked up in the bathroom of one of the empty suites. One of the cleaning crew found her early this morning. Thought it might dovetail with the psycho you're looking for, you know?'

Paris was speechless for a moment, his mind reeling, his heart thrumming a little too quickly, a little too loudly in his chest. 'Is the *Plain Dealer* on it yet?'

'Cicero's around here somewhere. His photographer, too.'

'What about TV?'

'No,' Murdock said. 'But any minute.'

Paris had to tell him. 'It gets better, Timmy.'

'What do you mean?'

'I was with her last night.'

Murdock went silent for a few moments. 'What the fuck are you talking about, Jack?'

'I saw her last night.'

'What? *Where?*'

'There,' Paris said. 'At the Radisson.'

'You knew her?'

'Yes,' Paris said. 'I mean no. I mean, I just met her last night. I met her at the Radisson to interview her about the multiple. She was a little hesitant at first. She thought she had met our boy and she was too scared to come in. So I met her out there.'

'And . . .'

'And we did part of the interview. She went out to smoke a cigarette and she never came back. I just figured she bailed on the whole thing.' Paris flashed on the woman's face, the way she flicked her hair from around her ear. He had known the woman less than an hour and he was mourning her little ways.

'What time was this?' Murdock asked.

'I don't know exactly. Why? You have a time of *death* already, Timmy?'

'Oldest known method,' Murdock said. 'Smashed watch. Looks like ten thirty-five. Presumptively speaking, of course.'

'*Fuck.*'

'What?'

'I was with her right around that time.'

Murdock waited a few beats, out of respect for the twenty years they'd known each other. 'Get down here, Jack. Room one-eighteen.'

*   *   *

The lobby looked much different in the daylight. Gray-suited men, blue-suited women, all name-tagged, all hustling, all doing some sort of commerce with one another. A suburban hotel in its midday swing. Conferences, meetings, luncheons. Paris wondered how many of these people knew that a woman had been sliced up in one of those tastefully appointed guest rooms. He also wondered if it would matter one bit. As long as all the widgets get sold, why should anyone give a shit?

When Paris cut short their lunch, he had told Diana Bennett only that duty had called, no details, knowing full well that she would learn of this homicide by the end of the day. They had exchanged phone numbers, made the usual promises.

Tim Murdock stood on the opposite end of the lobby, folding over his notebook, wrapping up an interview with one of the housekeepers. He noticed Paris with his cop's third eye and walked leisurely across the quiet carpeting. 'What a world, eh?' he said softly.

Paris said nothing.

Murdock flipped to a clean page of his notebook, clicked his pen. 'What happened, Jack?'

Paris related the details of the previous night, walking the chronology as he remembered it. Even though he anticipated each and every one of the detective's questions, he let Murdock ask them anyway. It just went a lot more smoothly that way.

'And you left the bar when?'

'Elevenish, I guess.'

'With anybody?'

'Timmy.'

'I'm asking.'

'I can't do that anymore. I'm an old man. Who the fuck's going to go home with me anyway?'

'If you're old, what the hell am I?'

'You're a perennial, Murdock,' Paris said. 'It's better than being young. But to answer your question, I left alone and I went right home. Thanks for the thought though.'

'All right,' Murdock said, putting his notebook away. 'Let's go in.'

The arterial spray that had resulted from the woman's throat being cut had decorated the shower curtain in the bathroom of room 118 to look like a Kmart version of a Japanese mountain scene. Red, snowcapped peaks against a light blue sky. Distant gulls.

The body had already been taken to the morgue on Adelbert Road and Paris was somewhat relieved to see only the taped outline remaining on the floor, sharp and angular at the base of the toilet bowl. He had not been looking forward to seeing Eleanor Burchfield's torn flesh scattered about the room after having sat and talked with the woman less than twenty-four hours earlier.

The blood on the floor had spread to a tortured circle about four feet in diameter and was already brown and sticky. A huge Rorschach on the smooth tile.

The room, Paris learned, had been vacant, and Nels Morrison had already determined that the electronic lock had been tampered with. The process was a lot easier than most people think, if you know what you're doing. Electronic locks in modern hotels were by no means tamper-proof.

Murdock and Paris agreed that whoever had carved up Eleanor Burchfield was either a professional thief or had been partnered with one. They also agreed that the new wrinkle narrowed the investigation considerably. Serial killers rarely came from the ranks of second-story men. And they almost always acted alone.

I think he may have come in with this woman . . .

'So is this where you tell me not to leave town?' Paris asked as he and Murdock stood in the doorway.

'Get the fuck outta here,' Murdock said.

Edgy tone, Paris thought. Not good. 'I'm serious, Timmy. I know how this looks.'

'You're not a fucking *suspect*, Jack.' Murdock leaned forward, lowered his voice. 'Jesus Christ, you're heading the task-force. This is probably going to be on *your* desk in twelve hours.'

13

They didn't talk about their escapade all week. Nor did the blond wig make another appearance. Andie had put the wig in an empty hatbox on the top shelf of the linen closet and that's where it stayed.

Saturday night it had been clear that they were still running on Friday night's leftover animal energy. Sunday afternoon found them on the floor of the living room, screwing like college students. Andie had put on her cheerleading outfit. It was a little tighter than it had been at Normandy High, but that was just fine with Matt Heller.

Monday took Matt to Buffalo and a project he was working on for their Port Authority. He spent the night at a Holiday Inn and made a cursory, hands-in-pockets stroll around the parking-lot at two in the morning, glancing at the few windows that were still lit.

Nothing exciting.

When he made last call at the hotel's small lounge, all he could think about was his wife on one of the bar-stools. He went back to his room a little bit buzzed and chock full of lead.

Wednesday morning, back home, as he absently buttered his English muffin, Andie got a phone call from her sister Celeste. She sat on the counter letting her skirt ride up her thigh as she talked, the lace edge of her slip peeking ever so coyly from beneath the hem, taunting him.

To his dismay, by the time Matt stepped out of the shower, Andie had already left for work. But she had left him a small *billet doux* to tide him over until that evening.

There, on her dressing table, perched on a velvet rostrum, sat the blond wig. Beneath it sat a white tea rose, a lone petal pierced with a ruby earring.

Enthralled, *engorged*, Matt Heller turned on his heels and walked back into the bathroom.

14

By eight o'clock Wednesday morning there had been a half-dozen confessions to the killings, spurred on, no doubt, by the *Plain Dealer* headline that screamed *Fourth Victim?* next to a rather unflattering picture of Eleanor Burchfield. The usual group of nut-house Napoleons had come in and spilled their guts, but none of them had known enough of the specific details to warrant the task-force following up.

The truth was, every alley Paris and the task-force had ventured up in the past seventy-two hours – the friends, family, co-workers, acquaintances and casual contacts of the victims – was blind. And for a string of homicides that had produced such copious amounts of human liquid, and thus the potential for a forensic banquet, there was nothing.

The weight of nothing was becoming unbearable around the sixth floor of the Justice Center.

At eight forty-five, Paris's phone rang again.

'Homicide, Paris.'

'I know where to find them,' a woman's voice said.

Paris knew right away that the woman on the phone was using a computer-generated voice-altering device of some sort. It had a soulless sound, flat and electronic. He had become very familiar with such devices when Cyrus Webber, a twenty-eight-year-old Wadsworth, Ohio, schoolteacher responsible for the death of five young girls, had used a small digital processor to make his voice sound younger when he telephoned his victims, claiming to be from their school, asking to meet them at the playground. 'What do you mean?' Paris asked.

Silence for a few moments, then: 'Look in the backyard. Next to the sandbox. What do you see?'

Paris should have known. 'Well, I'm not sure *what* I see,' he said, rapidly losing interest. 'I don't have my glasses with me. Why don't you tell me what I'm supposed to see?'

'Four girls gone,' the woman said, her voice changing pitch, up and down, as the synthesizer cycled.

'Right. Okay,' Paris said. 'Thanks.' He absently made a note about backyards.

'Four roses cut and laid to rest in long, white boxes.'

The word sat him upright. The rose tattoo information had not been made public. 'What about the roses?' he asked, pressing the record button on the tape machine connected to his phone via an in-line microphone.

First came the loud hiss of the woman's voice device, followed by a low, warbling sound. Finally, she said, 'The one you seek is like the Rose of Jericho, Detective Paris.'

'Tell you what, why don't you let me have your name and phone number and I'll call you back in a little bit,' Paris said, but even before he had finished the sentence, he knew the woman – if it indeed was a woman – had hung up.

Reuben called at nine-ten. 'I got good news, I got better news, I got great news,' he said. 'How do you want it?'

'Ascending, Reuben,' Paris said. 'Always ascending.'

'The good news is that Eleanor Burchfield had a large piece of skin missing. Of course, that isn't good news for *her*, but damned if the pattern of the rectangular cut isn't the same as the other three. I'm positive this is the same cutter, Jack.'

'Do you have the skin?'

'No. It wasn't found at the scene.'

'Where was it?' Paris asked. 'I mean, where was it cut from?'

'It was about two inches wide by four and a half inches long and it came from the back of her neck.'

Paris had looked for a tattoo on Eleanor Burchfield but of course he hadn't seen the back of her neck. Her hair was down.

'What else have you got?'

'We have a match on the face powder for the first three. Haven't gotten to Burchfield yet. Brand called Chaligne. An import of Cinq, Limited.'

'Who?'

'*Cinq.*'

'How do you spell that?'

'It's French for the number five, Jack.' Reuben spelled it for him as Paris erased what he had originally written on his pad: S-o-n-k. Eventually he would also revise his spelling of S-h-a-l-e-e-n for the face powder.

'It's a moderately expensive powder,' Reuben continued. 'But the other stuff is cheap. The lipstick and blush and mascara. Strictly bargain-basement shit, so it's going to take a while to pin down the formula. Need the feds for that one, though. Anyway, Cinq has a field office in Cleveland, if you want to talk to them or get a client list. Over at Tower City.

But there's no doubt about it. All of these women were made up post-mortem.'

'You're positive on that?'

Silence.

'Reuben?'

Nothing.

'Okay,' Paris said, moving on, remembering that silence was one of the many endearing ways Reuben Ocasio had of saying, 'Fuck you, I can do *my* job, can you do *yours*?'

'I also found something else on two of the victims' upper lips that I can almost guarantee they didn't put on before leaving the house,' Reuben said, letting Paris off the hook for the moment.

'Lay it on me, babe.'

'Spirit gum.'

'Lay it on me again, babe.'

'Jac*quito*,' Reuben said. 'You are so uncultured.'

'What? I watch PBS.'

'The main use of spirit gum is in the theater. It's used to keep on beards and eyebrows and sideburns and birthmarks and—'

'Mustaches.'

'Yep.'

'You *have* something for me, don't you, Reuben?'

'I would say that we've got a psycho in disguise out there. Your boy's mustache is a phony.'

'I *knew* it,' Paris said. 'Anything available in there?'

'In the spirit gum?' Reuben asked, incredulous. Ever since DNA testing had begun, cops expected MEs and labs to find it everywhere. 'I doubt it. But we still may be able to get something anyway.'

'What do you mean?'

Pause. A long *dramatic* pause. 'Got the mustache, Jack.'

'Say *what?*'

'It was tangled up in Karen Schallert's hair. Nobody saw it until last night. We'll have to send it out, but I think there may be something we can use on the mesh backing.'

'I love you, Reuben.'

'Should I start shopping for a dress?'

'I don't think you can wear white.' Paris looked through his doorway, into the common room, and caught Greg Ebersole's attention. He waved him into his office.

'I'll call you as soon as I have brand names on the other cosmetics and the details on the mustache,' Reuben said, clearly pleased with himself. 'In the meantime, tell your partner that he has won, hands down, the Cocksman of the Year award.'

'Tommy?'

'He didn't tell you yet?'

'Tell me what?'

'Connie Maitland – you know Connie, right?'

'Do I know Connie . . .'

'Yeah, stupid question,' Reuben said, considering that Connie Maitland, one of the assistant MEs, looked exactly like Anne Hathaway. Everybody in the department wanted to jump her bones so, for Tommy Raposo, it was like a mission. 'Anyway, Connie's on third shift last night and she's walking through the fridge and she sees a light on. She opens the door and there's Tommy Raposo nosing around a couple of stiffs.'

'What do you mean "nosing"?'

'I guess he had a couple drawers open or something,' Reuben said. 'So anyway he tells her that he's working a case, yak, yak, yak. Connie comes in this morning walking like a penguin and speaking Italian. Kenny Mertenson saw them leave together last night.'

'You're telling me Tommy bagged Connie Maitland?'

'That's the way it looks, *amigo*. The Formaldehyde Princess herself.'

'Unbelievable.'

'I've seen men go to great lengths,' Reuben said. 'I've gone to a few myself. But over a fucking stiff?'

Paris said goodbye and hung up, thoroughly envious, once again, of Tommy Raposo's astounding prowess with women.

It was that quiet time of the afternoon, that brief corridor between lunch and dinner when the calm before the deluge flattens out into silence on the sixth floor of the Justice Center.

By noon Paris had talked to every major wig and barber-products distributor in the North-east. He was told time and again that mustaches – high-quality, professionally woven, real-hair mustaches – had not been in demand since the height of the disco era. The cheaper ones were available locally at Cleveland Costume and a few other theatrical supply houses, but the type of mustache found in Karen Schallert's hair, he was told by virtually all of the firms, was not even being manufactured anymore. The most recent wholesale shipping record anyone was able to fax him was from a decade ago. And that was to a wig supply-house in Dayton.

Blind alleys. Dead ends.

'Who the hell you gotta know to get arrested around here?'

Paris, who had been daydreaming at his desk about slamming the iron door shut behind his clean-shaven psychopath and receiving a ticker-tape parade held by all the women in Cleveland, looked at his watch – already three o'clock – then looked up to see the owner of the surprisingly sweet voice.

It was Rita the Barmaid.

'*Hi*,' Paris said. 'Come on in.'

Rita looked even younger than she did at the bar. She wore faded denim jeans, white Reeboks, a short leather jacket. Her wild brunette hair was pulled back into a ponytail, secured by a black-leather holder with silver studs. She wore very little make-up. She took off her jacket to reveal a white T-shirt with the logo for Ketel One emblazoned across the front.

'I just got done with the sketch artist, but I don't know how much good it did. I never really got that close to the guy and it's pretty dark in there. Plus, I never wear my glasses at work.' She tapped her forehead. 'It's just that I know a hunk when I see one. Radar, I think.' She helped herself to a handful of microwave kettle popcorn from the bag on Paris's desk. 'But I had no idea it was all done with computers these days, you know?'

'Yeah, well, we're real modern up here in the big city.'

She helped herself to a sip of his Coke.

'Can I *get* you something?' Paris asked, more than a little charmed by Rita's forthright, familiar manner. And the way she made everything sound like a question.

'Why? You wanna *wait* on me, Detective Paris?' She leaned over his desk, smiling broadly. 'Is that it?'

Paris smiled back. Zoomed by a ninety-eight-pound waitress. 'Let's just say I owe you one. I appreciate your getting involved. And if you want something to eat—'

'I'm fine.'

Paris shifted gears. 'Let me ask you something. Did you notice anyone suspicious hanging around the bar, either before or after I was there that night? Somebody watching me, or maybe someone who might have followed Eleanor out of the bar?'

'Sorry,' Rita said. 'There wasn't much of a crowd, as you know. When it isn't busy I tend to zone out. I just remember a couple of the regulars and a busload of little old ladies with cheap raincoats.'

'Did you remember anything else about the first woman?' Paris asked. 'The one our boy may have come in with that first night?'

'No. Sorry.' Rita narrowed her brow. She looked out into the hallway, closed the door to the office. 'You know, that other cop was asking about you.'

Tim Murdock, Paris thought. 'What cop?'

'Big guy? Smells like a warm day at the animal shelter?'

'Murdock.'

'Right. He asked me a lot of questions about you.'

'Yeah, well, it's just routine, Rita,' Paris said. 'There *was* a murder after all and I *was* there. He's just doing his job.'

'Well, I had to tell him the truth, you know? Like how you were in the bar with her, then she left, then you left for a while, then you came back, but she didn't. Doesn't *look* good for you. But I still don't think you did it.'

'Gee thanks,' Paris said, hoping she was kidding.

'But it freaks me completely the hell out. At the fucking *Radisson*.' She brought her hand up to her mouth. 'Sorry. I keep swearing around you. Not very ladylike.'

'It's okay. This is a police station, it's mandatory to say that word a hundred times a day here or we all lose our jobs.'

'I've never even seen a *fist-fight* at the place,' she said with a nervous flip of her hair. 'Cheese Louise. It could've been *me*.'

'I don't want to alarm you, but I would keep an extra cautious eye out until we catch this guy. If he saw me talking to her, he saw me talking to you. Now if you like, I can have a patrol car drive by your place every few hours.'

'I'm on the twentieth floor at Fenton Place on Lakeshore. Unless they drove down the hallway, I don't think it would help.'

Paris smiled. 'Okay.'

'I grew up with five brothers, Jack. I've kicked *much* ass in my life.' She put on her jacket, rescued her hair from beneath the collar, opened the door and stepped into the hall. 'I can take care of myself, eh?' She blew him a kiss. 'But thanks for worrying about me. It's sweet, you know?'

'No charge,' Paris said. 'Let me ask you one more thing.'

'Sure.'

'Have you ever heard of something called the Rose of Jericho?'

'Rose of Jericho . . .' she said, thinking. 'Sounds like grandma perfume. Like Jungle Gardenia. Is it?'

'I have no idea,' Paris said, having run it through the police databases and come up empty.

'Well, don't be a stranger, okay?' Rita said, shaking a finger at him. 'Gotta run. See you.' She turned on her heels and was gone.

And as Paris listened to her footsteps head down the hall – the unmistakable gait of a young woman – it touched him with sadness.

Or perhaps it was just nostalgia.

Rita sounded a lot like Beth had at her age, and it made Jack Paris miss his family all the more.

'What can I tell you? It was a profoundly moving experience.'

'For who?' Paris replied into the phone.

'For her,' Tommy said. 'For me it was just another mission, of course.'

'Gonna give me details later?'

'Only if you can stand them.'

Paris looked at the doodle he had unconsciously been drawing for the past ten minutes. Considering his lack of sleep and level of frustration, he was not at all surprised to see that he had rendered a fairly passable sketch of an Irish walking-hat on his paper blotter. 'Where are you?' Paris asked.

'Across the bridge. West Side Market.'

'Listen, two things. One, we're probably going to have a better sketch by the end of the day. The barmaid from the Radisson just left.'

'Weissman?'

'Weisinger,' Paris said. 'Rita Weisinger.'

'Weisinger,' Tommy echoed. 'What'd she say?'

'Said she didn't get that close to him, but maybe she was able to fill in a feature or two.'

'Think she could ID him?'

'Not sure,' Paris said. 'And there's even better news from Reuben.'

'What's that?'

'He found our boy's phony mustache.'

'What? The mustache is phony?'

'Yeah. It was tangled up in Karen Schallert's hair. Can you believe it? Reuben says there may be something we can work with on the mesh backing. The mustache was applied with spirit gum, and something like that yields trace evidence.'

'Fuckin' Reuben, huh?'

'Why don't you follow up the two west-side guys from

Karen Schallert's wallet,' Paris said. 'And I'll take the guys in the Heights. The doctor and the other one.'

Silence.

'Tommy?'

'Okay . . .'

'And if you want we can—'

'. . . kick *yat*.'

'What?'

Paris heard a bus pass Tommy's location.

'Said I'll see you later,' Tommy replied.

'I didn't—' Paris began, but he already had silence.

15

Samantha had seen the man in the store three or four times in the past year, but she had never had the courage to wait on him. Mr Hendershott had always taken care of him while she straightened merchandise on the other side of the room, peeking around the rows of aerosol cans and plastic tubs of blue and pink and yellow gel. She never seemed to be able to muster the necessary fortitude to walk across the store and actually speak to him.

Although she *had* wanted to.

Because he was one of the handsomest men she had ever seen.

Every other Wednesday Mr Hendershott took a three-hour lunch so he could see his acupuncturist about his back pains, and Samantha was left alone to hold the fort at Allied Salon Products on West Forty-fourth Street. This had been the routine for eleven years. So, on this particular Wednesday, when the bell on the door jingled and Samantha looked up, she nearly fainted.

'Hello,' the man said. He wore a dark overcoat and a tweed hat.

Samantha clutched the hem of her dress as the man smiled, doubling her anxiety, and walked to the other side of the store. He stopped by the color rinses. Samantha swallowed once, brushed her hair from her forehead and charged across the store.

'However, if it's important that it washes right out, you want the EZ Color line,' Samantha said for what she was hoping was no more than the fifth or sixth time. 'Otherwise it takes two or three weeks of washing your hair to get it out.'

'This *is* a community theater group,' the man said, holding a pair of EZ Color boxes with 'deep chestnut' written on the side. 'Almost all of us have day jobs and it's important that we all show up for work looking like we did the day before, if you know what I mean.'

'What play are you putting on?'

'We're doing *Guys and Dolls* this year.'

'That's one of my *favorites!*' Samantha said, a little too loudly. She had seen the revival twice when the touring company had stopped at the State Theater the previous winter. 'Who do you play?'

'Why, Sky Masterson, ma'am,' he said with a slight New York accent, a touch of his brim and a smile.

'I *knew* it,' she said. An awkward silence passed. Samantha tried to fill it. 'Well, will there be anything else today?'

'Mr Hendershott showed me something once. I believe it was a display rack called the Penrod Collection.'

'The Penrod Collection,' Samantha mused, trying to put a product to the name.

'Yes, it was in the men's grooming section.'

'Mustaches!' Samantha said with the zeal of an amateur sleuth finding the key clue to an unsolved murder. 'Of course. For the *play!*' She walked behind the counter, through the curtains and into the back room. She soon emerged with a dusty two-foot-by-two-foot display card of real-hair mustaches on fine-mesh backing.

Samantha knew the mustaches were priced at fifty dollars, but they had been lying around the store for so long that she felt it would be ridiculous to charge such a sum. Impulsively, amazed at her temerity, she said, 'Pick any one you want. On the house.'

'Oh I couldn't.'

'I insist,' Samantha said, not really knowing what had come over her, or what she'd tell Mr Hendershott if he ever found out. 'Special for our good customers.'

After a little more prodding the man said he would take Samantha up on her most gracious offer. But only if she agreed to have lunch with him sometime in the near future.

After ringing up the purchase, Samantha scrawled her name, address and home phone number on the back of an Allied card. All she would remember later that night was the man's smile.

And his movie-star eyes.

16

When Paris walked into the Stone Oven café on Lee Road, and saw her sitting near the front windows with her legs crossed, her auburn hair down around her shoulders, he almost didn't recognize her.

Those *legs*.

Cyndy Taggart's dress was spectacularly short.

'You look great,' Paris said.

'In this old thing?' she replied, smiling. 'I just throw this on when I couldn't care less *what* I look like.' Her dress was a black knit and she wore a small silver crucifix on a chain around her neck. She had on dark stockings.

Cyndy stood up and straightened her hem — which seemed determined to stay about mid-thigh no matter what she did — and in her high heels she was nearly as tall as Paris, who strained to make five eleven on a good day.

'Where to first?' she asked.

There were five hotels close to I-271 and the dozens of corporate headquarters that line Chagrin Boulevard. Four had lounges.

'Let's go to the Impulse,' Paris said.

'Oooh, the *Impulse*,' Cyndy said. 'Just don't know what a girl might do at a place like that. I may not be responsible for my actions, Detective Paris.' She walked ahead of Paris, out the back door and across the parking-lot, purposefully swinging her hips in a wide arc, her spike heels clicking loudly on the asphalt. She stopped, opened Paris's car door, turned and said, 'Too much caboose?'

'Not for me,' Paris replied, laughing. 'Not for me.'

The Impulse was the lounge in the Embassy Suites Hotel on Mission Parkway, one of the commercial-park ingress routes. It was decorated in an art deco style with a lot of banquette tables, stained glass, indirect pink and white lighting and an elevated dance-floor against the back wall of the huge rectangular room. There were two bars. The music was mostly techno-house, provided by a deejay who was ensconced in a raised smoked-glass cubicle behind the back bar.

According to the placard in the lobby, Wednesday night was Ladies' Night at the Impulse and, at ten-thirty, the place was hopping.

Cyndy had gone in first, and as Paris leaned against one of the brass railings, next to a long line of banquettes, he scanned the room and found Cyndy sitting at the front bar, stirring what looked like a Screwdriver but was really just orange juice. They made eye contact, setting their positions.

Although Cyndy was an attractive woman, from that distance, Paris thought, in those clothes, she looked like a knockout. He tried to recall Cyndy Taggart's marital status.

'Can I get you something?' one of the barmaids yelled to him over the music. She was tall and spidery and sported a white shirt and lemon-yellow bow tie.

Paris had to think about it. He had never had to come up with a non-alcoholic choice in a bar before. For a few moments, his mind went blank. He couldn't even recall what he liked. 'Do you have ice tea?'

'Long Island ice tea?'

'No, regular ice tea.'

'I don't think so.'

'Let me have a Coke then. With a swizzle stick.'

'Pepsi all right?'

'Pepsi's fine,' Paris said.

She wrote down his order, and began to weave her way toward the bar.

Paris smoothed the sleeves of his blazer, a navy blue Armani he had borrowed from Tommy a few months earlier when they had hit the Warehouse District bars one night. Paris had never been one to spend a lot of money on clothes – he figured the jacket had cost northward of a thousand dollars – but standing here, feeling the luxurious texture of the fabric, he understood for the first time difference between buying cheap, and buying a designer label. He had to admit, he felt good.

'Nice jacket.'

The woman's voice came from his left. It didn't sound like Cyndy. He turned around and found that it wasn't. The compliment came from a shapely, well-dressed woman in her mid- to late-twenties. She had wild, curly blond hair, full red lips, and was leaning against a banquette, holding a drink that may have been a Brandy Alexander.

Her smile gave way to dimples at either side.

'Thanks,' Paris said. He glanced over at Cyndy. She was talking to a short black man in a three-piece suit. Paris turned his attention back to the blonde, already wishing he had a cold Budweiser in his hand at the very least. 'But I must confess, I borrowed it for the evening.'

The blonde nodded in understanding and sipped her drink through the straw. 'It looks good on you,' she said. 'You have nice friends.'

'You really think so?' Paris said, standing up a little straighter, throwing his shoulders back.

'Oh absolutely. Turn around for me.'

Paris turned around slowly, feeling a little stupid. By the time he had turned 360, the woman was smiling broadly.

'Definitely *L'Uomo.*'

Paris smiled, having no idea if that was a compliment or not. The deejay kicked into an upbeat song.

'You dance?' the woman asked, already swaying to the beat.

Paris's heart immediately doubled its rate. 'To this?' He hadn't been to a bar where there was dancing in so long that he had forgotten the abject horror lodged in the notion of fast-dancing in front of people. Sober, no less. In his time as a patrolman, he once stared down a gang-banger who was jacked up on PCP and twirling a Mauser .380 on his index finger. Didn't bat an eye. Fast-dancing in front of total strangers scared the shit out of him 'Maybe the next one.'

The blonde smiled and stepped closer. 'Not a dancer?'

Her perfume was deliriously sexy. 'I'm more of a slow dancer, I guess.'

'My favorite kind.' She stepped even closer, and as she did, she glanced to her left for what Paris imagined to be the third or fourth time. After a few moments, Paris looked in that direction and caught the glance of a man standing near one of the emergency exits. The man was in his thirties, brown hair, conservatively dressed.

When Paris made eye contact, the man looked away.

'Next slow dance, maybe you could show me a few moves,' the blond woman added.

'It's a date,' Paris said, wondering about the man's connection to this scene.

'By the way, my name's Abigail.'

'Jack. Jack Partridge.' What the *hell* was he thinking about? Jack Partridge?

They shook hands briefly and Paris could not help but notice the shift of the woman's breasts beneath her blouse. He looked back into her eyes.

She had caught him looking. She smiled.

Paris decided to look into this high-fashion thing in earnest. He didn't need a car or rent money anyway, did he? Before he could say another word, a slow song started. Some oldie by Whitney Houston. There was no avoiding Abigail's look. She arched one eyebrow. *Well?*

Paris decided to give the lady a whirl around the dance-floor. All in the line of duty, of course. He could get a better view of the room from the elevated dance-floor, he told himself.

He glanced over at the bar.

Cyndy was gone.

They had agreed that neither of them would make any moves without giving the other a high sign. And now he didn't see her.

'*Shit!*' Paris rushed into the crowd, jostling elbows and arms, spilling a few drinks in the process. He unsnapped his shoulder holster. He knew he might be overreacting, that Cyndy could take care of herself, and that just because she wasn't in her seat didn't necessarily mean a thing. She was a cop, she was armed, she had experience, so there had to be a really good reason.

He knew and he charged ahead anyway.

Halfway to the door one of the larger lounge monkeys – big blond kid, muscular, maybe twenty-four – tried to detain him, something about an apology from Paris for bumping into a girl the kid had known probably all of ten minutes. When Paris opened his coat sufficiently to show him the butt of his weapon, the kid backed off and let him pass.

But the exchange delayed him, eating seconds. It took him a full minute to bull his way to the front. When he arrived he found Cyndy's seat occupied by an obese man with a pair of margaritas already on call in front of him.

Paris looked left and right, into the angled mirrors above. He turned toward the room and scanned the crowd, the women on the dance-floor. There was no sign of her. The deejay mixed into another slow song as Paris found himself momentarily hemmed in by what had to be three or four of the Cleveland Cavaliers. He fingered the badge attached to his belt, considered using it to clear a path, but managed to push his way to the lobby door without it.

He looked through the etched glass. A few couples scattered around the brightly lit foyer. A bellman crossing with a pair pf rollaways.

No Cyndy.

Paris exited the lounge and crossed the lobby. He waited near the rest rooms for a few minutes, witnessed a parade of rather women entering, exiting. None of them police officers.

He moved down the main corridor, toward the convenience lobbies, the pool, the banquet facilities. He peeked into one of the meeting rooms. Nothing moving.

Paris stood in the doorway, watching and listening, sensing people nearby but not being able to pin them down. Muted conversation floated by, a man and a woman, rapid-fire talk.

Paris stepped into the hall and tilted his head to the sound. And that's when he heard Cyndy scream.

*   *   *

At first, Paris couldn't tell if it was a shriek of pain or delight, danger or pleasure. It may even have been laughter, but the sound remained in the air, chilling him. He drew his weapon and held it tightly to his side. Flat against the wall, he rounded the corner and found more alcoves for service and house-keeping. The passageway was quiet, empty.

At the end of the hall Paris noticed an oversized swing door bearing a 'Hotel Employees Only' plate. Through the small, frosted-glass panel he could see movement. Light, dark, light, dark. More voices, closer now. Paris strode silently to the door, crouched, edged it open.

Cyndy Taggart was up against the wall at the far end of the long service corridor, partially obscured by a tall man in front of her and to her right. The man was lean, but broad-shouldered. He held a black overcoat in his left hand.

Before Paris could react, the man raised his right hand high over Cyndy's head and the track lighting above him caught a reflection of a . . . watch? Bracelet? Keys? *Razor?*

'*Police!*' Paris yelled.

He sprinted the length of the hallway, taking the distance between them in eight or nine long strides, and blindsided the man at full speed. He heard the air rush out of the man's lungs as they locked arms momentarily and slammed into a vending machine. Somebody's knee smashed the glass into a hundred sparkling pieces.

For a moment, the edge of Paris's world went red as the right side of his face, in direct contrast, went white-hot. He recovered from the impact first, righted himself and kicked the man's feet out from under him. Although he was already breathless, Paris's upper-body strength prevailed. He wrestled the bigger man to the ground and managed to get one arm behind him in the process.

'*Jack!*' Cyndy screamed, for what was probably the third time.

Paris dropped his knee into the middle of the man's back and leaned forward, gasping for air. He looked down at the man's profile and immediately recognized the cheekbones, the hair, the earring.

It was Danny Lawrence. Danny lived in the city, but sometimes stayed with his brother in Beachwood. The hotel bars on Chagrin were his natural hunting grounds.

'Aw fuck me to *tears*,' Paris said.

He had tackled a fellow police officer in what would certainly become the 'middle-of-a-hotel lobby' when this story started to make the rounds in about an hour. And according to the blood that was coming from somewhere, he had probably fucked him up too. This was going to dog Jack Paris for as long as he knew cops.

Maybe longer.

'*Shit*, man,' Paris said, regaining his breath. 'I'm sorry, Danny.' He rolled off, onto his side, every muscle in his body now starting to howl in response to such rapid and unexpected abuse. To add salt, he barked his elbow on the edge of the soda machine.

'It's okay, Jack,' Danny replied. He stood up and straightened his clothes. A thin trickle of blood ran from his nose to his lower lip, then onto his shirt. 'It's our fault, man. We weren't thinking.'

'I thought you were going to be talking to that blonde for a while, Jack,' Cyndy said, helping Paris to his feet. 'I thought I got your attention. I thought you saw me leave.'

'*Jesus*, Cyndy,' Paris said, brushing bits of broken glass from his pant-leg. 'We're on the *job*.'

Paris turned, remembering where they were. The door to

the hallway was wide open and a crowd had begun to gather. He flashed his badge and asked them kindly to disperse, effectively blowing his cover at the Impulse Lounge for the rest of the evening. Probably, he thought, for the rest of the detail.

His face was killing him. Paris figured that he had banged his right cheek on the top edge of the vending machine when he slammed into Danny. But nothing seemed broken. He hoped.

He held the kitchen towel with the ice in it up against his face, pushed the play button on his remote, put his feet on the coffee table. He had left the movie cued up where he always had, right before the scene in which Woody Allen's character, Alvy Singer, visits Annie's parents. Whenever Paris saw the cutaway shot of Woody dressed up like a rabbi he all but died laughing. *Annie Hall* was one of the first videos he and Beth had rented as a married couple. They had seen it at least a half-dozen times since. Right now, Paris needed a laugh.

But when he saw the FBI warning flash across the screen, followed by some coming attractions, he realized that the DVD was starting from the beginning.

That was impossible.

Had someone been in his apartment?

Paris jumped to his feet. A quick glance around the room and the fact that he was sitting there watching television told him that his valuables, what few there were, were still on the premises. He bounded over to the bedroom — wedding ring, a pair of cheap watches, his Saint Christopher medal. All intact. What else was there?

Nothing.

He checked the windows, the back door into his apartment. No signs of entry, no nicks around the door locks. He walked back to the living room and stared blankly at the simple black-and-white credits to *Annie Hall* rolling by.

But he hadn't ejected the DVD, hadn't gone to the Scene Selections menu. He'd paused the DVD at a particular point, and left it there.

Hadn't he?

Another glance around his small apartment confirmed that everything was where it was supposed to be. And besides—

Hang on.

Had he seen Manfred on the way in? Of *course* he had. Manny was always at the door. What dog doesn't run to the door when his master gets home?

He couldn't remember. He panicked.

'Manny!'

The dog, who had been bunched up on the La-Z-Boy just a few feet from his master's booming shout, snoozing beneath a pair of deliciously pungent flannel shirts, levitated briefly before crashing back down on to the chair. In a moment, he shook the dream from his head, leapt on to the couch, into Paris's arms.

'Oh *man*,' Paris said, catching the dog. 'You had me going for a second.' The dog licked his face with sloppy abandon. 'Don't know what I'd do if something happened to you.'

Manny stuck his nose inside Paris's shirt pocket, instantly snapping in two the solitary cigarette his master had allowed himself to bring home.

'By the way, champ,' Paris said, holding the dog's head

between his hands and staring into Manny's lively brown eyes. 'Was somebody here today?'

Manfred yawned.

He dreamed he was in a porno theater. Sweaty purple walls, damp seats, the smell of fortified wine and urine and come and mildewed plaster.

Paris knew that the pain in his face had something to do with his presence on West Twenty-fifth Street. Payment for something, penance for something. His head throbbed. Felt oversized.

There were three or four other afternooners in the theater with him; slicked-back humps in the darkness. Paris found a seat in the back row.

He sat down, drew deeply on his dream-pint of Crown Royal and unzipped his dream-pants.

The movie that was unreeling was standard fare, a couple in the missionary position on a royal-blue bed-spread. The woman was blond and pretty; the man, in profile, Euro-swarthy. Handsome. Paris only saw them for a moment before the camera moved down their bodies, but they looked familiar, as if this was some sort of home movie footage he himself had shot years ago.

The thought made him hard. In the dream, he freed himself.

The camera panned to their glistening bodies, poring over the man's hips, tanned and muscular, silhouetted against the whiteness of the woman's thighs, gyrating, grinding. The woman's breasts rippled from side to side with each thrust; her sighing became more pronounced with each successive parry.

As their lovemaking grew to a frenzy, Paris finally recognized the woman's hands, the manicured fingernails that dug into the man's back, the very rhythm of her breathing.

When the man brought the woman to a deep, shuddering orgasm, Paris *knew*, and the knowledge filled him with rage and dark excitement.

The man was Tommy Raposo.

The woman, Paris acknowledged as he reached his own dream-climax, was Beth.

Karen Schallert's business cards produced nothing in the way of leads, nor had Wednesday night's undercover dry run yielded anything useful. Except, of course, the fable of Jack Paris's now legendary blind-siding of Danny Lawrence. There was already a photocopy circulating the Justice Center that showed a team photo of the Cleveland Browns defensive line with Paris's head stuck on to one of the linebackers' bodies.

Funny, funny shit.

Paris picked up the phone, called the Fourth District desk. He asked for Officer Daniel Lawrence.

A minute later: 'This is Officer Lawrence.'

'Danny, Jack Paris.'

'Hey killer.'

'How's the face?'

'It's okay,' Danny said. 'A little sore, maybe. But not too bad, considering that I got blitzed by a strong safety on a dead run last night.'

'Tell me that fucking team picture of the Browns is over there already.'

'What do *you* think?'

Paris shook his head. 'Anyway, I just wanted to apologize again.'

'Don't worry about it. I'd have done the same thing. Cyndy Taggart's worth saving, you know?'

'Got that right.'

'But you're going to be a legend around here for a while, I'm afraid.'

'What can I do to make it up to you?'

'Buy me a scotch and something someday and we'll call it over. Maybe I'll see you at the Caprice later.'

'You got it.'

'Listen, I got to hit the street. I'll talk to you.'

'Okay, Danny,' Paris said, and hung up, the pain beneath his bandage beginning to swell with its own remembrance of the previous night's acrobatics.

By Friday morning the trail had come full circle. With a ton of pressure from city hall, the files on all known sex offenders began to circulate the Unit for the second time in a week, even though there wasn't a cop in Cleveland who had ever run into a pervert like the one they were looking for.

Paris was willing to bet that there weren't too many cops anywhere who had.

The *Plain Dealer*, at least, had taken the story of the murders off the front page and put it in the Metro section, but still they persisted in running something about it every day. The phone had not stopped ringing since the Burchfield murder Sunday night and all the major tabloids were beginning to set up shop at the downtown hotels.

A short item had already run on page three of the *Inquisitor*.

The entrance to Cinq, Limited was impressive – light gray marble, plush carpeting, brushed-chrome appointments – and behind the posh retail store-front that graced the upper level at Tower City sat the quiet wealth of a successful international concern. Paris was met by an immaculately groomed woman of fifty or so named Rhonda Salinger. She was tall and slender and had radiant white hair that fell to her shoulders. Paris showed her his detective's shield and asked to speak to whoever was in charge of local distribution of Cinq, Limited products.

'That would be Andrea Heller. She's our regional sales representative,' Rhonda Salinger said. 'If you'll have a seat, I'll see if she's available.'

Paris sat in one of the dozen or so black leather chairs that were carefully arranged around the dimly lit reception area. Instinctively, he picked up a magazine, one he would have certainly been willing to read had it not been written in Italian.

'What can I do for you, detective?'

They locked eyes, and in that instant, they both knew. It was the blonde from Wednesday night. The one who had tried to pick him up at the Impulse. But her hair was now a reddish brown and she wore far less make-up.

As a detective, Jack Paris had a failing in that he really wasn't all that good with people's faces. Never had been. He was far more adept at reading behavior, body language. So, at first, he was only 75 per cent sure about the woman. They shook hands and Paris saw it in her eyes.

The rabbit look. Scared beneath the cool.

He glanced at the woman's left hand, saw her wedding ring, and decided to keep the obvious questions to himself until they were alone.

'This way, please.' She led him silently down a series of

corridors whose walls were decorated with large, rear-lit slides of lips and eyes and cheeks and every other body part to which one might apply cosmetics. And each photograph bore the distinctive Cinq, Limited logo of a five that turns into a white bird, wrapped in a circle.

'Abigail, isn't it?' Paris said, once they were ensconced in her spare but tastefully outfitted office. There were five windows and a spectacular view of the river.

'Andrea,' the woman said. 'Andrea Heller.' She sat behind her desk and beckoned Paris to sit in the chair opposite her.

'It's not Abigail?'

'I think you have me mixed up with someone else, detective.' The woman reached into her purse and took out a pair of glasses. She put them on and looked back up at Paris, as if they might hide a significant portion of her face and therefore obscure her real identity. 'My name is Andrea.'

'You weren't at the Impulse Lounge Wednesday night?'

'Uh, no,' she said. 'I was home that night. With my husband. I've never even heard of the – what did you say the name was?'

'The Impulse Lounge. The bar at the Embassy Suites Beachwood.'

'No. I played Scrabble that night with my husband,' she said, committing the cardinal sin of offering up too much information without being asked.

Paris figured that the operative word here was 'husband', so he decided not to press her on this point. Yet.

'Well,' Paris said, 'in the course of a homicide investigation we've run across a product of yours that was used by more than one of the victims. What I need is a customer list. Where the product is available retail in this area.'

'What product is that, Detective Paris?'

She was back in control, Paris thought. She's a pro. Kinky, but a pro. 'A face powder called Chaligne. That's one of your products, isn't it?

'It is.'

'Would you be able to give us a customer list for Chaligne?'

'That would be no problem at all.'

She rose from her desk, crossed the room. 'There's coffee on the credenza,' she said. 'Help yourself.'

When she left the office Paris poured himself a cup, did a casual nosing around of the room. Scandesign, high-tech furniture: gray and white. A quick glance at the photo on the desk neither confirmed nor denied the fact that the man in the picture was the guy hanging around the perimeter of the Impulse Lounge. This man had a long, straight nose and wavy hair. Paris studied it. Could have been the guy.

Which led Paris to two questions.

One: What kind of sex game were these people playing?

And two: If it had nothing to do with the murder investigation – which he fairly was certain it had not – why the *hell* was he so interested?

'Here we go,' Andrea said, striding silently into the office and handing Paris a short stack of photocopies. 'I gave you all of Ohio. I wasn't sure how far you wanted me to go.'

'Ohio is just fine for now,' Paris said. 'And I really do appreciate your time.'

'That's quite all right.'

'By the way, how much does this particular powder retail for?'

Andie sat on the edge of her desk. 'Chaligne retails for anywhere from sixty to eighty dollars, depending on the store.'

'Is that a lot?'

'Not really. We have other lines that retail for much more. They're sold online, and in Saks, Bergdorf, Neiman-Marcus. Because Chaligne is more affordable it is available in a lot of places. Over fifty stores and catalog outlets in northern Ohio.'

'Is *that* a lot?'

'Yes, it is,' she said, smiling. 'We have a very aggressive sales force.'

Paris saw a flash of the man-eater she was when she tried to pick him up at the Impulse.

Back, he thought as he stood to leave, when she was a blonde.

Paris pulled the car over at the corner of West Thirty-fifth and Franklin just as the rain began to come down in sheets. Tommy, who had been standing in the doorway to Minerva Beauty Care, made a dash for it with a newspaper over his head, cursing each drop of water that hit his Zegna suit.

'*Fuck* this weather.' Tommy slid in, slammed the car door behind him.

'We've got two left,' Paris said. Chaligne was available at nine Cleveland locations in all. They had visited seven. 'Allied Salon Products on West Forty-fourth, and DeQuincey's on Clark and Fiftieth. We could almost walk.' Paris handed Tommy the list and looked over his shoulder at the traffic. 'I'll tell you what. I'll drop you off at Allied and swing by to pick you up when I'm done with the other place.'

'No,' Tommy said.

'No?'

'I'll take DeQuincey's.'

'What's the difference?' Paris pulled out into traffic.

'I want to hit Clark News. It's two doors down from there and I want to pick up a *Racing Form.*'

'I'll get it, Tommy.'

'Jack, I owe Benny DeMarco for like six months of forms. Gotta be up to a three hundred-fifty bucks by now. I was gonna take care of him today, but if you want to pay him for me.'

'Um, no.'

'A'ight, then,' Tommy said, doing his wiseguy thing, shooting the monogrammed cuffs of his shirt like a mobster. 'Drop me off close, though. I'm not walking in this shit.'

Paris opened the bell-clad door to Allied Salon Products and immediately noticed a rather plain-looking woman in her late thirties running a feather duster over a long row of aerosol cans. She had dishwater-blond hair that drooped into her face and wore a pale-lavender cotton dress, tan Rockport walkers.

'Hi,' Paris said, shaking off the rain.

The woman looked at the floor, as if he had shouted at her. Her name tag said 'Sam'.

'Hello.'

'I was wondering if—'

'Can *I* help you?'

The man appeared to Paris's left. He was loud and fragrant, overdressed for the warehouse ambience of his showroom. He was fiftyish and balding, but impeccably groomed and accessorized. His tag said 'Mr Hendershott'.

Paris turned open the wallet bearing his shield and got right to business. 'Do you carry a product called Chaligne?'

'Of course,' Hendershott offered, snapping to attention, energized by the intrigue of having a policeman in the store.

'Would you have a recent customer list handy?'

'It's all on the computer,' Hendershott said. 'Right this way.'

Hendershott moved with a feminine grace through the labyrinth of shelving. He reached the back counter and tapped a few numbers into his computer terminal. He brought his bifocals to his face and grimaced. 'Just six this month. Not good.'

'All to one person?'

'No, no, no. Six separate sales,' Hendershott said. 'Chaligne is relatively expensive. For us, anyway.'

'Can you tell me who bought them?'

Bifocals back up. 'Five of them are cash sales. No record of their names, I'm afraid. One's a credit-card sale, but she's a regular customer.'

'Her name?' Paris held his pen expectantly over his pad.

Hendershott frowned but, after a few moments, gave in. 'Dorothea-with-an-e-a Burlingame. But Miss Burlingame has got to be eighty-five years old if she's a day.'

'That's okay,' Paris said. 'You never know where a lead is going to come from.' He replaced his notebook and handed Hendershott a card. 'If you think of anything.'

'Certainly.'

Paris turned to leave — the weight of having to ask the same questions a thousand times suddenly draining him of all energy — and smiled perfunctorily at Sam. He placed his hand on the worn brass knob, and saw it.

It had been propped against the top of a wooden bin full of small shampoo samplers the entire time, daring him to notice, mocking him like the old arcade steam-shovel games that never gave you a really good grip on that pack of Luckies with the lighter strapped to it: 'The Penrod Collection', it read in faded blue and red type. 'Mustaches of Distinction for Men of Action.'

Freddie Mercury, Paris thought as he walked back to the counter. The man in the Penrod Collection logo looked just like the late Freddie Mercury.

'Let me see,' Hendershott said. He keyed something into his computer, scrolling through screen after screen. 'Nope, haven't sold one of these mustaches in, well, I haven't sold one this year. Last year either. Not a one.' He looked over at the display card, wrinkling his nose. 'Nobody really wants them anymore, you see. In fact, I don't even know why they're out here. I haven't seen the Penrod Collection in a very long time.' He shot a reproachful look at Samantha, who reacted by lowering her eyes and dusting a little faster.

'Could one of these mustaches have been sold recently without having been recorded on your register?' Paris asked.

'Absolutely *not*,' Hendershott said, somewhat indignantly. 'Everything is rung up.'

'I'll need to take two of them with me. I'll sign a receipt, of course.'

Hendershott rolled his eyes, as if he had been asked to donate a few thousand gallons of perfume to an old-hookers' charity.

'Will the department reimburse me if something happens to them?' he asked as he reached beneath the counter and retrieved a narrow plastic box with a thin block of Styrofoam along the bottom. He put the mustaches inside and clicked the box shut.

'Of course,' Paris answered. He signed the receipt, took the box, dropped it into his pocket and headed once more for the door.

'They're fifty dollars, you know,' Hendershott added. '*Each*.'

Paris stopped, turned in the doorway, glanced back. 'You know, I'm going to go way out on a limb here and suggest that's why you haven't sold one in two years.'

18

Until the Blue Lantern, I hadn't been completely sure.

We had dared the semi-public venue on a few occasions. Like the time she sat on my lap, wearing a full peasant skirt, sans lingerie, on the crowded RTA. During the twenty-minute ride I was able to work myself out of my zipper and deep into Saila. As we sat in the corner fold-down seat — lost in a forest of overcoats, elbows, umbrellas and briefcases — the rhythm of the train and the nearness of those sweaty strangers brought us both to a silent, blazing orgasm as the car roared through the East Fifty-fifth Street station, the lights dimming and flashing and strobing above us.

But that night at the Blue Lantern was the first time she ever went violent.

She wore a lemon silk dress.

We had eaten only appetizers, so we were still rather frisky, not too weighed down by the food. Friskier than usual perhaps because of the bottle of Wan Fu wine we had polished off and the half-joint of *sensimilla* we had smoked on the way to the restaurant.

'Fuck me in the bathroom,' I said.

Her voice dropped a half-octave. 'Bad little *tomcat.*'

I moved closer, ran my eyes over her chest, her shoulders, up to her mouth.

'Go into the bathroom,' I said. 'Take off everything under your dress and walk back to the table. I want to watch every man in here get hot.'

I glanced at the 'Rest Rooms' sign at the back of the restaurant and then at Saila, who was beginning to color. I moved my hand between her legs and squeezed gently. Saila responded with a short gasp and a slight arch of her back, thrusting her breasts up against me. She clamped her thighs around my hand and smiled.

'What do I get out of this?' she asked.

I grabbed her hand and brought it under the table. I moved it a few inches down my leg.

'And what about later?'

A few more.

'I think I'm going to order us a brandy,' I said. 'This is a brandy caper, don't you think?'

She looked at me, her eyes full of a mischief, and said, 'Make mine a double.' She slid out of the booth, grabbed her shoulder-bag and started toward the back of the restaurant.

A full five minutes passed.

Then, a glimpse of silken hair in the dim light of the hallway told me that Saila was coming. The sexy, confident click of her heels on the hardwood floor kept time with my accelerating pulse.

Ten minutes later, in the car, she placed a perfect leg over the front seat and whispered my name. But before we could consummate our passions, we saw Emily Reinhardt walk across the parking-lot.

And everything changed forever.

*   *   *

If there was a kick to it all, besides the obvious, it was getting ready to go out. Because, despite the danger, despite the *forever* of it all, the foreplay was *my* end of things, and I could never get enough.

It may have been too early in the season but I selected a cream-colored ventless linen sportcoat by Valentino, flat front black slacks. My shirt was a straight-collared white Ike Behar. I wore no tie. My shoes were black Santoni.

Friday.

Saila had said, 'look smart,' on the phone and, in British vernacular, one of her favorites, that meant *dress*.

19

At 12.40 a.m. Saturday morning, while Jack Paris stood at the bar at the Emerald Lounge on Euclid Avenue dressed in his borrowed jacket, chatting with a short, thrice-divorced woman named Laurel Bettancourt, the man and woman responsible for the recent wave of killings in Cleveland, the ones who called themselves Saila and Pharaoh, but only after sundown, figured out precisely what they had to do. They knew how risky it was, of course, but they agreed, without discourse, that they had no choice.

Soon.

Two

Tantrum

20

Paris wanted Melissa to give the woman the benefit of the doubt. But, like all young girls of her age (almost twelve) and delicate position (child of divorce), Paris knew that she lived for the day her parents would come to their senses and realize that they just couldn't live without each other, that they had made a huge and terrible mistake and that from there on in, the divorce would be over and every Easter and Christmas and Halloween and Thanksgiving and birthday would be spent together, cross-legged, in their pajamas, on the living-room floor, like families are supposed to. And they'd take a lot of pictures and laugh themselves silly at something Daddy did. And they'd have their old house back.

Jack and Beth and Melissa Paris.

Maybe a brother for her to pick on.

But until then, if she had to put up with the Dr Bills of this world, Paris hoped she would warm to the women her father brought around too.

Paris swung into a parking-space and stepped out of the car, straightening the front of his brand-new sweater. His casual-date sweater. One hundred and twenty bucks he didn't have. He started anxiously toward the door to the theater.

'Wait for me, Dad,' Melissa said.

She called him 'Dad'. It sounded so *teenaged* to him. He

was counting on 'Daddy' for at least a few more years. 'Sorry.'

They grabbed each other's hands, instinctively, as they had in every parking-lot since Melissa had taken her first rambling steps out of the stroller. Paris wondered if his daughter was embarrassed yet. Most pre-teenagers would rather be eaten by sharks than even be *seen* with their parents, let alone *touch* them.

But neither of them let go.

Not yet.

At least three times during the movie there was some kind of sexual reference that made Paris squirm. He couldn't believe what was passing for PG-13 these days. He'd picked the movie because the reviews said it was okay for twelve and up, but every ten minutes or so there was some kind of sex thing.

He was dying.

To make him even more uncomfortable, each of those times, as if on cue, Melissa and Diana glanced at each other and giggled. They seemed to be sharing 'girl' moments, and the thought both scared and intrigued him. He wanted Melissa to like Diana, but he didn't want to feel excluded.

Later, as they sat in the Food Court finishing their Cinnabon pastries, Paris couldn't get a word in edgewise. But it wasn't as if he had anything to contribute anyway. The talk between Diana and Melissa ricocheted from boys to clothes to music to boys to school to boys to movies to martial arts to *colleges*. None of the topics were a part of Paris's knowledge base. Except college, perhaps. When he joined the force nearly eighteen years earlier, he had been one of only a handful of four-year college graduates — most of the recruits then had high-school or two-year degrees, many coming out of the military.

But Missy? College? That was still years and years and years away.

Please God, let it be years away, Paris thought.

He watched the two of them chatter away as he sipped his coffee, and wondered if he was doing the right thing.

When he heard them making a tentative date for the Home and Flower Show in a few weeks' time – plans that didn't seem to include him – Paris almost said something.

But, for reasons unknown to him, at least at that moment, he kept silent.

A swath of early hyacinth bordered Shaker Square: a soft, lilac quilt straining for the sun. The air was thick with the fragrance.

Beth sat at one of the dozen or so tables on the patio in front of the Yours Truly Café on the Square, scanning a *USA Today*, nursing a cappuccino. She wore sunglasses with burgundy frames and lipstick that matched.

'So how was the movie?' Beth asked, holding out her hands to Melissa but directing a concerned look at the bandage on Paris's cheek.

Missy ran across the sidewalk and gave her a hug. 'It was good.' She sat down. 'Daddy got a little embarrassed at some of the sex stuff, but otherwise it was okay. We had Cinnabons.'

Paris looked at Beth, shrugging his shoulders. How had Missy known that he was embarrassed? *God*, he was an open book.

He sat down across from Beth. 'You look really nice,' he said.

'Why thank you, Patrolman Paris,' Beth replied. She had called him 'patrolman' when they were courting. It was a long-shelved term of endearment that, from the look on Beth's face, had just slipped out.

Missy, having witnessed the exchange with a look of measured hope, slipped a five-dollar bill off the table and skipped over to the pharmacy.

'What happened to your face, Jack?'

Paris fingered the gauze. 'Bad guy threw a cigarette machine at me.'

Beth shook her head, remembering living with it day in and day out. 'Stitches?'

'Nope,' Paris said. 'Not this time.' He snapped off a corner of her raspberry scone. 'So how's, uh, *business*?' It sounded so strange when he said it out loud, but he was determined to change the subject.

'Business,' Beth replied, 'is *fantastic*.' She had gotten her real-estate license the year she met Jack Paris, but had put it on hold when Melissa came along. In the time they had been separated Beth had gone back to work and risen to the number-two slot at Hallsted Davidson, Cleveland's largest realtor. 'Closed on a house Friday in Rocky River. Iranian engineer and his wife. *Cash*, Jack. Can you believe it?'

He couldn't. 'I can,' he said. 'Who can resist you?'

They went quiet, looking around the square, feeling the sun on their faces, sensing the impending change of seasons in the air. When Jack looked back at Beth, she was smiling at him.

'What?'

'Nothing.'

'Right.'

Beth caved in with no further prodding. 'I saw you the other night, you know.'

'*What*?' The words sounded like another language for a

moment. He felt oddly violated but, ever the law enforcement professional, managed to calmly ask the next logical question. 'Where?'

'The bar in the Embassy Suites in Beachwood.'

'You *saw* me?' He really hoped she wasn't talking about his tackling of Danny Lawrence.

'Uh-huh.'

It was that playfully accusatory tone that only two people with a deep sexual history could recognize in each other. She even sounded a little jealous.

Paris smiled, felt himself redden a bit. 'What was I doing?' He crossed mental fingers.

'Forget *doing*. Let's talk about what you were *wearing*.'

Tommy's jacket, Paris thought. Here we go. 'What about it?'

'You looked really handsome.'

'I did?'

'Oh, *please*,' Beth said. 'You had to know that you looked good. It's just that I don't remember you ever looking so *GQ* when we were married.'

Paris debated about whether or not he should tell her that he was undercover. Seeing as Beth hadn't brought up the task-force, neither would he.

'So how'd you do with that blonde?' she asked.

Paris was stunned. It was one thing to be divorced and not know what your ex was up to. But here she was asking about his sex life. Something was definitely afoot. He felt a hopeful stirring deep inside.

'How'd I *do*?' Paris replied, thinking about Andrea Heller, still uncertain what game the woman had been playing. 'Not really my type.'

Then it dawned on him that he had a big, fat, nosy, diversionary, yeah-we're-unbridled-but-what's-up-with-this-shit question of his own. 'And what brought *you* to the Impulse Lounge, if I may be so bold as to inquire?'

Beth smiled. 'Just stopped in for a drink. Business.'

'So we're doing business in hotel bars now, are we?'

'I have to go where the *clients* are, Jack,' she said. 'Just like you have to go where the bad guys are.'

'Okay.'

'Get it, big guy?'

'Touché, already.'

Beth stirred her coffee, even though the cup was almost empty. She put down the spoon, took a few more moments.

'You know, Missy's going to tell me all about her,' she finally said.

'Who?'

'The one you bought the new sweater for. The one you took to the movies today.'

'Really?'

'*Oh* yeah,' Beth said. 'Girl code and all.'

'Is that right?' Paris hoped she was just kidding. He didn't ever want to do battle for Melissa's loyalty.

'So why don't *you* tell me about her?'

Paris gave Beth a basic description of Diana, down-playing Diana's looks. He still knew what he was doing, it seemed.

'Is it serious?'

'I don't know. How are you supposed to know?'

'Well, you just left her, right?'

'Yeah.'

'Are you still thinking about her?'

Paris found that he was. He told the truth.

'Then it's serious,' Beth said with what Paris read as a forced smile. She *was* a little jealous, after all.

'Well, it looks like you're going to get a chance to check

her out yourself. She and Missy made plans to go to the Home and Flower Show. Without me, I think.'

'I'll be gentle with her, Jack. I promise. I won't tell her how you use toothpicks and leave them lying around the house.'

'I never did that.'

'Or how you can't light a barbecue to save your life.'

'Who can't?'

'Or how you'll wear a pair of sweatpants until they drag themselves to the washer.'

'Hey. I'm just doing my part to save water.'

'But I appreciate the mini-profile. Every little bit helps. The serious stuff, though – like how she *really* looks – I'll hear that in about thirty seconds.'

'From Missy?'

'Yep,' Beth said as she arose from the table and smoothed her skirt. 'We'll be gossiping like fishwives before we hit the lobby. I'll get the lowdown on what she wore, how much jewelry and make-up she had on, if she colors her hair. Standard dossier stuff.'

Paris hung his head, clearly outgunned.

'You can't escape the scrutiny of two nosy women,' Beth added. 'Don't even try.'

'She doesn't tell me all that much about Dr Bill, you know.'

'I rest my case.'

Paris swung his legs out to the side, and when he stood up he found himself inches from Beth's face.

'Do you really have to go?' he asked.

Beth nodded. 'Got some work to do. I'll talk to you next week.'

As she leaned forward Paris turned his cheek, as was their custom. Instead, this time, she turned his head and kissed him gently, soulfully, on the lips, the first time in more than two years.

'See you,' she said, and walked toward the pharmacy.

Jack Paris could only stand mute.

21

She was ashamed of herself. She knew it was wrong. It had haunted her all weekend and she was *going* to do something about it in very short order.

But, Samantha had to admit, there was something about the whole matter that was kind of exciting, too. Sexy, in a perverted kind of way.

Morbidly fascinating.

Yet when the policeman came into the store that day, Samantha looked at him and just *knew* what he wanted, what he was going to ask about. It all made sense somehow, although she really didn't want to believe in the sense that it made. The rinses, the Irish walking-hat, the mustache. The sketch she had seen in the *Plain Dealer* didn't show much of the man's face, but it was enough. She would have known him from behind.

Because for more than a year, in her dreams, she had touched every part of the man's face — had kissed his forehead, his lips, the small, almost-cleft in his chin. In her dreams she looked like a young Michelle Pfeiffer, soft blond hair cast seductively over one eye, pinning the object of her desires helplessly to the bed.

Her Mr Faroh. Or Farrow. Or Pharaoh. She didn't know how he spelled it.

When the policeman asked Mr Hendershott about the mustache, though, Samantha knew that she would have to tell the truth. And soon. As much as she would hate to have anything happen to him, there were all those other women to think about.

But how could it be? How could her Mr Faroh be the man who killed all those women? No. His eyes were *kind*. Cultured. He was an actor, for heaven's sake. An *artiste*.

She knew that sooner or later the police were going to catch this killer, and if they found out that he got his phony mustache for free at Allied Salon Products . . .

Something would most assuredly happen, Samantha thought. Something bad.

She picked up the phone, looked at it, as if expecting it to dial itself, then replaced it on its cradle. All for the fiftieth time. She stroked her tomcat, Giacomo, debating.

But it wasn't *really* a debate at all. Because, who was she kidding? Did she really think that a man like her Mr Faroh would ever call her? Would ever date a woman like her? With her plain face and mousy hair and flat chest and knobby knees and crooked front tooth.

Fat chance, Sammy, she thought. The only reason he wanted your name was because you had to be so stupid as to give him that mustache. And then, for him, there was no turning back. He wanted to know where you lived. *Had* to know. Just in case.

He's a clever one, that Mr Faroh.

She ran a tub, scorchingly hot, dropped her robe to the floor. She stared at herself for a few resolute moments in the bathroom mirror: droopy and lined and puffy in the harsh light thrown by the single bulb hanging from the ceiling.

Thirty-seven, Sammy. Thirty-eight in three days.

She settled into the steaming tub, coming alive, feeling rejuvenated and aroused, hoping that this would be the very last time she would ever fantasize about him.

She grabbed the worn, plastic shampoo bottle and closed her eyes.

'Hi, this is Detective John Paris. Please leave your message after the tone. If this is a police emergency, hang up and dial 911.'

Beep.

'Uh, hi. My name is Samantha Jaeger and I work at Allied Salon Products on West Forty-fourth Street, and you were in the other day and you were asking about mustaches and Mr Hendershott said that we hadn't sold one in a really long time and while that is in fact true it is not exactly what you might call the truth. Call me.'

She left her number, hung up, grabbed a full breath, exhaling slowly. It had been relatively painless, she thought, this 'notifying the proper authorities'.

'See, Giacomo?' she said to the cat. 'If you just *do* things, it's so much easier than stewin' and stewin' and stewin' about them until your stomach gets all edgy and you can't eat anything.' She gently shook the rather portly cat. 'Which has never been *our* problem, has it?'

She put the policeman's card on the coffee table, walked into the kitchen and scanned the contents of her refrigerator. The same as yesterday, save for one less Diet Coke. She absently checked the cupboards, even though she knew there were no two things in the apartment that could be combined to make anything resembling a meal. Cocoa Puffs and evaporated milk. Hamburger Helper with absolutely nothing in the freezer to help. She ambled back to the living room, muted the goofy voice of Mr Howie Mandel, then dialed Domino's Pizza, her third time in three days.

Which is one of the reasons why, when the buzzer rang about twenty-five minutes later, she didn't ask who it was.

22

Sergeant Robert Dietricht and Sergeant Thomas Raposo were late for their 7.45 a.m. Monday briefing. The task-force started without them.

'We've run the name Farrow through the computers, spelled just about every imaginable way. There's sixteen Farrows in Cleveland. Ten Farohs. Three Faros,' Paris said to the handful of detectives scattered around the common room, including Tim Murdock, who was now on shared duty with the task-force, and an attractive woman Paris hadn't yet met but who looked a lot like a shrink. She had the posture, the confident bearing of education. 'We have paper on six of them,' he continued, writing the names on the chalkboard. 'Nothing bigger than a B and E, though. The rest are mostly traffic. No violence.

'Eleanor Burchfield told me she had not asked the man about his name, having assumed it was spelled F-a-r-r-o-w. It didn't occur to her that it may have been Pharaoh, with a P-h. Regardless, there's no "Pharaoh" in the databases. The FBI is currently running it through VICAP to see if there are any serial wackos out there with an Egyptian bent. On the other hand, he said his name as if it were just one word. I'm inclined toward "Pharaoh".'

'What about the make-up?' asked Greg Ebersole, who

looked to Paris about as alert on a Monday morning as he could remember seeing him. His unruly red hair was moussed and combed, his suit pressed. He looked like a cop. 'Did we get any matching MOs on any earlier victims being made up post-mortem?'

'Nothing yet. Or nothing that hasn't been closed, I should say. As for fingerprints, we've got everybody accounted for at the four scenes. The few errants that were picked up belonged to police officers. Carl McCracken, a rookie from the Fourth, dropped one at the Red Valley Inn.' Paris scanned their faces for more questions, found none. 'Cyndy?'

Cyndy Taggart stood up, flipped open her notebook. 'No connection yet between Reinhardt, Milius and Karen Schallert,' she said. 'They went to different high schools, different colleges, worked at different ends of town, they even banked with three different banks. Different health clubs, different gynecologists, different social circles. These three women did not know each other.'

'What about boyfriends? Exes?' Paris asked, finding it hard, after seeing Cyndy all dolled up the previous Wednesday night, not to look at her legs. Today she was wearing *very* tight jeans, making it even more difficult for him. 'Any crossover?'

Cyndy shook her head. 'Phoenix PD comes up negative on Milius's ex-husband. No record. Burchfield had been seeing a guy named' – she flipped a few pages – 'Peter Heraghty. But he was in New Orleans. Got his signature on a VISA receipt the day of the murder. The other two were real loners, I'm afraid. No steadies.'

Paris nodded at Greg Ebersole, who stood up, cleared his throat.

'All the women appear to have followed a similar routine, including Eleanor Burchfield. They all went solo to a club after work, had maybe one too many chardonnays and ended up leaving with our boy. All blood-alcohol levels were high, indicating that they probably had been drinking for at least a few hours.'

'Is there any evidence that they hit more than one bar on the evening of the murder, that they may have met someone and gone bar-hopping?' Elliott asked.

'No one has ID'd them at any other bars in the area. None of them smoked, so we didn't find matchbooks. No phone numbers on cocktail napkins.'

Greg Ebersole sat down.

Captain Elliott stepped forward and introduced the woman who had been standing at the back of the room. 'This is Dr Gayle Wheaton, Associate Chief of Psychiatry at Johns Hopkins. We're *extremely* fortunate to have her, but just for the week, I'm afraid.' Elliott said. 'Dr Wheaton?'

'Good morning all,' she said.

Dr Wheaton looked to be in her early forties – short red hair, fine-featured. She wore a navy blazer and pleated white skirt.

'I'm not here to subject you to Serial Murder 101,' she said. 'I'm sure you've all been well briefed on the basics of the deviant sexual mind. The reason I *am* here is to fill in a few gaps in the recent research.'

Despite her promise, Dr Wheaton proceeded to explain the very cardinal elements of the serial murderer's MO. Shrinks always have to start at the beginning, Paris thought. That way they can bill a few more hours. He listened to her explain how there is always a pattern, each murder followed by a cooling-off period, which can last from just a few hours to months and longer. She discussed how, many times, the killer would take a memento from the victim or the scene. She spoke about how they almost always act alone.

Paris knew the rudiments. He took the opportunity to slip away, check his voice mail, and find Tommy.

Eleven messages!

Message one was from Stan Azzarello of the *Midnight Beacon*, perhaps the trashiest of the tabloids. If such measurements could be made. Paris often thought that making such comparisons was like trying to judge which piece of dog shit smelled the best.

Message two was from the woman who worked at Allied Salon Products. Something about the mustache. Paris jotted down her number and made a note to call Reuben to see if FBI Hair and Fiber had gotten back to him about the mustache found in Karen Schallert's hair.

Messages three through nine were all from either national tabloid reporters or the regular group of sleazebags. The calls had come in all night. Out of habit, Paris copied these numbers down as well.

Number ten was from Melissa, who had called him at 7.05 a.m., before she left for school, to remind him about her upcoming play.

Message eleven was a hang-up.

Paris glanced at his watch and determined that it probably would not be too early to return Samantha Jaeger's call, seeing as she was a nine-to-fiver. He dialed the number, noting that she lived in Lakewood. He got her machine, left a message.

Ditto for Tommy.

He then dialed Kasimir's on Lorain, where Tommy had breakfast three or four mornings a week, but neither Kas Jaroz nor his wife, Bette, had seen him. Paris retrieved the Allied Salon Products card from his folder and was just about to dial when he noted that the shop was closed Mondays. He called anyway, but there was no answer, no machine.

Four for four, he thought.

With practiced ease he stood up, tossed the reporters' phone numbers into the wastebasket, and rejoined the meeting.

'. . . is the sort of man we're looking for,' Dr Wheaton said. 'The make-up, the mutilation caused by the removing of the tattoos . . .'

'So what does it all mean?' asked Cyndy Taggart. 'I mean, they're dead, why the lipstick and blush and mascara? The reports say there's no intercourse taking place after death. What's the *attraction*?'

'Well, the killer seems to be obsessed with the application and removal of adornments,' said Dr Wheaton. 'These are, of course, generally thought of as games young girls play. Dressing-up, putting make-up on dolls, that sort of thing. I'd say there's a good possibility that he was raised in an all-female home.'

'What about an only child, raised by his mother?' Cyndy asked.

'Certainly possible.'

The question had been bothering Paris since Rita the Barmaid had raised the possibility the previous week. He asked while the asking was free. 'What are the chances that we're looking for a woman? I mean, that this guy is partnered with a woman? As in, he's luring them to the motels and she's killing them and putting on the make-up. What are the chances we're looking for a couple?'

Greg Ebersole and Randall Elliott glanced at each other, exchanging incredulous looks, but remained silent.

'According to FBI stats, about nil,' Dr Wheaton answered.

'Less than one percent of criminals designated as serial murderers are female.'

'I'll bite,' Paris said, instantly regretting his choice of verb. 'Why?'

'We're not quite sure. The prevailing theories tend to lean toward the maternal instincts. Women tend to kill out of passion, not obsession. Men still commit most of the homicides in this country.'

Paris glanced over at Cyndy Taggart, who stuck her tongue out at him as punishment for asking such a sexist question.

'But don't think women can't be just as sadistic as men,' added Dr Wheaton. Paris returned Cyndy's sneer. 'The Aileen Wuornos case in Florida is an all too graphic reminder of the growing incidence of female serial murder.'

Paris knew all about Aileen Carol Wuornos, the road-house prostitute who was thought to have committed a string of murders along Florida's I-95, the basis of *Monster*, the film starring Charlize Theron.

When he was looking up the details about Wuornos he had also googled 'Rose of Jericho.'

The Rose of Jericho was a Middle Eastern flower that had a tendency to roll up when dry, then once again expand to full bloom when moistened. The Syrians and Egyptians had another name for it, Paris discovered, an ancient name he hoped would not be a portentous sign.

They called it the resurrection flower.

The EMS Unit was parked directly in front of 11606 Clifton Boulevard. The arched doorway at the front entrance to the twenty-four-suite apartment building was propped open with a stone pot bearing a few sadly neglected twigs, hollow stalks begging water.

The inner door was held open too – this one with a triangular wooden wedge – and as Paris scanned the mailboxes, found Samantha Jaeger's name and apartment number, and began to mount the stairs, he found himself tempted to look into whatever it was that had drawn the paramedics to 11606. Besides being a detective, he was a terrible snoop. Born to nose.

Instead he focused on his duties, grateful to be pursuing something that had even a nodding acquaintance with a lead in this case.

The hallway on the second floor was narrow and medicinally clean. The floor beneath the carpet runner had been painted a dark brown enamel and it looked as if it had been buffed once a week for years. The sconces and floral wallpaper gave the corridor a 1930s-hotel look. Warm and inviting. Paris wondered about the rent.

Maybe, he thought morbidly, the presence of the EMS boys meant there was going to be an opening.

He shook his head, amazed at the perverse nature of his thoughts sometimes, and knocked on the door to number 206.

'Are you with the police?' The voice was nicotine-raspy, frightened.

Having given up on Samantha Jaeger ever answering the door, Paris was nearly through the doorway to the stairwell when the woman opened her door and spoke. He spun around to see a short, frail woman in her seventies, bunching the top of her robe together at her throat. She held a rhinestone-encrusted cigarette holder in the other hand.

'Yes ma'am,' Paris said, producing his shield. 'What can I do for you?'

'There were two of them, you know,' she said soberly, as if passing along a government secret.

Paris walked toward the woman, who took a cautious step backward as he approached.

'Two of who?' He stopped short, not wanting to spook her. 'Two of what?'

'Two *people*, of course. A man and a woman.'

Paris could see a half-dozen cats perched in various positions through the slightly ajar door to the woman's apartment. He smelled the aroma of simmering onions and tomatoes.

'What two people would that be?' Paris asked, sensing a crackpot answer coming. Ben and Jerry, maybe.

'Two of them,' she repeated. 'They came for her last night.'

'Who?'

'And now they've found her at the bottom of the basement steps, her neck snapped in two.'

'*Who*?' Paris said, straining to keep his temper in check.

'Why, Sam, of course,' the woman said matter-of-factly. 'Sammy Jaeger. She's dead, you know.'

The words were like a roundhouse blow to Paris's gut. He heard *dead*. He heard *a man and a woman*. He turned on his heels and headed for the stairwell, hoping to catch the paramedics before they moved the body. He glanced over his shoulder. 'I'll be back up here in a few minutes,' he said, feeling winded, shaken. 'Please don't go anywhere, Mrs . . .'

She wasn't getting it.

'What's your *name*?'

'Estelle,' she said. 'Estelle Estabrook.'

'Please don't leave the building, Estelle,' Paris said, feeling lousy about barking at an elderly woman. His father, rest his soul, would have gone upside his head.

'Yes sir, sergeant,' she answered, saluting.

Paris headed down the steps toward the basement, wondering how much of what Estelle Estabrook had told him, or would tell him, was born of this planet.

As for Samantha Jaeger, and *her* relationship to this life, he would soon find out.

Samantha Jaeger's apartment was small and uncluttered, haphazardly furnished with a worn camelback sofa of indefinable color and a matching, overstuffed chair. The chair was draped with a green and white afghan and sported a sleepy, long-haired cat. The other pieces of furniture in the living room – a wobbly blond coffee table, a tatty ottoman, a braided oval rug – were all Salvation Army specials.

The only warm touch in the room – indeed the only real clue that any human lived there, besides the stack of Domino's Pizza boxes – were the bookshelves that contained row after row of brightly hued paperbacks. All romances, all dog-eared, many boasting covers with windblown muscular men and busty raven-haired women. There had to be hundreds.

He sat down at a small short-legged desk by the front door and surveyed the room. A woman's place, but only barely and then, perhaps, by default. The room had a palpable scent of loneliness.

Had she entertained men in this room? Paris wondered. Had she had parties and Christmas gatherings and birthdays and baby showers with her friends and family?

Paris thought about his own small apartment across town, with its mismatched furniture and its noisome smells of disinfectant and long-boiled coffee. Is this how his life would look to someone else? If he was taken out on the job one day, not given the chance to clean up the detritus of his existence, would some cop sit at his dining table and pity him like this?

During his formal interview with Estelle Estabrook, she had told Paris that a man and woman had knocked on Samantha's door at exactly 7.30 p.m. the previous night. She told him that she knew the precise time because it was just at that commercial break after *America's Funniest Home Videos*.

And no, she added, she didn't actually see the couple. But after forty-four years in the same apartment, she confessed, her ears had become rather highly attuned to the comings and goings and family disputes and midnight lamentations of the people in 206 and the people in 210, the apartments with which she shared walls.

She was certain there were three distinct voices. Samantha's, a voice she'd know anywhere. A man, whose baritone was deep and spooky. And another woman, who more than once had shouted something unintelligible at Sam.

Something, Estelle Estabrook believed in her Christian soul, that contained the f-word.

Paris rose, tried to plug Samantha Jaeger into this picture. She certainly wasn't the attractive career woman who fitted the killer's profile. But she *had* called and left a message on his voice mail. What had she wanted to tell him about the mustache? On the other hand, maybe the man and woman had nothing to do with anything. Maybe they were bill collectors. Maybe it *was* simply an accident. Happened all the time. He decided to head back into town, maybe send a lab team to work the hallway and the basement stairwell.

But what he saw when he glanced into the apartment's tiny bedroom nearly took his legs away.

Samantha Jaeger had built a shrine to a madman.

23

Andie didn't tell Matt about the cop. She knew that the very idea of police and courts and the very suggestion of trouble would have spooked her husband, and she wasn't done playing yet. After all, the detective's questions had nothing to do with their little game, right? *They* weren't involved with the murders, were they? So why rock the boat?

Matt wouldn't have liked the idea of her being questioned by the police, so he didn't have to know. She didn't like lying to him, but it was the only way she could think of to maintain the status quo.

The cop who called himself Jack Partridge, then Jack Paris, had looked a lot more ordinary at her office than he had at the bar, but he was still rather sexy in a rumpled kind of way. A little rough around the edges, maybe, but he had great hair, big hands. Wise, confident eyes.

Matt was out of town for two days. Ashland Oil had him on the road, a scenario that seemed to be unfolding more and more frequently at this point in their marriage. Their *childless* marriage, Andie amended, a little annoyed at her husband but not knowing why. He *was* working hard, wasn't he? So that they could live in Shaker and maintain their one luxury car and their one all-American colonial on a hill.

She was just about to open a bottle of sauvignon blanc, put her feet up and see what was on HBO, when the phone rang.

'Hello?'

'Hi.'

She didn't recognize the voice. 'Who is this?'

'Who *is* this? You know who this is.'

'No I don't. That's why I asked, see? It's what we in the profession call a *question*.'

'Don't play games.'

'*I'm* playing games?'

'Yes.'

'Five . . . four . . . three . . .'

'Don't hang up, either.'

She was sure that she didn't know the voice. Clearly it was a man, and it wasn't Matt. Unless of course Matt had a bad cold and had put a pair of Huggies over the mouthpiece. The voice had a strange electronic sound to it.

'Last chance, Sparky.'

Silence. Light breathing.

'Bye.'

She hung up.

The movie wasn't very good, something with Will Farrell. But she actually sat and watched two-thirds of it. Matt would have been proud of her.

She missed him, thought about calling him in Ashland, but it was late.

She left a few lights on downstairs, brushed her teeth and was halfway under the covers when the phone rang again. 'Hello?' Andie said, fully expecting to hear Matt's voice.

It was the breather. She had almost forgotten.

'Oh it's *you*,' she said. 'How've you been?'

'Why do you show me this disrespect?'

The voice was clearer than before. Softer, somehow. Like a breezy whisper. It actually *could* have been Matt. There was some hissing behind the voice. It sounded like long-distance static.

'Matt?'

Pause. 'I saw you at the nightclub.'

Andie wasn't sure, but she decided to play along for a little while, not wanting to kill the game if it was Matt, but not wanting to play along with some pervert, either. The sauvignon blanc put in its two cents, and it voted for the game.

'Yeah?' she said. 'Which one?'

'The hotel bar. Beachwood.'

It *had* to be Matt, she thought. Who else knew?

'Is that right? And what was I wearing?'

'You looked like a vixen. Tight career-girl suit. Underneath *that*? God only knows.'

'God and me,' Andie said, starting to sound a bit too eager. 'I can imagine though.'

Andie heard something in the man's voice that told her it wasn't Matt. The voice was too deep and authoritative. Then again, Matt Heller was always the one at the party who did the impressions, told the dialect jokes. The idea that it might *not* be her husband both excited and frightened her. A bit.

But not enough to make her hang up, she discovered.

'Can you?' Andie untied her robe, flicked off the table lamp on the nightstand and lay back on the bed.

'Yes.'

'And what do you imagine?'

'I imagine expensive silk,' the man said. 'I imagine the feel of the silk against your nipples.'

'Yeah?'

'That's why you wear it, isn't it?'

'Maybe.'

'Don't play with me.'

The voice commanded the truth.

'Yes,' Andie said. She pulled open her robe and ran her hand over her inner thighs. Her skin was supple, smoothed with lotion.

'Does it happen often?' the man asked.

'What?'

'Your nipples, standing erect. Does it happen on the elevators at work?'

'Sometimes.'

'Say it.'

'Sometimes my nipples get hard while I'm at work.'

The man exhaled. He sounded pleased with the fact that he had gotten her to talk dirty to him.

'Do you think the men notice?'

Andie licked the tips of her fingers. 'Oh, I'm certain they do.'

'Do you think they want you? Want to fuck you?'

'Yes, I think they do.'

'Think?'

'I know they do.'

'How does it make you feel?'

'Good,' Andie whispered, her breath coming in shorter and shorter gasps.

'I know *I* do.'

'You do what?'

'Want to fuck you.'

Andie liked the way the man said the word. 'Yeah?'

'Yes.'

'Tell me,' Andie said.

'Tell you what?'

'Tell me what you want to do to me.'

After Andie was certain that the man had come, that her *husband* had come, she fell silent; hushed in this strange after-glow of telephone sex.

Finally, he spoke.

'I have to go.'

'Okay,' Andie replied.

'I have work to do.'

'At this hour?'

'Yes,' he said. 'Before I leave you, let me ask you something.'

'Yes?'

'When you see me, will you know me?'

Andie thought for a moment.

But before she could answer, the man laughed softly, and hung up the phone.

Let me tell you about women. I know them, love them, adore them, couldn't imagine myself living without them for one day, one hour, one minute, one second. It is the pursuit of women that makes life endurable.

I say this because I have always been good with women. 'Good' in the seduction sense. Have you ever spent any time in a nightclub, watching a well-dressed man talking to a beautiful woman, making her laugh, getting her to slow-dance, then walking out of the club with her, only to return alone an hour or so later and start all over again?

That was me.

And it's not just about looks, you see, it's not just about clothes — although I think I might be dead myself without them — it's about *style*. And confidence. If you give a beautiful woman the impression that you couldn't care less if you got between her legs, you'll drive her crazy with desire. How *dare* you not fall over yourself to pursue me? she thinks. How *dare* you not call? Who do you think you *are*?

I'll tell you who I am. I am a most prolific lover of women; the bane of every working husband. Yet, when I give myself over to one woman, I am just another slave.

Just like every other man.

I trust my woman with my life.

The hole in the center of his forehead was less than a half-inch in diameter. Clean around the edges, except for the ash-white of the powder, the deep violet streak of the burn.

The back of his head told another story altogether. A story punctuated by the dried clumps of pink and gray tissue that clung to the lampshade and stereo receiver behind the chair.

The .38 Smith and Wesson Police Special was taped to his hand and wrist with a huge ball of silver duct tape, lest there be any frantic searching for the weapon when the team arrived, lest there be any spasming that might have flung the revolver out the window. At his feet lay an empty fifth of Absolut Citron Vodka and a pair of Gucci slippers, neatly tucked under the base of the couch.

But there was no note. No confession.

Reuben was positive, going on appearance and smell alone, that the corpse was at least seventy-two hours ripe. Which made it Friday night. Which made sense, if everything was as it appeared to be.

And Paris was far from convinced of that.

Yet the shock of the scene was still enormous, even to the so-called seasoned veteran. Cops say they get used to it after a while, but there are some things you never get used to. Dead kids. Maimed kids. Mutilated bodies. *Brains*.

You can't be seasoned enough for this, Paris decided as they zipped the plastic body bag around the man's broad shoulders.

The police officers walked silently around the living room for the next forty-five minutes, doing their respective duties, sidestepping each other, averting eyes, trying to deflect the anger and guilt they all felt, the sense of shame at not having been able to prevent this.

Paris knew he was putting it off.

He walked slowly into the bedroom and began the ritual scavenging of the dead man's treasures.

The bedroom furniture was Japanese in design: black lacquer finish, red-tasseled nylon sash cords, silver hardware. The bed was huge, easily a kingsize, probably a special-order job, which looked as if it could sleep four across. To the right of the bed stood a dresser bearing a large collection of expensive colognes, cut-crystal sentries standing guard on a carved wooden tray. Acqua di Parma, Clive Christian, Burberry, Bond No. 9 New York. Paris remembered when there were only three colognes to choose from: Aramis, Obsession, and Old Spice. This was all so foreign to him. Another world.

He pushed the bottles aside.

At the back he found a small vial of spirit gum.

The bathroom was spotless and fragrant, hardly a bachelor's strong suit, Paris thought as he pushed open the door. Gray curtain, black carpet, white fixtures. He rummaged through the drawers and cabinets and found just what he expected to find, the usual minutiae of an unmarried man: nail clippers, Bic razors, airline soaps, mint-flavored floss. He looked into the wicker wastebasket. A pair of used Band-Aids they would bag for blood type. There was also a brightly colored box bearing the words 'EZ Color Fashion Rinse'.

The closet. A dozen suits, as many brilliant white shirts, all carrying names Paris knew only from the magazines: Armani, Valentino, Hugo Boss, Prada. There were a dozen pairs of shoes all filled to their welts with cedar shoe trees, all reflecting back a funhouse-mirror face at Paris. At least a hundred ties, thirty or so belts.

Paris stepped back, stood on his tiptoes and, within a few moments, found what he was looking for.

On the uppermost shelf, perched atop a quartet of meticulously folded Ralph Lauren and Dior Homme sweaters, sat an Irish walking-hat.

Paris knew where he would find the patches of skin.

The rose tattoos.

He just didn't feel like opening the freezer yet.

26

When the buzzer rings at one o'clock in the morning at the Candace Apartments, it is never good news. Pick one: some crazyass, some *drunk* crazyass, or one of Jack Paris's long list of junkie informants in need of a cure.

He was a third of the way inside his own evening's whore, a fifth of Jameson, when he finally marched over to the intercom. He shushed Manny and pressed the button, expecting anything.

The last person he expected was Diana.

'I heard, Jack,' she said. 'I'm sorry.'

She took off her coat. She was wearing an oversized white shirt and denim skirt.

Paris didn't know what to say. He was so full of rage and sadness and impotence. He felt the same debilitating weariness he had felt the moment he knew his marriage was over.

Diana took the cue and pulled him to her. She grabbed the bottle from his hand, placed it on the end table and held him close.

Within a few moments, she kissed him for the very first time.

* * *

'Cindy Crawford.'

'Okay,' Paris said. 'Good one.' He looked at the ceiling, lost in thought. 'Okay, how about Dale Bozzio?'

'Who?'

'Dale Bozzio.'

Diana looked at him sceptically. 'I thought we were just doing women.'

'Dale Bozzio *is* a woman.'

'Never heard of her.'

'She's real, I'm telling you,' Paris said. 'Hers is right where yours is.'

'Sorry. I think you're making it up.'

'Are you challenging?'

Diana thought for a moment. If she challenged, and was wrong, she'd have to take a drink. 'Yeah.'

'Google her.'

'How do you spell her last name?'

Paris told her. Diana entered the information on her Mac Book Pro. Seconds later she had a photograph of the former lead singer of Missing Persons on the screen. 'Damn.'

'Told you,' Paris said. 'Bottoms up.'

Diana obeyed, taking the bottle in hand, tilting her head back in deference to the smooth Irish whiskey.

They were sitting on the couch, facing each other, their hands from time to time finding each other's knees and thighs and shoulders as they told their stories. They had talked for what seemed to be hours – about the case, about themselves, about the nature of life and death. Somehow, they had drifted into this drinking game. They were about two inches from the bottom of the bottle of Jameson, but that was okay. Paris had another.

The game was naming famous women with beauty marks.

'Your turn,' Paris said.

Okay. 'Lil' Kim.'

Paris hadn't the slightest idea who Lil' Kim was. 'Okay,' he said. How about—'

'You don't know who she is, do you? You're just trying to get me drunk.'

'What are you talking about? I've loved every single one of her movies.'

'Albums.'

'Albums.'

Diana laughed. She handed Paris the bottle. He swigged. It was getting to be a very loopy game.

She waved it playfully in front of his eyes, then tossed it to him. A latex condom. 'Don't even *say* it,' Diana warned, the color began to rise in her cheeks.

'What was I going to say?'

'Some kind of Girl Scout joke' She stood up, unzipped her skirt, stepped out of it. 'Something about being prepared.'

She sat on the coffee table in front of him, the tails of her big white shirt between her thighs. Paris looked down and saw that her toenails were painted a blood red. Diana reached into her shirt pocket and produced a perfectly rolled joint.

'Ms *Bennett* . . .' Paris said. Surprised but not shocked.

'Yes, detective?' She batted her eyes demurely, licked the end of the joint, lit it.

'Are you aware of the fact that you are endeavoring to use a controlled substance in the presence of a police officer?'

'Yes,' she said, releasing the smoke slowly. 'But it's just that I'm trying to get control *of* the police officer.'

'Is that right?'

'It is.'

She leaned forward and put the joint to Paris's lips. He drew on it deeply. Immediately the pot found the booze in his system and put an entirely new, euphoric perspective on the evening. He let the smoke leak out of the corners of his mouth in thin gray ribbons. It had been ages.

Diana sat back, unbuttoned two more buttons on her blouse, the tops of her breasts now visible through the folds of white cotton. She ran her hands slowly up his thighs, back down.

'I'm afraid I'm going to have to place you under arrest,' Paris said, slurring the word 'place' so that it sounded like 'plaish'.

'I don't see that you have any choice,' Diana said, hitting the joint again, passing it back to Paris. 'I'm completely incorrigible. Irredeemable in the eyes of this court.'

Paris took another hit, nearly coughing it out. 'You have the right to remain sexy,' he said.

'Uh-huh.'

'Anything you hold against me,' Paris continued, 'will be held against *you*.'

'Fair enough.' She finished unbuttoning her shirt and pulled it down over her shoulders, letting it drop to the floor as she worked her way between his legs.

'You have the right to be an attorney.'

She unbuttoned his shirt and kissed her way down his face, his neck, his chest. She kissed his stomach and pulled open his belt.

'And . . .' Paris continued.

Finally she worked his pants open and started running her tongue around the tip of his penis. She sat back on her heels.

'Jack.'

'Hmm?'

'Tell me about the first time you saw me.'

'What do you mean?'

'The first time you saw me. What did you think? Did you want me?'

'*Oh* yeah.'

'When I questioned you on the stand. Were you thinking about it then?'

Paris didn't have to think about it. 'Yes.'

She leaned forward, this time taking him fully in her mouth, but only for a few seconds.

'*Tell me what you want, Jack,*' she whispered.

She flicked her tongue out once, twice.

Paris could not answer.

She gently pulled Paris to his feet and steadied him at the foot of the couch. She reached behind her and lifted the venetian blind to the top of the window, displaying the two of them dimly to the night, to the parking-lot that faced Eighty-fifth Street and the handful of cars that grew out of the darkness there.

'*Say my name,*' she said.

The next thing Paris knew he was on his back in bed, and Diana was on top of him. He was deep within her.

'*Jack.*'

A whisper.

To Paris, her voice was floating somewhere between the smooth jazz coming from the radio and the traffic noise below. A voice from his past, it seemed. Patches of sound. The room decided to spin again.

Diana leaned forward, lips close to his ear.

'*Do you still think about her?*'

Too much booze. Four-o-five, according to the bright green numbers of the clock radio. She was leaving.

'Don't go,' Paris said.

He wanted her to stay, to be there in the morning. Because this time it felt different. Of the handful of times he had had sex in the past two years he had not wanted any of them to stay.

He tried to sit up, but his body deserted him. His mind was working overtime.

Tommy.

Diana stood at the foot of the bed for a while, darkly silhouetted against the now drawn blinds.

'Lie back down.' She prodded him gently, her voice calming, her hands now so familiar. She zipped her skirt, put on her shoes. 'Come on. I'll help you.' She lifted the covers and pulled Paris's feet toward the foot of the bed, covered him. 'I have to go, baby.'

Paris rose unsteadily on to one elbow. He tried to put the day's events in order. As much as he wanted to push the horror of what had happened earlier away, it kept rushing back with brutal, debilitating force.

Tommy Raposo was dead.

Moments later, when Diana closed the door behind her, Paris rolled on to his back, his body flat against a wall of fatigue, his mind a dark deadfall of questions.

Three

Furore

27

In the photograph her mother was beautiful. Her complexion looked perfect in the early morning sunlight, her hair, a symphony of reds and browns and rusts and silvers. Hairdresser hair. But then again, she was only twenty-eight years old at the time the photograph was taken, brash and still defiant, her rose tattoo brazenly exposed on her stomach, just below her midriff shirt.

And why shouldn't she look good?

Why shouldn't she look like a movie star?

She was standing in the doorway to their apartment at Holly Knoll, the ever-present menthol cigarette growing out of the V between her painted fingernails, the ever-present purple bruises mottling her thighs and arms. She was off to work at some beauty parlor or another, the longest stint being the one she'd had at the Hair Force on Victorville Road, next to the Cork and Bottle.

And although she had long ago completed her two-year course in cosmetology and had the most extraordinary cheekbones, she'd never quite gotten the hang of putting on make-up. At the distance from which the photo was taken, her cheeks appeared to be slashed with a thick streak of crimson, giving her the painted look of a warrior-squaw.

* * *

Lois Bentivegna liked to dance naked for her boyfriends, and she did so, with a remarkable amount of vigor, right up until the cancer stopped her at thirty-four. She never danced professionally in any sense – her Christian upbringing would have squarely prevented that – but once in a while, on a Friday or Saturday night, after she'd had a few tumblers of Southern Comfort, she would put on an old Kool & the Gang tape and strut around the apartment, Styrofoam cup in hand. She'd usually make a sexy outfit out of whatever she had available, whatever was clean and wasn't too elastic-worn.

All the while she believed her daughter to be safely stashed away in her room with a pizza, along with her own TV and her very own Princess phone. Sometimes she'd let her daughter have a friend stay overnight and the two girls would covertly slip out of the bedroom window and sneak around the apartment, peeking through the living-room window, hiding in the hedges, at once repulsed and deliriously stirred by the acts unfolding in front of them.

Then, one day, came the blood.

And there was change.

Because it was Lois at the door to her daughter's room that very first time, just a few years after the photograph was taken, the same year the cancer began to eat at her lungs. It was Lois, unexpectedly home early from her station at the second chair at René and Julian's at Burton Center, stepping lightly, the sounds of sex drawing her silently toward the door, the unmaskable sighing of a young woman, inexperienced to the touch and rhythms of a man, drawing her closer, closer.

Lois Bentivegna didn't throw a tantrum like other mothers might have. Lois didn't burst into the bedroom that day, or any day thereafter, seething with righteous indignation, threatening years of groundings and the absolute denial of junior prom tickets.

Lois watched. Lois crept up to the slightly open bedroom door, her eye to the jamb, and watched her daughter take this young man into her hands, her mouth, her body. A fifteen-year-old girl and her sixteen-year-old lover.

Lois stood by, her own hand violently between her legs, a woman of barely thirty-one years herself, and thought of the afternoons, not all that long ago, when she had entertained a series of inexhaustible sixteen-year-olds of her own.

28

Nicholas Raposo lived in a three-bedroom bungalow in Garwood Gardens, a pre-Second World War residential development in Garfield Heights, on Cleveland's south-east side. There were no gardens to speak of, no greenery rimming the fifty-foot lots, as the northern end of the street, once a part of the MetroPark system, now gave way to I-480. It was a gray, working-class street on an even grayer day.

Paris had only met the man twice, once at the Justice Center and once at Tommy's service, three weeks earlier. He knew that Nick Raposo had been a cement worker most of his life, and his hands proved it – rough planks of flesh that seemed to swallow Paris's hand when they shook.

'Nice to see you again,' Nick said, a deep sorrow limning his eyes. Paris knew the man had lost his wife a dozen years earlier, and now his only son. The grief hung upon his shoulders like a tattered cardigan.

'Nice to see you too, Nick.'

'Come on in.'

Paris stepped into the small living room. The walls bore the odd grouping of religious pictures and gold-framed photographs of Tommy and his sister, Gina. The worn sofa boasted an orange and brown afghan – Cleveland Browns colors – and a disheveled pile of *Time* and *Sports Illustrated* magazines. Paris instantly smelled the aroma of Italian staples: Romano cheese, basil, garlic. Nick Raposo was making sauce.

'Coffee, Jack?'

'Only if it's already on,' Paris said. 'Don't go out of your way.'

'I make the espresso,' Nick answered. 'It's no problem?'

Paris held up his hands as if to say yes.

'Come on in the kitchen.'

Paris followed him into the kitchen. Although he knew Nick Raposo was still a physically powerful man, he looked small at that moment, a sketch of the man he was before death stalked his family.

Paris sipped the hot, sweet coffee. It warmed him. The house, the kitchen, the way the small Formica table butted on the wall beneath the window, the way the dish towels cascaded over the handle on the oven door – these things warmed him even more. Unlike his apartment, with its smells of transience, this was a *home*. He noticed a row of plants sitting on the windowsill over the sink, patiently waiting for spring: parsley, oregano, tarragon, chive. Things move on, Paris thought. Things grow back.

'You get Tommy's belongings from the station all right?' Paris asked, even though he knew the answer.

'Oh yeah,' Nick said.

'The stuff from his apartment too?'

Nick just nodded. The two of them were quiet for a while, the tick of the wall clock the only sound in the room. Finally, Nick spoke.

'Tommy didn't do it. You know that, don't you?'

Paris didn't know what to say. He said what he thought he should. 'I know.'

'I'm not going to tell you he was squeaky clean. I don't have that sixty-inch TV in the basement or that big Buick in the drive because of my IRAs, eh? He took care of me, Jack. He took care of his sister.'

'I know, Nick,' Paris said. 'But it's—'

'But what?'

Paris met Nick Raposo's eyes and found a deeply wounded man there. 'The case is closed, Nick. I'm afraid everybody wants it that way.'

'Not everyone.'

'You know what I mean.'

'But you can do something about it, no? You can still ask questions, can't you? You can still ask around.'

Paris realized then that he was talking to a man who still believed in a fundamental order to things. A man who still clung to the notion that if you play fair you always win. But Paris also knew that the reason he was in Nick Raposo's house in the first place was because he also knew something was wrong. He simply couldn't shake the notion that the Pharaoh case – as it had come to be known – had closed a little too quickly with Tommy's death.

'Everything I do I gotta do on my own,' Paris said. 'After hours, off the meter. You know that, right? I push too hard somewhere, hit the wrong buttons, I'm back handing out parking-tickets in Hough.'

Nick nodded in understanding. Then he looked deeply into Paris's eyes and said, softly: 'Clear my son, Jack.'

The basement was cool and orderly. On one side was a large TV and sofa. On the other, a tradesman's refuge. There was a wall of tools, along with a workbench, smooth and worn and black with years of spilled 3 in 1 oil.

The small room off the main reflected the systematic habits of the son. White boxes were stacked floor to ceiling, wall to wall. They were mostly the kind which store legal papers. All were all precisely labelled in green block letters. It did not take Paris long to find the box containing Tommy's personal papers.

On top was a stack of Playbills, mostly from the Palace or State theaters, mostly musicals: *Les Misérables, Wicked, The Jersey Boys.* Beneath them were postcards from what had to be a hundred different women. Crystal and Denise, Jackie, Barbara, Peggy, Lydia, Sarah, Junie and Annette. At least a dozen were signed, simply, 'me'.

He picked up a plain white business envelope, open at the top, jammed full of photographs of various sizes and vintages. There was a pair of Tommy and his sister in Atlantic City, a few with his mother and father at his police-academy graduation, Tommy with girl after girl after girl. There was Tommy with cops, Tommy with citizens, Tommy with crooks.

Next there was a layer of softbound books, textbooks from the feel of them. Paris lifted out three or four. *Leisures and Pleasures of Roman Egypt. A Handbook of the Ancients. Arabian Nights.* They looked like they had been opened, but not necessarily pored over for any great length of time.

At the very bottom of the box was a series of maps and travel brochures, along with a nine-by-twelve-inch brown kraft envelope that was clasped and sealed. Paris flipped it over and saw the familiar rooster scrawl of Tommy's signature over the seal. It appeared that Tommy had signed the envelope in black ink, right over the flap, so that if anyone ever tried to steam it open and then reclose it he would know. It took Paris all of five seconds to decide to tear off the top. He coughed as he did it to mask the sound of ripping paper, lest

Nick think he was doing exactly what he *was* doing: destroying evidence. If evidence is what it turned out to be. He folded the pieces of the envelope into quarters, placed the pieces in his pockets and looked at the contents.

The only thing in the large envelope was a banded stack of photographs. Both sides of the stack of photographs faced inward.

The appearance of the envelope and the feel of the photographs filled Paris with apprehension. What didn't Tommy want him to see? What secrets? What was he going to find on the other side of these seemingly benign white cardboard rectangles?

And yet, Paris thought, if Tommy knew he was going to kill himself, why didn't he just destroy them?

Paris glanced around the corner, up the yellow-and-gray-linoleum-clad steps. He could hear Nick making kitchen sounds, preparing another espresso for them.

'You need any help up there, Nick?'

'No,' Nick said. 'I'm okay.'

'You sure?'

'I can still make a cup of coffee, eh?'

Paris walked to the far end of the workshop and stood directly beneath the fluorescent swag lamp. He removed the rubber bands from the stack, and as soon as he flipped over the top photo, he realized that his vigilance had been warranted after all.

The top photograph was of a woman in S&M leather drag, her back to the camera, kneeling at the foot of a bed. It was taken in a standard motel room, with no regional clues in the decor. The bedspread looked to be dark green or dark blue. The woman's body was perfect, her waist was thin, her hips rounded and smooth. Her leather bustier crossed her back in a spiderweb of thin lines that seemed to cut deeply into her flesh.

The second photograph showed a side shot of the woman from the waist up. She had the flushed look of a woman fresh from lovemaking, but her face was once again turned away. Of the ten photographs, only one showed any degree of the woman's face, but even that shot was a profile, and she wore a thin, black-lace mask over her eyes.

There was one photograph taken outdoors, in a wooded area, a side shot of the woman with her white camisole pulled to her waist, her hands bound to a tree with what looked like electrical cord.

Tommy was not to be found in any of the pictures.

Paris turned the photographs over, one by one, looking for any writing that might have been on the backs. There was a faint pencil mark on one, something like a check mark, but nothing decipherable. He was about to flip two at a time when something caught his eye, and he had to go back a few. There, written in pencil at the bottom right-hand corner, printed in a rather childlike manner, were three words. It looked like: 'Saila does qualify'.

Saila does qualify?

What the hell did *that* mean?

Paris looked around for some sort of magnifying glass and saw that Nick had a swing-arm magnifier attached to a small table against the wall. Paris switched on the light and ran the photograph beneath the glass.

'Saila does *quality*,' he corrected himself immediately. And who the hell is Saila? And quality what?

He turned over the photo with the writing and found that it was the one picture that didn't seem to be of anyone or anything in particular. It was a photograph of a slightly opened closet door, with just the hint of something that looked like a white shoe — a white high-heeled shoe, maybe — visible at the bottom.

Paris placed the photos into his pocket, and searched the remaining boxes, finding little else of relevance, if any of this was indeed relevant. Certainly nothing to match the impact of the photographs. There were, to Paris's surprise and dismay, no financial records of any kind.

'You want this down there?' Nick asked, calling from the top of the steps.

'No, I'm coming up,' Paris said. 'I'm finished.'

'Okay. Don't forget to close the light.'

Close the light, Paris thought, smiling. Was it just Italians, or did other people say *close* the light? His own grandfather, Angelo Parisi, who had somehow managed to lose the i on the end of his name in the noise and confusion of Ellis Island, had said *close the light*.

Although it was past the middle of April, winter still roamed the streets of Cleveland. When Paris had driven to Garfield Heights, the sky had dusted the city with a light powdering of snow. Now there was blinding sunlight. Paris headed into town up I-77, getting off at the Broadway exit. He came to a stop at a red light, directly in front of the entrance to the old McCrory's five-and-dime.

Saila does quality.

He held the photograph up to the sunlight. It had been perched on the front seat beside him since he left Nick's house, taunting him, begging his glance at every stop light. This one was a low-angle, dominatrix-type shot of the woman.

Saila does quality.

I'll bet she does, thought Paris, wondering about the where, the who, the what, the why and the when of it all. Who *was* this woman? Where did she come from? Why did he have a nude photograph of her in his hand? When did she—

The man who suddenly appeared at his window and the sound of the car horn from behind him registered at the same instant.

It was the hulking gray shadow to his immediate left that unnerved him more.

Paris turned quickly and saw that it was a homeless man, part of the Broadway squeegee brigade. It looked as if the man had come over to approach Paris about a quick wipe job, but he must have seen the photograph in Paris's hand decided to just enjoy the view. As Paris pulled away he looked in the side mirror and saw the man shake a finger at him and display a wide, toothless smile.

Quality, he thought as he cut the engine.

How about 'quality' as in Quality *Inn*?

Emily Reinhardt had been killed at the Quality Inn.

'Sorry about your friend,' she said.

'Thanks,' Paris replied. 'But it's not like, I don't know like I can say I *knew* him now, you know? It's still pretty hard to believe.' Paris sipped his coffee. 'My *friend*.'

John Q's was jammed with the lunch crowd, the impending spring giving license to everyone to speak a little more loudly, a little more animatedly than they had all winter. On this day, for Jack Paris, it was just an annoying wall of noise.

But Rita the Barmaid had left a rather urgent-sounding message on his voice mail and said that she would be at *this* table, at *this* restaurant, at *this* time, and if he wanted to talk . . .

He knew exactly what was on her mind.

'I'm afraid I was as fooled as everyone else,' he said.

'You don't sound too convinced, if you ask me.' Rita gave her hair a quick toss over her shoulder and bit into her sandwich. As she continued to speak, Paris noticed a drop of mayonnaise that had made its way on to her chin. He was going to point it out to her but he already knew enough about Rita Weisinger to wait until she had made her point. 'I guess what I'm trying to say is, that's not the guy. The guy in the picture that was in the newspaper and on TV? The cop they say did it? Tommy . . .'

'Raposo.'

'Raposo,' she said, rolling the r. 'Anyway, I don't know how to put this. It's just not the guy I saw with the Burchfield woman. Definitely not.' She paused, placing her sandwich on her plate, waiting for Paris's reaction to this case-breaking bit of evidence.

'I know,' Paris said. He absently waved his finger near his mouth, hoping Rita would catch the vibe and wipe her chin. After a few beats of silence, she did.

'You *know*?'

'Yes.'

'How?'

'Well, number one, why else would you ask an old flatfoot like me out to lunch unless you had something you wanted to add to the Pharaoh case? And two, if you look at it with any objectivity, the sketch doesn't look like Tommy. It could be him, but it could also be a hundred thousand other guys in this city.'

'Exactly.'

'But the bad news is that all the evidence was there, Rita. It was way too pat for me but it was still a grand jury's wet dream. The hat had bloodstains tied to two of the victims. The make-up kit was found in the trunk of his car. And the patches of skin, for God's sake.'

'I don't know. It just isn't in your friend's *eyes*, you know? I mean, I can tell a lot from looking into a man's eyes. And even in that shitty photo they published in the newspaper, I could tell.'

'Well, the case is frozen shut. Captain Elliott is happy, the prosecutor's office is happy. Tommy Raposo was this unknown, up from Summit County four months ago, nobody really knew him well. A real department outsider.'

Rita shook her head, new to the machinations of institutional politics. She asked a few more why-not-and how-come-there-isn't-type questions as they finished their lunch. Halfway through coffee, Rita waved for the check.

'So, what are you going to do?' she asked.

'Now? Well, I'm going to go back to work, Rita. I've got three unsolveds on my plate and I have no partner,' Paris said. 'Anything I do about the Pharaoh case is going to be off the meter. And probably very stupid. Not to mention a huge waste of time.'

Rita looked at her watch, stood up to leave. 'Well, if you need any help with any after-hours sleuthing, you let me know. I'm really good when it comes to these sorts of things.' She reached into her purse and dropped a pair of twenties on the table. Then, anticipating his reaction, held up a hand to deflect Paris's protest about her paying the check. 'By the way, this is the last time I'm going to fling myself at you like a wanton woman. Ball's in your court, officer.' She swung her bag over her shoulder, the early afternoon sunlight rushing through the windows, painting her hair with highlights of gold.

'And me with this wicked forehand,' Paris said, surprised at his burst of wit, his sports reference. He had never played a game of tennis in his life.

Rita leaned forward, kissed him on the cheek, then smiled as she thumbed away the lipstick. 'Call me.'

She turned, left the restaurant, trailing a long wake of rubber-necking men – young, old, and those of Jack Paris's rather ill-defined vintage: somewhere in between.

The Homicide Unit was beginning to recover from the media blitz that began about twenty minutes after Tommy's body hit the freezer and didn't even begin to abate until two weeks later. But now, despite the best efforts of the tabloids, the cop-haters and the loyal political opposition, the story was being eclipsed by other, more pressing problems facing the Best Location in the Nation. The Unit averaged about eighteen homicides per month and usually maintained no more than twenty detectives at any given time. So, given the average daily shitfall in a city like Cleveland, the shitstorm eventually passed.

And then there was a threatened garbage strike which, in a purely sensory capacity, eclipsed everything.

Yet any time a police officer is directly involved in a big-time felony, or some kind of sex crime, it was always a huge embarrassment for the department. When you combine the two, the fallout is devastating and, considering the longevity that sex gossip usually has, politically far-reaching.

After a few thousand missiles from all corners, the department's new whiz-kid spin doctor, a PR flack named Teddy Dahlhausen, had somehow managed to put the Pharaoh case into manageable media blocks. The grand jury was satisfied with the evidence that linked Sergeant Thomas Anthony Raposo to the deaths of Emily Reinhardt, Maryann Milius, Karen Schallert and Eleanor Burchfield, and that seemed to be that.

Paris reached his desk and was relieved to find only three messages waiting for him: Diana, Cyndy Taggart, and Beth.

Three women. Could be much, much worse, he thought as he picked up the phone, then pecked out his wife's number. Could have easily been three guys named Rasheed, Nunzio, and Hector.

He left a message on Beth's cell phone, then dialed Cyndy's number.

'Got some stuff of yours,' she said. 'You must have left it in my car that day we staked out the Versailles.'

Paris hadn't touched base with Cyndy Taggart since the debriefing. Cyndy worked out of the Fourth.

'Thanks, I'll pick it up at the station.'

'You all right?'

'Yeah,' Paris answered. 'Barely.'

'If you say so, Jack. Anyway, maybe I'll drop it all off to you tomorrow. I'll be up around Eighty-five and Carnegie after dinner.'

'Okay,' Paris said, distracted. He decided to trust her. 'Hang on, Cyndy.' Paris looked into the duty room, into the adjacent offices. The floor was very light with detectives and other personnel. Greg Ebersole was in his office with his feet up, sawing logs. Paris closed his door, picked up the phone.

'You know I'm not happy with how fast this was all shut down.'

'I know,' Cyndy said.

'I'm going through Tommy's things at his father's house, and I found these photographs of a woman. And it's wild stuff.'

'What do you mean?'

'Well, it's sadomasochism. Costume stuff.'

'Tommy is in them?'

'No.'

'Can you identify the woman?'

'No. Can't see her face in any of them. But believe me, you sure can see everything else.'

'And why do you think this woman is tied to the murders?'

Paris wasn't sure. He told Cyndy that.

'Tommy *did* get around, you know.'

'Yeah, but there wasn't any S&M stuff in his belongings,' Paris said. 'No magazines, videos, books. No whips and chains. Certainly nothing like this.' Paris fell silent for a few beats. 'So tell me, Cyndy. Why can't I shake the idea that there is a woman involved?'

'Because now you've got photographs.'

'I suppose.'

'Okay, Jack,' Cyndy said. 'I have a few minutes. Gimme the list.'

'Okay. One, the make-up kit. Just doesn't fit with Tommy Raposo, does it? He's cutting up women, wiping their faces clean and putting make-up on them like he works a cosmetic counter at Macy's? Make sense to you?'

'Nope. Next.'

'Samantha Jaeger.'

'What about her?'

Paris hadn't told anyone about the Jaeger woman's bedroom. He wasn't going to start now, either. The Jaeger woman's death was ruled accidental, so there was no homicide investigation. 'I know her death was an accident, but the older woman next door said she heard a man and a woman arguing the night Samantha took the fall.' Paris heard someone walk by his door. He waited a few seconds. 'I don't know. There's a woman around here somewhere.'

Paris went on to tell Cyndy about the 'Saila does Quality' message on one of the photographs. Cyndy said that the name held no significance for her either, but was much quicker to pick up on 'quality' as meaning a possible location.

'You think "Saila" is the woman's name?' Cyndy asked.

'Don't know. But I'm going to run it anway.'

'Okay. Anything else?'

'Well, last but not least, of course, is the fact that we have no razor. If someone was setting Tommy up, why not leave the murder weapon? I mean, with all that neatly placed evidence in Tommy's apartment, why not give us the weapon? You can pick up a straight razor for twenty-five bucks. Why not leave it?'

'Unless.'

'Unless you weren't done with it.'

'So . . .' Cyndy began, knowing full well the answer, but playing the game all detectives played: Saying It Out Loud. 'What's the next step?'

'Next step is to revisit the Quality Inn and see if the photo matches up with the guest room where Emily Reinhardt was killed. If we get a match there, I think we can get the DA to consider reopening the case. We've got an accomplice.'

'Makes sense.'

'We'll talk later,' Paris said as Bobby Dietrich knocked on his door and then entered anyway.

'All right,' Cyndy said. 'But now you've got me thinking.'

'Good.'

'I'll stop by with your stuff tomorrow.'

'Thanks.'

'Maybe I'll go with you to the Quality.'

'Even better,' Paris said, and hung up the phone.

After Dietrich left, Paris called Diana.

'Are you going to make it to the Home and Flower Show with us?' she asked.

'Us,' Paris repeated.

'Melissa and I are going tomorrow? Remember? We talked about it?'

'Yeah, sure,' Paris said. 'I remember. I just don't think I can go, Diana. I'm buried down here.'

'Are you sure this is going to be okay with Beth? This strange woman doing something like this on a Saturday afternoon with her only daughter?'

'Believe me, if you're okay with me, you're okay with Beth. I'm a cop, remember?'

'You're right. I just get a little paranoid. There's three people I want to like me now and it's too much.'

'You'll wow her,' Paris said.

'Kowloon Garden afterwards? On me?'

'I'll do my best.'

Paris hung up the phone, awash with Dad-guilt. He hadn't seen Melissa for more than a few minutes in the past two weeks, although it was certainly understandable in the light of the Pharaoh case aftermath. He had caught the last five minutes of Missy's play, but when he went backstage afterwards he immediately saw that he wasn't fooling her into thinking he had seen the whole thing. If pressed, she would have asked him specifics anyway, and he would have caved.

Missy was a very bright girl, very worldly for her age. She read the newspapers and she watched the local news and she knew full well what had happened where her father worked.

She knew that the man who had killed those women had worked with her father.

The information, unfortunately, was not lost on some of Melissa's schoolmates, either. 'M. P. is a pervert' showed up written on the blackboard in her homeroom one morning. Another creative young artist had ripped an illustration of an Egyptian mummy out of a school encyclopedia and drawn a rather obscene appendage between the figure's legs, then taped it to Missy's gym locker. The 'Pharaoh' aspect of the case had been well publicized.

Paris put his feet up and attempted to catch a nap.

He tried to remember if there really *was* a time when art class meant white paste, construction paper, and safety scissors.

It was Friday and this glorious stranger stood a few fragrant inches away from me. We were in a quiet, multi-roomed nightclub called Whitney's.

Saila and I knew that we shouldn't have been out playing so soon, but spring was in the air, I guess.

'You look like a very young Jeanne Moreau,' I said. 'Around the time she made *Five Branded Women*, I'm thinking.'

The edges of her mouth turned up slightly, but she wasn't quite ready to release the smile just yet. Her eyes betrayed her, telling me that my reference was not lost on her. Nor were my looks. She was dressed conservatively in a burgundy tailored suit, cream blouse and navy heels, yet there was no concealing the fullness of her breasts, the firmness of her upper thighs. She was a working woman, a citizen, and the very idea sent my blood to steam.

The fact that Saila was standing right behind me, sipping her drink at the bar, made the moment all but unbearable.

'Do I?'

'*Oh* yes. But sexier,' I replied, moving closer to her. She didn't flinch or pull away in the slightest. 'Jeanne Moreau was so, how should I put it, two-*dimensional*.' My knee touched hers, a delicious shiver. 'You, on the other hand, are flesh and blood.'

Her hand trembled a bit as she reached for her nearly empty glass, betraying her resolve to remain in complete control of the situation. I was intimidating her somewhat and, as always, that pleased me.

I imagined her to be about twenty-eight or so, probably married, probably a suburban mommy, although she wore no wedding ring. Her blond, permed hair was obviously a wig, but perhaps that was part of her appeal for me. She was out to play. She fancied herself the conquering bitch, and for the moment, I let her believe it.

She called herself Abigail.

After a very erotic slow dance, we returned to the bar. Saila was on the loose. I didn't see her.

'Can I get you something?'

'White Russian,' she said.

I motioned, ordered. Out of the corner of my eye I could see her looking me up and down, further cruising my wares, as it were. She was very well accessorized herself, tasteful, with moderate-to-expensive jewelry, just a few show-pieces. A very pretty Piaget watch. Her make-up was flawless.

She was also petite in just the proper, most appealing ways: small hands and feet, a tiny, turned-up nose, a narrow waist.

Our drinks arrived. I clasped mine, an Absolut on the rocks, with my cocktail napkin – in case a quick departure was forthcoming – and raised the glass.

I recited: '*Hold fast thy secret, and to none unfold. Lost is a secret when that secret's told.*'

We touched glasses, sipped.

'What does that mean exactly?' she asked.

'It's a caveat. It's from the *Arabian Nights*.'

'That's odd.'

'What?'

'You don't *look* Arabian.'

'I know,' I said. 'I'm very aware of my appearance.'

'I'll bet you are,' the woman said, fashioning her mouth first into a smile, then around her straw. Her lips were scarlet. I imagined them doing all sorts of things.

'So, what's an intelligent, cultured woman such as yourself doing in a common roadhouse such as this?' I asked. 'And why on earth would you entertain a villainous lout like me?'

'Oh,' the woman said, searching for a morsel of wit. 'You could say I'm slumming.'

'Really?' I asked. I put my hand upon her leg. She tensed the slightest bit but did not resist me. Instead, her eyelids fluttered once and I knew that she was mine. 'And just what is it that you're used to?' I moved closer.

'I'm used to the best.'

'The best.'

She looked at my lips. 'Yes.'

'And what if I told you that you had never once *had* the best?'

'I'd say . . .' she began, her hands finding my waist, giving in to me. 'I'd say *show* me.'

She leaned forward, ran the tip of her tongue over my lips, then pulled away.

God, I loved a challenge. 'Come with me,' I said.

'No.'

'Come with me now. Just for an hour.'

'No.'

'You're going to play with me, aren't you?'

'As long as I can.'

'I think your time is running out, kitty-cat.'

Without further talk the blond woman in the expensive

suit and the harlot's wig took me by the hand and led me toward the lobby, full of sass and self-possession.

I knew we were being watched, of course.

My only hope was that, for everyone's sake, he was part of the game.

30

Paris did his best to block out the conversation around him, even though it was quiet, piano-bar talk, cool and important: Land Rovers, stocks and bonds, the films of Miranda July, smart drugs.

He had other things on his mind.

So many things didn't fit. For instance, the time of Tommy's call the night of the Schallert murder. Tommy had taken the call at 1.12 a.m. Saturday, and called Paris at the Caprice Lounge at 1.18. Tommy had indeed called from Berea.

The coroner's office was able to do a liver-temperature reading on the body and the reading put the time of Karen Schallert's death at very close to twelve-thirty, which made it at least *possible* for Tommy to have driven to Red Valley.

The woman Tommy was with that night – one Arlene Ward – said Tommy had gotten to her place around a quarter to one, maybe one o'clock.

And then there was the fact that Tommy's hair was dark brown, so why on earth would he *dye* it dark brown? Yet, the lab had found traces of the EZ Color Deep Chestnut in Tommy's hair.

And then there was the matter of Samantha Jaeger's bedroom. A sick little ditty known only to Jack Paris and Mr

Larry Goldblatt, the super at 11606 Clifton Boulevard.

Paris conceded that he might never understand the significance.

Because, of the 140 photocopies Samantha Jaeger had tacked to her bedroom walls – photocopies of the killer's sketch that had run in the *Plain Dealer*, blown up to an eight-by-ten size – fifteen of them had been drawn upon. She had smeared lipstick on the man's lips, rouge in the hollow beneath his cheek-bones. The lenses of his glasses were tinted yellow and orange and amber, some gradient. The rest of the black-and-white images were untouched, showing the same idiot repetition of the grayed-out tweed of the man's Irish walking-hat, the same cleft in his chin. Paris imagined the woman furtively visiting a Kinko's Copy Center at three in the morning with her *Plain Dealer*, running off all those copies of the composite sketch, taking them home, mounting them carefully on the walls, drawing on them and then . . . what?

Something twisted, he was sure.

The bottom line was that the department had lacquered the case shut the moment the story had moved to the Metro page.

Bullshit.

Paris had seen Diana three times in the previous weeks, but it had never matched the first night. Or maybe it was just the stress of the case that made him think so.

Why was he so worried about it becoming something?

He dropped a twenty on the bar, made his way to the men's room, did his business. He stepped out of the bathroom and was just about to cross the lobby when he saw her. He knew who it was, even before she turned and showed him her profile.

It was Andrea Heller.

And she was once again decked out in her B-girl-blonde regalia.

Abigail.

Paris stepped back into the men's room, his heart pounding. He waited a few moments, pushed the door, peeked out. Andrea Heller was standing in front of the hotel, arms crossed, shivering in the chilly night air. Finally, a white BMW pulled up and she got in.

Paris followed.

31

Matt Heller thought: *What the hell am I doing?*

None of this had been planned to his satisfaction. Not really. Control was a very important part of his fantasy life and Andrea, it was clear, had just decided to wrest it away from him. Part of it was very exciting. Part of it scared the crap out of him.

She had leapt up from her stool and walked out of the bar with this attractive man, without even giving him a high sign of any sort. What if he hadn't been watching them at that precise second? What if he didn't think it was such a good idea? What if the car hadn't been able to start?

What if Andrea was a lot more involved in this game than he had ever known?

Regardless, there he was, following his wife and another man to God knows where, to watch them do God knows what. He had always wondered what Andrea would be wearing when this finally happened; what he would finally, after all these years, see some other man unsnap, unzip, unhook, undo.

Matt Heller had also thought that what was about to happen to him would happen just once in his life, then they would go back to their marriage as if it had never happened. Each to their own private fantasies. And although he had planned it a thousand times over, now that it was unfolding in front of him like some steamy off-off-Broadway show, now as he drove four car-lengths behind his wife and another man, now that he was so furiously aroused, he wasn't at all certain he could go through with it.

Because, besides being the most outrageous thing he had ever concocted, wasn't this also the most dangerous? Didn't that psycho-cop who killed himself prove that you can never tell about people?

Matt followed the white BMW from a safe distance, not knowing that yet a third car was a few lengths behind *him*, heading to the same destination.

Matt thought: Why does it have to be a fucking BMW on top of it? Couldn't he look like that and drive a Kia or something? Or a Focus?

Matt decided to call it off. The minute he found out where they were headed, he would find a way to call it off. He would say he is Andrea's brother or something, in from Waukeegan, with the sad news that Uncle Conway had died and that his six Akita pups needed a home.

Fantasies, unlike reality, Matt Heller thought as he rounded the exit ramp, are a lot more manageable.

And probably, he was all but certain, a whole lot safer, too.

32

Paris parked on the berm of the road and walked back the quarter-mile to the single-story, rust-red building that formed the L-shaped Motel Riverview in Russelton, about thirty-five miles east of Cleveland. It was a mostly rural area, and while the motel had a small neon sign on Townshend Road, it was virtually hidden from the highway, set back a few hundred yards and bordered on three sides by a gravel parking-lot that quickly gave way to the forest.

From his position behind the first layer of second growth, Paris found himself completely obscured, yet no more than forty feet from the building. The two windows to the right were dark, but the third window, the window that corresponded to the BMW parked on the other side, was illuminated, perhaps by a light left on in the bathroom. The glow gave the impression of a diaphanous curtain drawn on a tiny stage.

Moments later a woman's hand flipped on the light in the main room. The bright rectangle of color in the darkness looked like a film unreeling, or perhaps some big-screen television that someone placed in the middle of the forest.

Because the shade was half drawn, Paris could only see part of the man as he stood against the far wall and removed his jacket, then his shirt. His abdomen was hard and rippled, his arms muscular. He wore black pleated trousers and a thin belt. Paris occasionally caught a glimpse of Andrea Heller's profile, she being by far the shorter of the two, but he could not see the man's face. He would have to get closer.

Paris argued that part of him was there, hiding in the woods like a Peeping Tom, because he felt in his heart that the Pharaoh case was not closed, and that this somehow would give him insight. He argued back that there was something about the prospect of watching this woman have sex that was driving him mad.

Hadn't he thought about Andrea Heller a number of times since they met at the Impulse Lounge that night? Hadn't he wondered what sort of game she was playing?

Now, it appeared, he was going to find out.

He watched the man remove her blouse and unzip her skirt, letting it slide to the floor. She wore a claret-colored camisole.

They kissed for a while, caressed for a while. Then, in one powerful movement, the man lifted Andrea Heller and put her roughly on to the bed.

As they made love, Paris could only discern the back of the man's head, his matted hair and the sinewy tiers of his back and broad shoulders. His face never came into view. As Paris stood up and tried to achieve a better vantage point, he realized that his left leg had fallen asleep. He immediately fell backward into a tree trunk, which, mercifully, was substantial enough to hold him. He righted himself, turned back to the room, and—

The explosion, the huge barrage of fireworks that Paris figured was located about an inch or so behind his eyes, came in bright orange bursts which, were it not for the pain at the base of his skull, would have been tolerable.

Then came the pain.

Then, the darkness.

Whoever had hit him from behind had been either a true professional or a true amateur. Paris had not 'seen the lightning' in a few years. Whoever had belted him had either clipped him just right – so he'd be out for only an hour or two – or had tried to kill him and missed completely.

But there was little doubt in Paris's mind who had hit him. He figured it was the guy he had seen hanging around the edges of the Impulse Lounge that night, the one he'd pegged as Andrea Heller's husband.

Either way, all things considered – the fact that it was four-something in the morning, the fact that he was lying facedown in a gravel parking-lot in Russelton, Ohio, the fact that he probably had it coming for being such a pervert – he *had* felt worse.

Paris sat up, focused on his watch, the ache sitting at the base of his neck like a full hod of bricks. His hands then instinctively tapped where his gun and shield should have been, and he was very pleased to find them in place. Then he tapped his jacket pocket and that gratifying sense of satisfaction left him just as quickly.

The photographs he had found in Tommy's belongings were gone.

Saila does Quality.

Shit.

He should have stashed them away somewhere.

The light in window number three was off now, as were all the other lights in the motel. A check of the parking-lot in front showed Paris that the white BMW was gone too.

He found his legs, then his car, then his car keys.

An hour later he was throwing up in his kitchen sink.

Five hours and six aspirin later he felt nearly human.

At 2.30 p.m. he got up and went to open his door for his newspaper. He found a yellow Post-it note stuck to the inside doorframe, and his paper lying on a nearby table. He brought the note over to the window, trying his best to focus. He didn't immediately recognize the handwriting. It read:

> *Stopped by, came in, decided not to wake you. (Why were these doors unlocked, detective??!!) Off to pick up Melissa for the Home & Flower Show. Hope Beth doesn't hate me (nervous). Had to change on the fly so please mind my overnight bag. Hope you can meet us at the restaurant as planned . . .*
>   *Diana*

Paris looked at the couch and saw the Louis Vuitton bag. It looked new. The desire to peek inside was overwhelming, but Paris bullied it back for the time being.

He had no idea what Diana had come by, but he did recall hearing Manny let out a few barks sometime early that afternoon. He had shushed him, and the dog, not exactly Conan the Terrier anyway, had curled up on the bed.

Paris poured a second cup of coffee and flipped open the paper. It was the first day since Tommy's death that the story wasn't mentioned, even in a short item.

Hallelujah, Paris thought, as he gulped his coffee and headed for another scintillating adventure in urban bathing – a cold, brown shower at the Candace – a session during which he would, unknowingly, wash all traces of blood off his hands.

*   *   *

At five-thirty the buzzer sounded. It was Nick Raposo. He was carrying with him a bulging plastic garment bag.

'Nick. What brings you here?'

'Got a few things,' Nick said, puffing from the four flights of stairs, handing Paris his hat and coat. 'Thought you might like to take a look at them.'

Nick caught his breath while Paris hung up the man's coat, then poured him a cup of coffee.

Paris explained to Nick that there were no leads yet, nothing to deflect Tommy's guilt in the Pharaoh killings, but that he had a few ideas he was going to follow up on. For the time being, Nick Raposo seemed satisfied.

'My brother's a tailor, Jack,' Nick said, crossing the room and grabbing the garment bag. 'Fuckin' genius at it, too. Always was. I figured you to be a forty-two long. Here. Try this on.' He held up the suit coat.

Paris slipped on the cashmere blazer, and it was a perfect fit. Right down to the sleeve length. He may have felt like a dirty dime, but he looked like a million bucks.

'The pants,' Nick continued, 'the pants we work on later.'

'Nick, I don't think I—'

'Hey, don't worry about this stuff being Tommy's. It's just things, you know. No soul, no heart. Why waste them? I sure as hell can't use them.'

'I don't know what to say.'

'Then don't say anything.' Nick waved a hand at the door. 'I got a box of stuff in the car, too. Books and CDs and other things I want you to have. Jazz and some other crap. R'n'B. Whatever the fuck that is. On the other hand, if it ain't Frank or Tony Bennett, I'm kind of lost, you know?'

'Thanks, Nick.'

'Not a problem. Now get your ass downstairs and get the box out of my car. I'm too old to be hauling shit that heavy up four flights of stairs because you can't live in a building with an elevator.'

In the larger of the two boxes Paris found some of the books he had seen when he went through Tommy's belongings in Nick's basement. He flipped open one book, *A Handbook of the Ancients*. It was inscribed: 'Happy Birthday from Marta, Danny, Chauncey and the rest of the crime-drones at the Fourth.' Paris knew them all. Marta was Marta Perez, the bombshell dispatcher. Danny was Danny Lawrence. Chauncey was Ed Chance, a lifer with a job-related limp and a pair of Great Danes the size of a loveseat.

Next was a stack of CDs and a pile of T-shirts from every major airport in America. Tommy had a thing for flight attendants. Underneath was a small leatherette photo album, one Paris had not seen before.

The first photo in the book was Tommy sitting on a concrete bench at Disney World, holding a plump little girl about two years old on his lap. The girl, who had curly blond hair and wore a neon-orange sun bonnet, didn't look anything like Tommy, so Paris figured she wasn't his child or even his niece. Paris marvelled. It wasn't as if there weren't enough single women in Cleveland. Tommy found a way to date women with two-year-old kids.

The second photograph in the book was of Tommy in a cream-colored suit, his arm around the waist of yet another gorgeous woman. It was taken at what looked to be the lobby bar at the Ritz-Carlton Cleveland. The woman had long dark hair, shapely legs. The moment Paris was able to tear himself away from the woman's legs he noticed something else about her.

It was Diana Bennett.

Midway through Diana's overnight bag, Paris got pissed off. Pissed at the world, pissed at his stupid fucking life, pissed that he had allowed himself to tumble even an inch for this woman, pissed that he was, at that moment, rifling her bag for the childish reason of finding not only more evidence that she had slept with Tommy Raposo – which was none of his goddamn business anyway – but evidence that she was tied to a series of homicides.

There had been nothing remotely kinky about the photo of Tommy and Diana. Nothing perverse at all. It was just a party shot of sorts; a posed picture, snapped through a boozy haze. All potentially explainable. Tommy was a cop, Diana was a prosecutor. Cops and lawyers hung out all the time.

You're losing it, Jackie-boy.

He reached deeper into Diana's bag, pulled out a short black slip and bra. Next, from the large pocket at the side, he retrieved a zippered, clear-plastic make-up bag. It was the same size and type as the make-up bag found in the trunk of Tommy Raposo's car.

'No,' he said aloud. 'God no.'

Paris dumped the contents onto the dining-room table and his eyes were immediately drawn to a powder compact. He picked it up, turned it over. Engraved in silver atop the slim ebony case was the understated logo of a bird morphing into the number five. Beneath it, a silver, engraved word:

Chaligne.

*   *   *

'I have to say, I'm a little jealous, Jack,' Beth said over the phone. 'I didn't think she'd be so, I don't know – what's the word I'm looking for here – beautiful? I guess that *would* be the proper one. If you like perfect looks, that is.'

'Beth.'

'Actually, now that I think about it, I'm jealous.'

'Are they back yet?' Paris asked, trying his best to mask any hint of fear in his voice.

'What is she, a size *five* for God's sake?'

'Are they back yet, Beth?'

'Not yet.' Her tone shifted, the playfulness gone. She had made him. She knew him well. 'Why? What's wrong?'

'Nothing,' Paris said. 'We were all supposed to hook up for Chinese food later and I don't remember if it was the Golden Dragon or Silver Pagoda. Some precious metal as I recall.'

'Jack.'

'I'm telling you, nothing's wrong. Listen, I gotta run, so I'll either meet up with them, if I can figure the restaurant out—'

'Kowloon Garden.'

'Thanks.'

'You sure everything's all right?'

'Yes.'

'Okay, then.'

She didn't sound convinced.

Paris rounded the corner and nearly knocked over Cyndy Taggart. She was still in uniform.

'As promised,' she said, regaining her balance. She held forth a pair of gloves and sunglasses, task-force leftovers that Paris, in keeping with most of his adult life, figured he had donated to the Land of the Lost Father's Day Gifts. 'Dig these Maui Jims, though,' she added. 'Almost kept them, except they're a little too big for me.'

'Knock-offs,' Paris said. 'Got them on Prospect somewhere. You of all people should know that I can't afford Maui Jims.' He turned on his heels. 'Come on up for a second.'

'What's going on? You don't look too good.'

Paris opened his door and they stepped into his apartment. 'I'm okay.'

'No sale, pal.'

She gave him that fellow officer/mom look that told him he should have his head examined rather than try and lie to another cop. He caved.

'You know Diana Bennett?'

'Sure,' Cyndy said, sitting on the arm of the couch. 'I mean, I've met her at the grand jury when I've testified. She's questioned me. Why?'

Paris told her the barest details of his past three weeks with Diana and how, without thinking about it too much, he had let her take Melissa to the Home and Flower Show. He told her about the Chaligne compact in Diana's overnight bag, as well as the photograph of her and Tommy.

'Well, number one, the Chaligne doesn't mean anything. Lots of women wear it.'

'Okay, but that just means—'

'Do you have the pictures you found at Tommy's father's house?' Cyndy asked.

'No,' Paris said, hoping Cyndy would buy it. 'They're downtown.'

'Exactly how kinky are they?'

'Nothing really hard-core. But I have the feeling these weren't the first pictures of that type she's ever had taken.'

'That's a long way from serial murder, Jack.'

'What I'm saying is—'

'What you're saying is that you somehow think this "Saila" might be Diana Bennett.'

Boy, did it sound stupid when she said it out loud. 'I don't know what I'm trying to say.'

'I think you're losing a little perspective here, detective. I mean, how do I put this delicately? You've been *with* Diana. In the biblical sense. Don't you—'

'Recognize her body in the photographs?'

'Yeah.'

'No. It was dark and I was drunk. There isn't quite enough in the pictures to rule her completely in or completely out.'

Cyndy shook her head. 'You men are unbelievable. We do this long, complicated dance for you, we finally give it up and you get so drunk you miss it.'

Paris shrugged. She was right. 'What can I say?'

Cyndy looked at him for a long moment. 'So where are you heading?'

'I guess I was going to stop at the Home and Flower Show and peek in at them. Just take a look from the upper deck at Public Hall and prove to myself that I'm a paranoid asshole. If I didn't see them, I was going to go to Kowloon Garden. Then I was going to head out to the Quality Inn.'

'I'll go with you.'

'No, Cyndy,' Paris replied. They stepped into the hallway. Paris locked his door. 'I can't ask you to give up your Saturday evening.'

'It's no problem. Personally, I think you're blowing this way out of proportion, but I understand your concern.'

'You sure?'

'Don't worry about it. Besides, we don't have any tickets to the Home and Flower Show and the way you look you won't be able to bull your way in with a badge.'

She was right. 'Thanks.'

'Just want to stop at my place and get out of my blues. Follow me. We'll take one car into town.'

Paris put a hand on Cyndy's arm. 'Is this little excursion going to remain between you and me?'

'You mean like me deserting my post at the Impulse that night?'

'Exactly.' They descended the steps.

'You're my kind of man, Jack Paris.'

'How long have you lived here?'

'Almost two years,' Cyndy called from the other room. 'Two years this July.'

'Nice,' Paris said, running his hand over the cherry credenza in the dining area, holding a well-groomed Persian cat in the other hand. Like everything else in Cyndy's tastefully appointed apartment at the Terrace View Towers on Cedar Hill, the cat looked European. It smelled of fresh lemons. 'I never knew you were such a decorator.'

'Let's just say my ex is doing pretty well.'

Cyndy swung out of the bedroom buttoning her short denim jacket, carrying an oversized shoulder bag. Once again, Paris was disarmed by her out-of-uniform looks.

Cyndy checked the action on a small, nickel-plated .25 semi-automatic pistol, snapped in a mag and put it in her purse just as Paris's cell phone rang. He answered.

'This is Paris. SIU there yet? Call me when they get there.' He clicked off. '*Fuck.*'

'What's up?'

'Got a warm one at King-Kennedy. And I'm up, damnit. I need coffee bad.'

Cyndy sat on the arm of the couch. 'Look, none of this Diana business is going to amount to anything anyway. You're just being paranoid.'

Paris considered his actions of late. 'You're right.'

'But if you like, I'll go meet up with them. I've met Diana, she knows me. I'll pick Melissa up and take her wherever you want. I'll say you decided to take Melissa to a movie, and it starts at whatever time et cetera, et cetera.'

'I guess that sounds okay.'

'Then you and I will go to the Quality Inn,' Cyndy said.

Paris knew he was overreacting, but he decided to take Cyndy up on her offer. 'Okay. Check the show, check Kowloon Garden. If you catch up with them, just bring Missy to my place and I'll stop there as soon as I can, all right?'

'You got it.'

'Thanks, Cyndy,' Paris said. 'Ring the super at my place and show him your shield. Name's Jimmy DeBellis. He'll let you in.'

'No problem,' she replied, opening the door. 'And relax. Everything's just like it's supposed to be. Make yourself coffee, wait for your call. Just close the door when you leave. It's already locked.'

'I owe you, Cyndy. Big-time.'

'Believe it,' she said with a smile, and left her apartment.

On one wall of Cyndy Taggart's dining room was a huge Georgia O'Keeffe reproduction, expensively framed. The floor was highly polished and the wall coverings were very subdued, very tasteful. Lots of beige and brown and brass and antique-type things. Paris flipped through her CDs. Oldies, jazz-fusion, show tunes.

He sipped his coffee, found the remote and clicked on the TV. He surfed the channels for a while, landing on the

Cavs-Knicks game on ESPN. But he found himself glancing at his watch far too often to concentrate on what the Knicks were doing to his beloved Cavs.

Ten minutes later, his call-back came.

The King-Kennedy homicide was a fifteen-year-old dealer named Ramon Jackson. He had been shot point-blank in the back of the head, twice, Scarface-style, and he still had more than $2,000 in his pockets. This was clearly no robbery. There wasn't much left of Ramon's face, but one of his cousins identified him to police based on the Raiders jacket he wore with the embroidered 'RJ' along the waistband.

The interviewing went surprisingly quickly – Paris suspected that no one had seen a thing, or would admit to it, and he was right – and he was in and out of the scene in less than an hour. He stopped home, found no one there, then drove back to the Justice Center.

Paris called Cyndy, got her voicemail, left a message. He paged her, drew a cup of coffee. After filing the report on the King-Kennedy shooting, he laid out the pictures of the four serial victims on his desk, and realized immediately how ludicrous it was to think that Diana was in any way involved in this. What was wrong with him? Was he *that* pissed off that she had taken a picture with Tommy Raposo?

Maybe that sap to the back of the head was worse than he thought.

The truth of the matter, Paris conceded, was that he was overworked. The truth of the matter was that he was never going to be comfortable with the idea that Tommy was solely guilty, or even guilty at all of the Pharaoh murders, and it was that feeling, combined with the lack of sleep, that was making him stupid. The truth of the matter was that Diana, Cyndy and Melissa were probably, at that very moment, sitting at Kowloon Garden with a puu-puu platter and three bowls of wonton soup in front of them, trashing the hell out of one John Salvatore Paris, Paranoid Supreme.

That was the truth of the matter. Still, even though he believed all of the above:

He dialed the Kowloon Garden and got a busy signal.

He dialed Diana's number and got her machine.

He dialed Beth's number and got her voice mail.

He paged Cyndy again.

He waited.

The kid had the stringy blond hair and multi-colored bicycle shorts that identified him as an urban surfer. As he approached, Paris saw that under his arm was a zippered nylon courier pouch, thus explaining his presence on the sixth floor.

'Are you Detective Paris?' the kid asked.

'Yeah. What's up?'

'Sign here, please.' He held forth a clipboard and a ballpoint pen.

'What, you guys are seven days a week now?'

'Yes sir. Twenty-four hours a day, too. Since Feb. one.' The kid checked his beeper, retrieved his clipboard and handed Paris the package.

Paris flipped him a pair of dollar bills and examined the outside of the cardboard envelope. Beneath the FleetGram logo it read, simply, 'Det. Jack Paris.'

'Have a good one,' the courier said.

'You too.' Paris was just about to open the envelope when

Brian Sands, one of the desk cops on duty, came lumbering up the steps, papers in hand.

'Message for you, Jack,' Sands said, clearly out of shape and out of breath. He put his hands on his knees for a few moments. When he recovered sufficiently, he said, 'Cyndy Taggart from over at the Fourth called and said to tell you she didn't see anyone at Public Hall. Said she's heading over to the Chinese place.'

'She called the desk?' Paris asked.

'Yep.'

'Why didn't she just call *me*?'

Sands just stared at him, as if the question could be anything but rhetorical. Brian Sands was fifty-seven years old, impatient by nature and tired as hell. 'I don't know, Jack. We didn't discuss it.'

'When did she call?'

'Ten, fifteen minutes ago, maybe.' Sands stood in the doorway and arched a single eyebrow, waiting.

'Oh, uh, thanks, Brian.'

'Betcha,' Sands said, and headed down the hall.

Paris sat for a few moments and wondered if Diana and Melissa were already en route to Beth's place, or if Cyndy was going to catch them at the restaurant. Then he remembered the package on his lap.

He tore open the top of the package and pulled out an envelope, white, unmarked. Inside that was a three-by-five index card with some typing on it. There was also a photograph. When Paris pulled out the picture and turned it over, he felt his breath suddenly lunge through his chest.

The photograph was of him.

It was outdoors, at night, and he was propped against a tree with what looked to be a pearl-handled straight razor in his right hand. Over his left shoulder was the neon Motel Riverview sign. He appeared to be just resting against the tree, as if he were looking down at the razor, but Paris knew for a fact that he was out cold.

On the index card, the message was also quite clear:

> Go to Shaker Square. Park directly in front of the florist.
> Bring all P files and this material. Speak to no one.

The *Hellers*? He was being set up by the fucking *Hellers*?

He didn't buy it for a minute. Andrea Heller might be a little kinky, her husband might be the kind of guy who drilled holes in the girls' shower wall when he was in junior high school, but they were no psycho killers.

But if not them, who the hell else was out there in the woods with him that night?

Paris looked at the typeface. It was a standard Times Roman 12-point. Common to just about every word-processing program out there. He found the number for Fleet Courier Services on the outside of the envelope and dialed it.

'Fleet.'

'This is Detective John Paris with the Cleveland Police Homicide Unit. I just received a package a few minutes ago and I'd like to ask you a few questions about it.'

'Sure thing,' the man replied.

Paris heard the plastic click of the keys and a loud burst of laughter in the background. Outside his own window, a cruiser went by at full speed and full siren. Finally the man said, 'Yep. Have it right here. Detective Paris at the Justice Center. What can I tell you about it?'

'I need to know who sent it.'

'I'm afraid I don't know that, sir.'

'You don't have a record of who sent the package?'

'Well, it's not required. I mean, if someone is paying cash, as they did in this case, we don't require a sender's name or address. We ask, but we don't demand. The important part is where the package is going.'

'Where and when was it picked up?'

Paris heard a few more key clicks.

'It was picked up at six-fifty this evening.'

'Where?'

'Six floors beneath you,' the man said. 'In the lobby of the Justice Center.'

The file boxes for the Pharaoh case took up the entire front and back seats of Paris's car. In all, it amounted to a cargo of nine legal-size storage containers. The boxes were empty of course, but Paris had to play the game, had to maintain appearances until he clamped the irons on this motherfucker. The complications of actually *bringing* the files with him — legal, ethical, logistical — were enormous, so that was never an option.

Besides, this operation wasn't going to take anywhere near that long, or get anywhere near that far.

Paris found a space directly in front of the florist on the northwest quadrant. He cut the engine. It had rained briefly and gotten completely dark during the ride out to the square. Except for a few window-shoppers and late RTA commuters, the area was relatively empty of activity. He positioned his rearview mirror and side mirrors to his best advantage and slumped down in the seat.

Soon, a woman approached the window at the florist. She wore an oversized tam-o'-shanter and an overcoat that looked to Paris to be a bit bulky for the fifty-degree evening. She perused the display of flowers for a few moments, hesitated, looking left and right, then moved on. She rounded the corner onto South Moreland and disappeared.

Five minutes later, just as unease began to set in, Paris noticed a white rectangle stuck into the hedges directly in front of the hood of his car. It briefly fluttered into view, then out. It looked like it might have been an envelope, but it was partially hidden in the dark recesses of the hedge. Paris got out, retrieved it and found that it was, in fact, an envelope, sealed, bearing the initials J. P. Inside was another typed three-by-five card, which read:

> Leave car unlocked and walk across the square. Stand in front of the theater. Will flash headlights when done.

Shit.

Paris looked around the quadrant, at the scores of shops, office buildings and apartment complexes. He was sure he was being observed, so he shifted to plan B. He closed the car door and walked the 100 or so yards to the far side of Shaker Square, crossing South Moreland against the light, counting his steps, calculating how long it might take him to sprint back across. He stood directly under the brilliant marquee of the Shaker Square Cinemas, and felt the temperature around him increase a degree or two.

Soon a figure approached his car, but due to the distance and the darkness, Paris couldn't tell if it was a man or a woman. The door swung open and the figure entered from the driver's side. Paris moved to the edge of the sidewalk. He could see a flashlight moving around inside the car, its beam playing off the white interior ceiling. Paris stepped out on to Shaker Boulevard and waited for the traffic to pass, hoping he could take advantage of that small window of opportunity between the time his suspect saw the boxes were empty and the time his suspect turned to bolt.

Paris drew his weapon and ran.

Before he had taken three steps, the car door slammed hard and the figure ran through the breezeway between the shops, toward the parking-lot on Drexmore.

Paris gave chase, racing across the square at full speed, nearly slipping twice on the rain-slicked RTA tracks in the process. By the time he reached the parking-lot it was dark and empty. Just a few cars scattered around. Nothing moving.

He caught his breath slowly. When he was satisfied that he had fucked up the one and only lead he was ever going to get in this case — a case that was officially closed — he walked back to his car and looked inside. A few of the cardboard boxes were slashed, as was the upholstery on both the front and back seats. Paris got in and pounded his fists against the steering wheel.

And that's when he saw the third white envelope on the dash-board. He opened it. Inside was a picture, a photograph that told Jack Paris that nothing was closed.

Nothing at all.

33

'Hi, how was the show?'

Beth found it hard to believe that she was sitting there chatting on the telephone with her husband's new girlfriend. What a difference a few years can make, she thought. At one point in their relationship she and Jack had even resorted to eavesdropping on each other's telephone conversations because of their petty jealousies, and here they were schmoozing with each other's significant others. As soon as Beth heard the woman's voice on the phone, with its take-charge aplomb, any and all doubts she'd had about the woman disappeared.

'It was wonderful. I think Missy has permanently moved into the model home they've built down here. You should see the little-girls' room.'

'Justin Bieber posters and lots of ruffles?' Beth asked.

'Yep.'

'Every entertainment device at the Apple store?'

'You've got it.'

Beth laughed. 'Did she behave herself?'

'Oh my, yes. You're raising a very polite and intelligent little girl here.'

'That's very kind of you to say.'

'Did you know she had an interest in pyramids? There's a

huge one here and Missy did five minutes on the history of the pyramid. I was *very* impressed.'

'I had no idea,' Beth said, not at all sure how she felt about her daughter moving from 'Melissa' to 'Missy' in two short afternoons. 'But, I have to say, she's been curious her whole life. Her father's a detective, after all.' Beth was *so* thrilled that she had brought Jack up at that moment. She flashed to the two of them in bed.

'I'm afraid we've cooked up a few more outings in the near future. I hope I'm not overstepping any boundaries.'

'No,' Beth said, lying through her teeth. 'Not at all.'

'Well, the reason I'm calling is that I'm afraid I won't be able to drop her off as planned. I just got paged and I have to rush back to work tonight. We're just about finished eating and I was wondering if it would be okay if I dropped her off at Jack's. I'm only a few blocks away.'

'Sure,' Beth said. 'I do appreciate you calling, though. Just tell Jack to give me a ring when he's ready to drop her off.'

'Not a problem. I know how mothers can worry. I also wanted to say thanks for a lovely afternoon with Melissa.'

'Anytime,' Beth answered.

Beth decided that she would sort out her feelings later For now, as she hung up the phone, she had to admit that she felt a little jealous and a lot surprised that Jack Paris – he of the endless litany of short con games – would end up with someone quite this nice.

Paris's hands trembled as he turned the photograph over and over in the red light thrown from the traffic signal. The image was of a girl – bound with rope, hand and foot – lying in the trunk of a car. A white car, by the look of the trim.

As Paris stared at the picture, even though the girl's face was turned away from the lens, it didn't take long for him to identify the red cardigan sweater and plaid kilt.

It was Melissa.

On the back was a message:

'Saila does Chinatown.'

Beneath that, an address he did not recognize.

Saila clicked off her cell. It was a burner phone, untraceable. Jack Paris's ex-wife was as gullible as she had hoped and it had given her more time with Melissa, more time to work Jack.

Because, you see, Jack Paris had fucked her at Shaker Square. Jack Paris had bent her over and fucked her like a common harlot.

And now it was time to pay the whore.

The woman making the wounded-animal sounds from the trunk of the BMW was beginning to wear down. Thank God. The little girl was now sitting in the front seat of the car, perfectly calm, burning holes in her with her fiercely defiant brown eyes. What a *beauty* she was.

Saila dialed another number.

'Hello?' the man's voice answered.

'Guess who?'

'I *know* who.'

'How is my Pharaoh?' Saila asked.

'I miss your cunt.'

'Bad little *tom*,' she replied. 'My cunt misses *you*.'

'Yeah?'

'My tail is *so* high.'

'When and where?'

'It's why I called,' Saila said. 'Not tonight.'

'But I—'

'What?'

'Sorry.'

Saila closed her phone. There was something fundamentally wrong with the deductive processes of a certain type of man, she thought.

She'd see about Paris.

36

The headwaiter at Kowloon Garden, a slight, nervous man named Anton Fong, said he had seated a girl and a woman matching Diana and Melissa's general descriptions earlier in the evening, but he also remembered clearly that they weren't alone, that he had seen a man and a woman sitting with them, but only from the back. Then, Fong said, he went into the kitchen. When he returned to the dining room, ten minutes later, they were all gone and a fifty-dollar bill tented on the table.

'Fifty dollar,' Fong said. 'Can you imagine? Fifty dollar for water and *tea*.'

None of the other five waiters were able to say for sure that they had seen the foursome actually leave the restaurant.

Paris headed down Chester Avenue to East Fifty-fifth Street. Then he turned south, toward Carnegie and University Circle.

Tarleton Street was an odd enclave of twenty or so small bungalows that sat atop University Hill, surrounded by scores of dormitories, classroom buildings and high-rise residences for the students and faculty of Case Western Reserve University. The houses were built in the early fifties to accommodate visiting faculty. Yet, despite the ethereal orange glow from the nearby RTA train stop, the street had a pretty active

crime element, consisting mostly of burglaries and reports
of radios being stolen from the cars that were forced to park
on the street. There had once been a series of rapes in the
long tunnel leading to the RTA stop. Paris had been in on
that collar as a rookie.

But this night, the incandescence from the train platforms
didn't even make it up the hill. At least half the lamps were
out and the remainder of the light seemed to be swallowed
by the hedges and trees. Tarleton Street was bathed in
darkness.

The address on the back of the photograph was 15203.

Paris found the house, third from last on the dead end
street, cut the headlights and the engine, then rolled quietly
to a stop. He checked his weapon and got out of the car.

The front door to the cottage was unlocked and slightly ajar.
Paris pushed it open with the barrel of his weapon and felt
along the wall for a light switch. Within moments he found
one and flipped it on. A table lamp, set on the floor directly
beneath the switch, blazed to life, showing him that the front
room was empty. He stepped inside.

The living room had a worn, shabby look to it. The furniture
consisted of a stained maroon couch against one wall, a coffee
table, a small desk with an all-in-one fax machine/phone/
copier, a crate with a TV. There was also a broken-down hutch
at the other side of the L-shaped dining room.

As Paris drew closer to the dining area, his weapon raised,
he noticed that the coffee table was seventies vintage, covered
with ash trays and magazines, a few condom wrappers, a
tipped wineglass. He also noticed a pair of half-smoked joints
sticking out of the forest of lipstick-stained filters in one tray.

To the left of the living room was the kitchen, small and filthy, also empty. Straight ahead Paris could see what looked to be a bedroom. He sidled up to the doorway, reached around the jamb and found another switch.

The bedroom was long and narrow. It had obviously been two rooms at one time. At one end was a double mattress on the floor; next to it sat a camcorder on a tripod. At the foot of the bed was a small pile of women's lingerie and night-clothes. The other side of the room looked like a smaller version of a Gold's Gym: exercise bicycle, rower, lat machine, as well as a set of free weights.

But the display in the bedroom didn't come close to the display inside the crudely crafted walk-in closet. Inside was an extensive pegboard array of oils and perfumes, handcuffs and leather restraints, whips and dog collars, a wall of hoods and masks and leashes and head-pieces. One side held virtually every sex toy that Paris had ever encountered in his life, as well as a good many he had not. Another wall held an elaborate collection of wigs and leather clothing: skirts, vests, chaps, thigh-high boots.

On the floor was a small cardboard box full of photos. Most were standard bondage fare, similar to the 'Saila does Quality' photo. Women in leather restraints. Men in rubber suits, clamped into a bizarre collection of devices. Most wore leather masks, and for that reason, no one was immediately identifiable. As Paris began to flip through the pile, he found the photos near the bottom to be increasingly more graphic and violent, more sadistic. Some were close-ups of lacerations and cuts; some, pictures of dark purple welts against soft white flesh, wounds most likely caused by a whip.

But it was one of the last photos in his hand that stopped him cold. Suddenly, in the midst of all this madness, Paris saw a room he recognized. It was the bathroom of room 118 at the Radisson. The photograph showed Eleanor Burchfield curled up on the tile floor, fetal, her throat laid wide open, a shiny pool of blood gathering beneath her head.

Although Paris had seen hundreds and hundreds of crime-scene photographs in his career, thousands of color and black-and-white images of carnage and violence and mayhem, the fact that Melissa was in the hands of a monster at that moment, a monster to which he could not put a face, made all the difference in the world.

He barely made it to the sink.

Three minutes later, the fax phone rang. The built in answering machine got to it before Paris did.

'Hi . . . *If you're sending a fax, send it now. If you'd like to leave a voice message, wait for the beep. Thanks . . .*'

'Pick it up,' came the voice from the speaker. Cold and sinister. Paris instantly recognized the sound of the voice scrambler. It was a woman, but Paris could not identify the voice. It sounded like computer speech.

Paris lifted the phone in a blind fury. 'Who the *fuck* is this?'

'Are you on the fax phone?'

'Diana?'

Silence.

'Saila?'

Silence.

'Answer me,' Paris said. 'Who *is* this?'

After a few moments, the woman said, 'I'm going to hang up.'

'No!'

He waited. The electronic hiss gave him hope that the caller was still on the line.

'Is Melissa all right?'

'Of course.'

'Put her on. Let me speak to her.'

'Right away, detective. Listen—'

'No, *you* listen. You're going to tell me where my daughter is, and I'm going to come and get her. One scenario, that's it.'

The caller laughed. 'I'm not going to hurt your daughter, detective. Not yet, anyway. Because there's still a way out of this. It involves the destruction of evidence, though. I hope you don't have a problem with that.'

'Not when it comes to my daughter.'

'Good. By the way, how *did* I look to you in those pictures?'

Paris wanted to snap the phone in half. He remained silent.

'I want an answer. I want the *right* answer.'

Paris took a deep breath. 'You looked good.'

'Did you want to fuck me when you saw them?'

He had to play the game. 'Yes.'

'Did you get hard?'

'Yes.'

Another fun house laugh. 'You said the right thing, detective.'

Paris heard a car pass loudly by the caller's location.

'Speaking of photographs, I'll prove to you that Melissa is fine. You see that table by the front door?'

Paris gripped the phone a little more tightly. 'Yes.'

'Open the drawer.'

Paris found that the phone cord nearly reached the table. He leaned over and opened the drawer. Inside was another photograph. It was a color picture of Melissa sitting on the couch, not five feet from where he stood. His daughter looked about eighteen in the photograph, make-up and teased hair having transformed her into a woman. She wore an oversized white terry-cloth robe.

'You sick *fuck*.'

'She looks really good there, doesn't she?'

'My hand to God, I will hunt you down. You touch her and you don't *see* a fucking courtroom. You hear me?'

'Like a little lady.'

'She's eleven years old!'

'She told me that she's nearly twelve. That's almost a teenager. Something tells me that you're not going to cope too well with the hormone years.'

Paris took a deep, calming breath. It had absolutely no effect upon him whatsoever. 'Do you have any idea what I'd like to do to you right now?'

'Girls just wanna have fun, Jack.'

'Who the fuck is this?'

'Back to business. I am going to say these things once. I want you to listen, do precisely what I tell you to do, and not to speak, not even one word. Can you hear me, kitty cat?'

Silence.

'Good boy. But you may answer me this one time.'

'Yes, I can hear you.'

'Good. And please don't think that I can't see you. I can see everything you're doing. Nod if you understand.'

Paris scanned the night-black windows of the kitchen, living room and dining room, confirming that every light in the house was on and all the window shades were up. She could have been in any one of ten different buildings. He did as he was told.

'I want you to hold up all the photographs and all the notes you've received this evening,' the woman said. 'I want to see them.'

Paris reached into his pocket and retrieved the three-by-five cards and the photographs. He held them high in the air.

'Tear them into very small pieces and drop the pieces on the table.'

Paris obeyed.

'Do the same thing with Melissa's photo.'

Paris had no problem destroying the picture. He let the jagged pieces fall to the table.

'Now, obviously, I can never set foot in that house again. On the coffee table you'll find two or three small tea candles. I want you to get them and bring them back to the phone. You have ten seconds. No tricks. Go now.'

Paris put the phone down, crossed the living room and did as he was instructed to do, a million bytes of departmental procedure flashing through his mind, an avalanche of rage in his gut. He brought the tea candles back to the table, picked up the phone and listened for further instructions.

'Light the candles and place them on the table in front of you, near the base of the fax machine, where the paper comes out.'

Paris found a match in his pants pocket and lit the candles. Before he could stop himself, he said: 'Done.'

'I told you not to speak.'

'I—'

'You say one more word and I cut little angel here in half.'

Paris shut his eyes tightly and bore the next fifteen seconds in complete silence, the image of Karen Schallert's neck wound flooding his mind, the scent of burning wax filling his nostrils.

'Now, go into the kitchen, under the table, and bring back the throw rug. Place it on the floor beneath the fax machine. Make it look like it belongs there. Ten seconds. Go now.'

Paris sprinted to the kitchen. He peered under the table but there was no rug. He looked frantically around the kitchen and was just about to grab a dish towel and go back out and say that he had the rug, when he spotted it, bunched up against the baseboard near the sink. He ran back to the phone, picked it up and breathed heavily into the mouthpiece, announcing his return.

'If everything is in place, say the word "yes".'

'Yes.'

'Good. Just one more thing to do. I want you to pull that bar cart next to the phone. Position it very close. Five seconds this time. Go.'

Paris found the bar cart just around the corner in the living room and did as the woman had instructed. He could smell the sour, grainy scent of rum coming from one of the uncapped bottles.

'Take the bottle of Ron Rico 151, open it, and spill half of it on the rug. Leave the open bottle on its side.'

Paris did as he was told.

'Now move the candles to the edge of the table. Like someone put them there at a party.'

Again Paris complied, making sure the candles would fall as planned. He figured there was no point in trying to sabotage this. The last thing he wanted to do right now was disappoint this woman. He knew what this set-up was about: destroying the evidence, collecting the insurance and beating the arson investigators, who were some of the savviest people in all of law enforcement. She would say that she'd had a get-together, she left the house with the candles still lit, she got a fax while she was out and the next thing anybody knew—

'Grunt if it's done.'

Paris grunted.

'Now, you know and I know that we can't have you walking out of there with anything, so what I want, right now, is for you to strip to the waist. Everything off. Do it.'

Paris decided that he couldn't take the chance that she was bluffing about being able to see him. He dropped the phone and pulled his shirt, jacket, tie and undershirt over his head as one unit. Unfortunately, his shoulder holster and weapon came with it. He picked up the phone again.

'When I see you run out of the house I want to see your hands empty and your pockets turned inside out. Front and back. If you understand, say so.'

'I understand.'

'Where is your cell phone?'

Paris nearly spoke.

'You may answer.'

'In the car.'

'Good. I'm going to give you exactly ten seconds from the moment I say go to reach your car. I can see it very clearly and I have a very good watch. If it takes you one second longer, bad things happen. Once you get to your car, take your phone out, then go across the street and wait on the RTA platform under the lights. Understand?'

Silence.

'Saila says talk.'

'I understand.'

'Oh, and there are two things you should know about me, Jack. One, I don't hurt children. And two, I'm no *fanatic* about that.' She paused, with Paris stretched nearly halfway to the door, trying to get a jump on her command. 'If I'm satisfied,' she continued, 'we'll proceed to step two in our game. I will call you, but we will not talk very long. We're not going to give anyone time to triangulate the call. Be sure you are somewhere there is a strong signal. Are you ready?'

Paris said nothing.

Saila laughed. 'Oh, just *go.*'

He made the trip in less than eight seconds.

The cold night air braced Paris as he ran, sweating and shirtless, onto the porch. About halfway to his car, Paris panicked for a moment, thinking that he had left his keys in his jacket pocket, inside a house that was set, at any moment, to catch fire. Then he remembered that he had stashed them under the passenger seat. He hadn't known what to expect when he went inside 15203 Tarleton Street, and because he had more than once physically engaged a criminal only to find that after the dust settled, things like keys and wallets and watches and rings and lighters had been flung into oblivion, he had decided to leave his keys in the car.

He reached his car, well within the time limit the woman had given him.

And that's when he heard the voice.

'Don't move.' It was a calm, confident request that came from behind Paris and to his left, just on the other side of the car.

Paris froze.

'Put your hands on top of your head and interlace your fingers.'

Paris did as he was told, a feeling of relief instantly washing over him. It was a cop. He waited for the next instruction, even though he knew what it was going to be.

'Now turn around, slowly, and face me.'

Paris spun slowly to his right. About halfway, he knew.

'*Jack,*' Danny Lawrence said. 'Jesus *Christ,* Jack.'

Even though they knew each other, Paris kept his hands raised. Paris was pretty sure that Danny Lawrence, and all the other cops in the Fourth, patrolled in one-man units, but you never knew.

It took Danny a moment to realize that he still had his weapon pointed at a CPD detective. 'Jesus. Sorry. Put your hands down, Jack.' He holstered his weapon.

Paris took the opportunity to glance at the house. No flames yet.

'Sorry, Danny,' Paris said, trying to formulate his story on the fly. 'I hope I didn't, you know, get the adrenaline pumping *too* hard there.'

'What's going on?'

'Actually, I was going to ask you the same thing,' Paris said, smiling, hoping his gold shield would carry the moment. It did.

'Well, what *I'm* doing here is that I caught a call on this street. Report of a burglary in progress – 15203 Tarleton.'

Danny had given Paris his out. He went for it.

'Yeah. I caught it too. I was dropping someone off at the RTA and I heard the call. So I swung the car up here and took a look.' Paris stole another glance at the house. He had to get rid of Danny. 'Nothing. False alarm.'

'You're a detective, Jack,' Danny said. 'Why would you handle a burglary call?'

'Reflex, I guess. I was here.'

'Is there anybody in the house?'

'No,' Paris said. 'I checked all the doors and windows. Looked in with the flashlight. Nothing. False alarm.'

'Well, maybe I should—'

'Danny. It's handled. It's done.'

Danny looked at him, a little more skeptically than Paris

would have liked. 'You'll call it in? You'll clear it?' he asked, turning his flashlight toward the house. He scanned the eaves, the porch, the bushes.

'Absolutely,' Paris said. He reached down and quickly turned his pockets back in.

'Well. . .' Danny began, now directing the flashlight toward Paris, '*okay*, I guess.' He finally produced a smile and, with it, all the tension immediately dissolved. 'You think you'll ever tell me why you don't have a fucking shirt on at this moment?'

Paris thought about it. 'Yes, Danny. I will. I promise. It's a good story.'

'Something to do with the friend you just dropped off?'

'Something like that.'

Danny Lawrence did a few more takes on Jack and the house. He clicked off his flashlight, turned toward his patrol car and said, 'Have a good night, detective.'

'You too, Danny. Thanks.'

As Danny drove off, Paris wondered why he had thanked him. Perhaps it was rooted in the feeling all police officers have after having a gun pointed at them and not getting shot.

37

The woman was very sexy for an older gal. Kind of curvy but still muscular and fit. Jeff liked them fit. He also knew that a lot of the women that came into the Kinko's on Mayfield Road didn't give him a second look because of his complexion and all. This woman had actually *smiled* at him.

She wanted to send a fax.

'That's a local phone number, right?'

'Yes,' she said, handing him three pieces of eight-and-a-half-by-eleven paper. 'The number's at the top.'

'Do you need a cover page?'

'No thank you.'

'Doesn't cost any extra,' Jeff said with his most winning eighteen-year-old smile. 'And we've got lots of interesting designs.'

'Just what I gave you is fine,' she answered, sounding very authoritative, and suddenly very much like one of his teachers. He took the pages over to the fax machine, feeling like a kid being sent on an errand by a beautiful woman.

So what was new?

He loaded the pages, dialed the number.

'Hi . . . If you're sending a fax, send it now. If you'd like to leave a voice message, wait for the beep. Thanks . . .'

Jeff Trimble pressed the send button with consummate

skill. After the pages made their rotation, he turned back to the woman, hoping he had exhausted his cache of really stupid moves. He had not.

'Will that be all?'

She smiled. 'Yes, that's it. Jeff.'

'That will be five-fifty-six,' he said. The woman had seen his ID tag and called him by *name*. She handed him the correct change. He rang it up, handed her the receipt. She stared deeply into his eyes, apparently waiting for something.

'Is there something else I can do for you?' he asked.

'The original?'

'Original?'

'The three-page document. The one you just faxed for me?'

'Oh, how stupid.' Jeff Trimble turned a bright and remarkably even shade of crimson. It seemed to devour him. He handed the woman her papers. 'Sorry.'

'It's quite all right, young man. You have a nice evening.'

She turned and left the store. As Jeff watched her walk to her car, a white BMW, he thought she was one of the most beautiful women he had ever seen in his life.

He could tell that her daughter, sitting out in the car, was going to be a knockout one day too.

38

Paris waited until he saw the fire before he dialed his cell phone. Danny Lawrence had barely turned the corner on to East 115th Street before the first flames began to appear. Paris knew that if he had called it in immediately after getting out of the house and the fire hadn't broken out for another ten minutes, he would have had a very hard time explaining it. He imagined that the woman had gone somewhere where there was a fax machine – Kinko's, OfficeMax, Staples – and called, sending a couple of pages down the wire and out of her machine, sending the tea candles onto the rug.

He didn't know if the woman was still in the area, still watching him, so he remained on the RTA platform across the street, out of sight. Paris hoped that she hadn't seen him talking to Danny Lawrence, or, if she had, that she had given him credit for enough sense to have kept his mouth shut around a cop.

Besides, he wasn't all that anxious to run into a burning building anyway. He would simply have to hope that the CFD would arrive in time to save some key piece of evidence to link her to the Pharaoh murders.

But as he heard the muffled pop of the liquor bottles exploding he knew it would all go up by the time the first engine company arrived. Within minutes, the roof and eaves were shooting bright orange flames high into the night.

Paris sprinted back to his car, opened the trunk, retrieved a damp, sweatshirt out of his gym bag, pulled it over his head. He also pulled out his backup weapon, along with a spare holster and a box of rounds. Although he had been forced to give up his revolver inside the cottage, he had, luckily, managed to get his shield and ID out of his pocket and down the front of his pants before running out of the house. He got in the car, turned over the engine, cranked the heat up to high and turned north on Murray Hill, not having the slightest clue as to why he was heading in that particular direction.

The coffee at Bengal's was rarely fresh, but it was always strong and hot. Bengal's was a soul-food place on Carnegie, about halfway between his apartment and the Innerbelt. He didn't know if he'd have to go east or west when he got the call, but he wanted to be ready when it came.

He got out, checked his phone for the tenth time, making sure he had good signal strength. He paced for a few minutes, got back in his car, sipped from the Styrofoam cup, tried to put this nightmare in order.

Who the fuck was doing this to him? Was it Diana? And if it was, how could he have been so wrong? Was it the Hellers? He still found that hard to believe.

And where the hell was Cyndy?

And where the hell was Beth?

He fingered the weapon in his shoulder holster and watched the slow, sparkling parade of hookers as they walked up Carnegie, swinging their purses like world-weary schoolgirls.

*   *   *

Saila called at nine-fifteen.

Paris looked at the LCD screen, at the caller ID and, for a moment, thought he was misreading the display. He turned on the interior light and found that he had been right in the first place.

It was his home phone number.

He flipped open his phone, but remained silent.

'I feel as if someone has stolen all my dolls, Jack.'

'Then just leave my apartment,' Paris said, trying to build some momentum. 'We're even. Leave Melissa there, take off, and we never did this, okay?'

The silence that greeted his seemingly reasonable suggestion was deafening.

'You really are a shitty housekeeper.'

The woman's voice was still synthesized, but it sounded as if the batteries were fading.

'I know, I know,' Paris answered. 'But let's—'

'I mean, you're a very attractive man, but this place is not going to get the job done. You know what I mean?'

'Saila.'

'And what have we *here*?'

Paris heard the sound of rustling papers and then, mercifully, a brief *woof* from Manny. At least *he* was okay and at the right place. The room then went quiet for what seemed to Paris like a full minute but in reality was no more than fifteen or twenty seconds.

'Some interesting reading material here. Aileen Wuornos? That roadhouse pig? You were actually reading up on this? You actually thought that there were similarities in these cases? What an insult.'

Paris could feel the conversation slipping away from him. He said nothing.

'What else do you have on the case?'

'Not a thing. I swear.'

'You fucked me over at Shaker Square. Why should I believe you now?'

'You think this job means more to me than my *daughter*? There was nothing in my car because there isn't any evidence. The prosecutor's happy with Tommy Raposo and that's that. The case is closed.'

'Then why won't *you* give it up?'

'I'm done,' Paris said. 'I'm off it.'

The woman went silent for a few beats, the digital processor filling the void with a hissing sound.

'Maybe I'll just walk into the kitchen, Jack. Maybe I'll just stroll into the kitchen and carefully pick up one of your sharper knives – one just loaded with your fingerprints – and stick it into Melissa's chest. How would that be? Leave her right in the middle of your living-room floor in a big, dark pool of blood. Then it's bye-bye Daddy. Bye-bye anchor around my fucking neck.'

'No.'

'Or maybe I'll just take this straight razor and send it off to the authorities. Anonymously, of course. Because I'm pretty sure that the state police are going to be very interested in it, considering the fact that there's the body of a Peeping Tom pushing up lilacs in the woods near the Motel Riverview.'

Paris's skin crawled. She was talking about Andrea Heller's husband. 'What do you mean?'

'I'm not sure how it happened, but your fingerprints are on one end of the razor and this dead pervert's blood is on the other. Can you believe it?'

'You can't possibly be *serious*.'

'And if that wasn't enough, detective,' she continued, her

voice dropping to a deep, almost manly whisper, 'how do you intend to explain away the woman you barbecued tonight on Tarleton Street?'

Paris felt his stomach turn. '*What?*'

'The exhibitionist. The Peeper's wife. She was *alive*, Jack. That's what she was. Tied up and chloroformed, but alive. Up in the attic.'

'You *mother*fucker!'

'The heat might have brought her to before she went up in flames though, seeing as she was covered in kindling and newspapers. Some oily rags too. I really can't see anyone sleeping through something like that, can you?'

The horrors were piling up faster than Paris could sort through them. He had to think, had to find her weakness. He went for the obvious.

'Look,' Paris said, 'I've got some cash, poker cash, it's stashed in the basement of the building. It's yours. Maybe five, six grand.'

'Men are so predictable. You think everything in this world revolves around your cocks or your cash flow, don't you. You amuse me so.'

It sounded to Paris like she might be ready to hang up. 'Don't—'

'But, on the other hand, I *will* take the money. Where is it?'

Paris described the location in the basement.

'Hang on.'

Paris heard the phone strike something soft, then fall silent. He heard the door to his apartment open, its familiar creak filling him with a rush of fear. When he figured she had begun her way down the stairs, he spoke.

'Missy. Can you hear me?'

Silence.

'Missy, if you can hear me, make some kind of sound.'

Nothing. Paris looked out at the street, at Carnegie Avenue, and calculated that he was twenty blocks from his apartment. He'd never make it.

Paris heard a quick snort of breath into the mouthpiece of the phone, then the rustling of material? Clothing? Paper? Was someone listening?

He was just about to call out again when he realized that it was Manny, trying to figure out why his master was inside the telephone.

'Manny.'

The dog barked once, but the electronic voicebox changed it into something birdlike. Then Paris heard the door creak again. Then, quick footsteps toward the phone and Manny's nails scampering away on the hard-wood floor.

'I've decided that I don't believe you about the evidence. And I've got to get going.'

'Wait.'

'I usually go out on Friday, but Saturday's okay too, I suppose. Especially now that I have a new partner. Right, Melissa?'

Paris's heart all but stopped.

'Oh, she'll come around. But she has a hell of a lot to learn, I think. Who better to teach her than me?'

'Just let me talk to Melissa for five seconds. Just let me know that she's all right.'

'I don't think so. We're leaving. Girls' night out.'

'Don't.'

'I know you're going to look for us. You could try looking in the backyard, next to the sandbox. Maybe we'll call you later, or maybe not. Maybe we'll hit the kiddie bars. Maybe we'll pick up a couple of sailors and head off to Atlantic City.'

The woman laughed and the sound frightened Paris to the bottom of his soul.

'Don't hang up.'

'Use your head, Jack. I want everything you have on the Pharaoh case. And if you bring anyone in on this, if you talk to one other cop, I'll hurt you for the rest of your life.'

'But there isn't—'

'Everything.'

Paris opened his mouth to speak but was met instead with a brief, antiseptic click.

Then, the coldest silence he had ever heard in his life.

How was he going to tell Beth? He decided he wouldn't, he couldn't. He decided he would call her, take the heat over being so late and tell her that Missy was going to stay at his place.

He was lucky. Beth was either on the phone or not home when he called, and he got her voice mail. He left what he thought was a fairly convincing message.

He turned his phone over and over in his hands. Who the hell was on his team? Tim Murdock was out of the question. Way too blue. Greg Ebersole would help him and keep his mouth shut, but Greg was probably two sheets to the wind by this time of night on a Saturday. Bobby Dietricht was far too ambitious to ask for this huge a favor. He would never be able to pay it off completely.

No. Paris knew he couldn't take a chance on another cop, not as long as this psycho had Missy.

He flipped open his phone and called one of the few people on the planet he felt he could trust.

* * *

'I have to tell you how thrilled I am that you know I have absolutely nothing to do on a Saturday night,' Rita said.

'Actually—'

'I'm usually working on Saturday, you know. It's not like I can't get a date or anything.'

'I've got problems, Rita. Big-time. I could really use your help.'

'On-the-phone help or in-person-and-I-might-have-to-leave-the-house help?'

'Leave-the-house help,' Paris replied.

'Okay,' Rita said. 'But there's no way I'm doing this with dirty hair. Give me twenty minutes. I'm at 2018 Fenton Place.'

Rita Weisinger's apartment was bohemian and funky. Inexpensive but functional furniture, with a few fairly interesting reproductions on the walls. On one wall was a bookshelf that held nearly as many romance paperbacks as Paris had found at Samantha Jaeger's flat. Rita may have had the same tastes in literature but, thankfully, was a lot more in touch with terra firma than the very spooky Miss Jaeger turned out to be.

'Before you fill me in, is this a drink-mission or a coffee-mission?' Rita asked.

'Coffee.'

'Black, one sugar, right?'

'You're amazing.'

'It's a gift,' Rita said. She poured him a cup, placed it on the coffee table and sat down. As she listened, she ran a wide-tooth comb through her slightly damp hair.

Paris began the story by relating the events of 21 October of the previous year, the night he had gotten the call to investigate a suspicious death. A woman named Emily Reinhardt.

He ended the story by placing a photograph of Missy on the table in front of Rita. He had told her everything.

'Plus, I can't get hold of Cyndy. I can't get hold of Diana. I can't even get hold of my ex-wife,' Paris said.

Rita put the comb down on the coffee table and stood up. She reached out her hand to Paris.

'Let's do it,' she said.

39

Every large city has its sexual underground, people who, for the most part, don't function very well in the sunlight. Paris was well aware that Cleveland, even with its high-profile escort services and suburban sex clubs, was essentially a blue-collar town. And that meant that while some of the games played may have lacked the imagination, the *élan* of New York or Los Angeles, they seemed to make up for it with the sheer depth of their depravity.

Paris stopped at his apartment and changed clothes while Rita waited in the idling car. As expected, every drawer and closet had been turned inside out, every bit of research he had done on the Pharaoh case was gone. Manny was fine, but seemed to be wandering around in a fog, wondering why every smell in his entire world had been relocated.

When Paris saw the loop of twine wrapped around the legs of one of the wooden chairs pulled up to his dining-room table, his heart trip-hammered. Had Missy been tied up at his table? Would she, could she, ever get over something like that?

He sponged himself off quickly and put on one of Tommy's Armani blazers. He ran a comb through his hair.

Rita, who was young-looking for her age anyway, had understood completely what they had to do, as well as the very nature of the danger they were about to court. She wore a short red-and-white-checked gingham dress and a matching ribbon in her hair. She wore white anklets and flat shoes. Considering the inevitably subdued lighting in the places they were heading, she could easily pass for sixteen.

Because, Paris thought, if this psycho was planning a run around town, trying to pass a twelve-year-old girl off as eighteen, he knew there would be only so many places she could go. She had to be at one of only two or three kiddie bars around the city. As far as Paris knew, they were all within a few miles of Public Square, but they always kept moving, for obvious reasons.

Paris phoned Dave Drotos in the vice unit. Drotos told him that there were two bars of this type operating somewhere between the Forties and Sixties off St Clair, but he wasn't sure where exactly. Drotos of course asked if he could help, but when Paris declined, he asked for no further details.

They started with the leather clubs, a series of blank-doored warehouses around the Fifties off St Clair and south toward Superior.

The first few bars were just getting rolling, with a handful of desperadoes staking out their territories for the evening. It wasn't yet eleven o'clock and the A-list players, it seemed, were still underground, still primping. Mostly they saw the younger hustlers, already pumped and primed and muscled up to the bar. The black-T-shirt boys.

There were places they visited where Paris got all the looks — no doubt, he figured, because of Tommy's $1,000-jacket, a dead man's blazer he had so cavalierly thrown over his shoulders — and there were those where Rita drew all the attention.

The fifth bar they hit was a place called Insatiable on East Fifty-seventh. It was mostly a transvestite hangout, but it had different specialty nights now and then, and it was more or less known to draw all sorts of people who could be loosely referred to as having an alternative lifestyle. The music was canned and loud and raunchy and seemed to Paris to be the same five notes repeated over and over and over again with somebody grunting in the background.

At least three times, as they cruised the huge room Paris looked over at the U-shaped bar and caught a Hispanic kid watching his every move. The kid was maybe twenty-one or twenty-two, tough-posing, decked out in the standard barrio uniform. He sported a blue flannel shirt buttoned at the top, baggy chinos. Big arms.

Had they crossed paths before? Paris wondered. Had he busted him, rousted him? He couldn't remember. Real *cholote*, Paris thought. He kept one eye on him.

Rita ran into some friends, hairdressers and manicurists mostly, plus a couple of people she knew from work. One, Paris overheard, was a tall blond kid named Vasily. They all disappeared for a few minutes, running up the steps to the upper level with a vigor Paris envied.

He scanned the bar and caught one more glance from the kid in blue flannel, who looked away immediately.

Paris decided that his proximity to the large, blaring speaker to his immediate left was merely compounding his already splitting headache. But before he could plot his course across the room to the stairs, he saw Rita weaving her way back through the crowd. She arrived nearly out of breath.

'My friend Robin from Mark Drury's Salon introduced me to this guy upstairs named Perko or Burko or something. Really freakin' scary-looking, let me tell you. Big head, nose like a busted anchor.' She was yelling into Paris's ear now, inches away. 'Anyway, we start talking and I ask him about after-hours-type specialty places, and at first he resists me, then he dials in on the way I'm dressed and he starts babbling on and on about these kiddie bars. I think he liked me, Jack. Or it might have had something to do with the two Johnny Walker Reds I had to buy him.'

'I'll take care of it.'

'Anyway, he said the woman to talk to is named Alida Witherspoon. He told me that she kind of holds court at this diner around the corner. The Good Egg or something.'

'I know the place.'

'He said she'd probably be there now.'

'Who's she supposed to be?'

'Some kind of pervert social director, I think. I guess she knows all, sees all.' Rita reached into her purse, pulled out a powder compact, checked her face in the mirror. She put it away. 'Anyway, this Burko guy said that if someone as young as Melissa showed up at the kiddie bars – even if it was just a couple of hours ago, even if it was across town – Alida Witherspoon would know about it.'

'Jesus,' Paris said. 'Let's go.'

Alida Witherspoon was a good deal of woman, taking up about two thirds of her side of the booth at the Good Egg, a twenty-four-hour greasy spoon on St Clair and East Sixtieth. The way things were arranged around her, it was easy to tell that she fancied herself to be Queen Alida, a subterranean sex maven of sorts. Paris thought that, at some point, she may even have been an attractive woman, but years of cheap food and pills and booze had taken their toll. Her whiskey-stippled face, broad shoulders and brittle, straw-colored hair gave her the appearance of one of those women who play the hardened prison guards in the 'chained heat' movies.

As Paris and Rita approached her, Alida Witherspoon somehow reckoned that they had business with her and raised a solitary index finger, freezing them in their tracks. She looked up. Her eyes were small and wizened, the color of wet sand. She pointed at Rita and beckoned her forward with one long red-and-white-enameled fingernail. Paris slid into a booth facing them.

After a few moments Rita reached into her bag and produced Melissa's picture, a photograph Paris had taken of his daughter in front of the Rainforest building at the MetroPark Zoo the previous summer. The two women talked for a while, and when they leaned forward to whisper, Paris knew they were digging in. He ordered coffee and something he theorized had passed for a plain doughnut at some point within the past seventy-two hours.

Ten minutes later Alida Witherspoon extracted herself from the booth, with no small measure of difficulty, and began walking toward the front of the restaurant. Rita followed her. The big woman did not even glance at Paris as they passed his booth, but Rita leaned over and whispered, 'Wait for me outside. I think she has something for us.'

Paris waited until they were in the ladies' room. He stood up, dropped a five-dollar bill on the counter. He walked out the door, hung a quick left, turned his collar to the night and marched a few feet up the alley.

Jack Paris stood in the darkness, leaned against the mossy brick wall and listened to the night sounds: the traffic on St Clair, the heavy bass of a rap song coming from somewhere above him and to his left, a parking-lot argument under way within a block or two.

Missy, he thought.

Please God.

No.

He decided he would pray, formally, the first time in years, probably the first time since Melissa was born. He would pray with all the 'thous' and 'thees' intact, like a Catholic, like he was raised. He would make his deal with God and agree to whatever terms were necessary in a situation like this.

He began with Hail Marys as he walked around the alley for warmth.

Rita had been gone for nearly ten minutes and Paris was beginning to worry. What had he gotten her into? Sure she was pretty savvy for her age, but he was using her to bait a psychopath. What had he been thinking?

Melissa, is what he'd been thinking.

He peeked back into the Good Egg, but neither Rita nor the corpulent Ms Witherspoon were anywhere to be seen. He walked to the far end of the alleyway and found a tiny, pitted asphalt-and-gravel parking-lot stashed between the buildings. There were five or six cars. One of them, a white BMW. It looked like the car that had picked up Andrea Heller at Whitney's.

Paris moved quickly across the lot and put his ear to the trunk. He heard nothing. He looked at the back seat. There was a pile of papers, balanced somewhat precariously on the edge of the seat. On top was a copy of the *Scene*, Cleveland's entertainment weekly newspaper. Beneath it Paris could see junk mail: catalogs, grocery-store fliers, insurance-company come-ons. He could also see the edge of a huge envelope, a clearinghouse sweepstakes package. The address was in gigantic letters but all he could read was the very end of the top line. The letter t but no more. The person's last name on the big beige envelope ended in a t.

Paris began to rock the left rear fender, jostling the papers and the envelopes around, sliding them toward the edge of the seat, revealing the address bit by bit. After a few moments, he bounced the fender a little too hard, and the pile of papers fell, facedown, on to the floor. 'God*damnit*,' he said in a loud whisper. He was just about to write down the license plate and call it in when a door opened behind him.

Paris spun around quickly, his hand on his weapon, but the shadows were upon him in an instant.

It was Blue Flannel, the *cholote*. And a big friend.

The two surrounded him with such exactness, such mechanical ease that it appeared they knew he was going to be standing in that precise spot at that precise moment in history and they were just making their appointed rounds. Natural-born predators. The kid flashed a knife, and before Paris could react, the blade was at his stomach.

'What d'fuck you *doin'* here, man?' the kid said, bringing his whiskey-sour breath within inches of Paris's face. 'You way d'fuck outside Pepper Pike, eh?'

'What do you want?' Paris asked.

'*I* do the talking, homes.'

'I'm a cop.'

'*Hah!* I don't give a fuck if you eff-bee-eye,' Blue Flannel said. 'Makes me wanna cut you even more.'

His partner, who wore a red bandanna and black wraparound sunglasses, found immense humor in the sentiment.

'So what you lookin' for, man? Maybe I can help, you know?

You lookin' for black girls? Is that it? Or maybe boys, eh? You like boys, man?'

The kid rubbed his knee against Paris's leg. He licked his lips.

'Or maybe you lookin' for a baby,' he continued. 'Maybe you like them *real* young, eh *padrone*?'

More laughter from Sunglasses.

'Because that girl you was with looked pretty young for you, man,' the kid said, shaking a finger at Paris. 'That your daughter?'

Paris said nothing.

'Niece?'

Paris just glared at him.

'So, where she at right now, man? I got somethin' for her myself, I think.' Blue Flannel reached down to his crotch and gave it a quick squeeze. 'She look *good*.'

'She went home,' Paris said wistfully, watching a black-and-white patrol car cruise past the other end of the alley.

'I don't think so. I think she talkin' to Alida, you know? I think you all gonna go somewhere and party and me and my homeboy Ottavio are gonna be left out. We don't like that, man.'

'Just take the money,' Paris said. 'I got two, three hundred dollars on me. It's yours.'

'I don't need your per*mission*, motherfucker.' Blue Flannel leaned forward, putting a slight pressure on the knife tip.

'Look,' Paris said. 'I'm on the job. We're stinging this place around the corner and there's maybe ten, twelve cops right around this area somewhere. Maybe there's one on the rooftop right above us, right now, dialing you into the cross-hairs of his rifle. Do yourself a favor. Take the money and run or—'

From over his left shoulder, Paris saw the nose of a .45 automatic suddenly, silently appear. The weapon was pointed directly at the kid's head. He then heard the cold, measured voice of a man who had probably scared the crap out of a *hell* of a lot of people in his life. A voice Paris found familiar.

'Get outta here, shitbag,' the voice said. 'Take your boyfriend with you.'

Paris didn't move. Blue Flannel eased the pressure on the knife, but didn't give any indication that he was getting ready to move.

'Looks like we got us a Messican stalemate here, eh, homes?' he said with a nervous laugh. 'Looks like we got us a wash.'

'We don't have shit,' said the voice. 'But I *will* tell you what happens next. I count to three, pull the trigger and detach you from your fucking head.'

The kid got the message, withdrew the knife slowly and began to back down the alley, his hands out to his sides, his partner behind him. They both stared, unblinkingly, over Paris's left shoulder.

Paris heard the hammer being pulled back on the .45. The sound seemed to echo between the buildings before disappearing into the clear black sky.

When the two men were near the mouth of the alley, Blue Flannel spoke. 'You real *lucky*, man,' he said, trying to wrest a modicum of machismo from this defeat. He spat on the ground directly in front of him. 'Next time we meet, it's gonna be a l'il dif'rent, you know?'

'Yeah, and next time I pay your sister *fifty* cents for a blow job,' came the voice from over Paris's shoulder. 'Now, get the fuck outta here.'

Paris remained still until the two disadvantaged youths had

turned the corner onto St Clair and disappeared. He spun around to meet his savior, his knight in shining armor, his cavalry, only to find that it wasn't John Wayne or Dirty Harry after all.

It was Nick Raposo.

'One more time, Nick.'

'Like I told you, I've been following you around, on and off, for three days,' Nick said. 'Almost lost you again tonight, though. Over at Fenton Place.'

'You followed me last night, too?'

'Yep. Except last night I lost you around South Russell or Bainbridge somewhere. Then I went home. I don't think I'm cut out for this private-eye shit.'

'How'd you get so good at sneaking up on people?' Paris asked, feeling some measure of relief that Nick didn't see him do the Peeping Tom bit at the Motel Riverview. He didn't need an eye-witness putting him at the scene. The fact that Nick Raposo knew he was in Russellton at all that would probably burn him to the ground one day anyway.

'Two tours in Nam. Special Ops'

Paris was impressed. He went silent for a few moments, the realization that he had very nearly been stabbed to death in an alleyway near Sixtieth and St Clair starting to sink in. He finally asked the question, although he had a pretty good idea what the answer would be. 'Why are you doing this?'

Nick looked at the sky, back. 'I know you gotta go by the book. I respect that. But the point is, I *don't*, see? I mean, we find the asshole who framed Tommy, you go home, I fuck him up. Done.'

'I can't let you do it, though, Nick.' He placed his hand on Nick's thick shoulder. 'Jesus, man, there isn't anything out here for you. Let me take care of things. Go home and I'll call you, I swear.'

Just then Rita came around the corner with a girl who looked to be about fifteen. The girl had on very high heels and a green sequined dress that was far too tight, even for her thin, wiry frame. Her blond hair was set in pigtails. She had her arms crossed over her chest and she was shivering in the cold.

Nick looked at Paris, raised his eyebrows, and Paris knew then that he would have to explain everything, and that Nick Raposo was going to be in this for the duration.

'This is the guy I was telling you about,' Rita said. 'Tell him what you told me.'

'*Could* be her,' the girl said.

This close, Paris could tell that the girl was a little older than he had originally thought. She looked to be around eighteen or so.

'I'm not sure,' she continued. 'I mean, she looks like a little *girl* in this picture you have.'

'She *is* a little girl,' Paris said.

'Right. Whatever.' The girl snapped her gum twice. 'Anyway, she was with this woman, late twenties, early thirties maybe. Weird set-up if you ask me.'

'When did you see her?' Paris asked.

'Twenty minutes ago.'

'Where?'

'Up the street,' the girl said, looking at Paris's hands to see if he was going to make a move to fork over a ten or a twenty for the information. When she realized that the move was not forthcoming, she sighed and spilled it anyway. 'Place called the Swing Set. It's a kiddie bar. Go right on St Clair and down a block. Brick building with a black door. Door's got a silver rose in the upper right-hand corner. The guy's name is Sandy. Tell him Angel sent you over.'

'Thanks, Angel,' Paris said, the name of the kiddie bar immediately triggering a recollection.

The Swing Set.

Look in the backyard. Next to the sandbox.

'You're not *cops*, are you?' Angel asked.

'Not tonight,' Paris said, and tossed her the twenty.

Sandy was huge, standing about six six, weighing at least two-eighty; bald and black and full of attitude for middle-aged white men who like to get drunk and play with little girls. Or women who dress like little girls. Sandy knew why they all came — welders, politicians, bankers, lawyers, cooks, teachers, businessmen of all sorts. The guy who owns the Quik Print franchise up the street. The guy who drives your children around in the morning. The guy who stands around the mall, outside the Merry-Go-Round store, sunglasses casually deployed, his hands in his pockets.

But Sandy St Cyr also knew who was in charge. He looked at Paris and Nick, then, very carefully, very thoroughly, at Rita. He smirked and shook his head, as if he'd seen the act a thousand times before. 'Fifty dollars,' he said. 'Each.'

He stared at Paris, who returned his gaze with a cool vengeance, but still reached into his pocket for the cash. Paris felt Nick idling roughly behind him, itching to get into it. He leaned back slightly and Nick got the message.

'Downstairs, to the right, gentlemen,' Sandy said, standing out of the way, placing the money in his pocket. 'And *lady*.' He reached down, lifted the ruffled edge of Rita's dress and ran his hand over her thigh as she passed him, all the while staring Paris down, defying him to react.

Instead, Rita reacted for both of them, swinging around in one smooth motion, positioning a small, razor sharp knife between the man's legs. Sandy pulled his hand away very slowly. 'Keep your fucking hands to yourself, Chewbacca,' Rita said. 'Unless you want to sing with the Vienna Boys' Choir. You hear me?'

Incredibly, the moment Rita put the knife back into her purse, Sandy broke out laughing and stamping his feet, clearly enjoying this start to another Saturday night at the Swing Set.

40

The volume increased geometrically as they descended the steps to the Swing Set. About halfway down the stairs the bass line became thunderous and the drums seemed to shake the sparsely plastered walls around them. Rita told Paris she thought she recognized the mix.

'The what?' Paris asked, shouting to be heard.

'The mix,' Rita said, yelling into his ear. 'All the best deejays have a certain style, a certain way they mix the songs together. A lot of them sample other people's stuff, make their own house music.'

'Okay.'

'I know most of the deejays around town. This sounds like it could be this guy Faustino, old friend of mine. Real twisto, though.'

'What a shock.'

'He's probably not real big on cops. In fact, I would almost guarantee it, seeing as how he's a Brazilian illegal,' Rita said. 'He likes *me*, though. If it turns out that it *is* him, let me handle it, okay?'

'Do you think he might help us?' Nick asked, looking more and more uncomfortable by the step.

Rita just shrugged.

'Did you turn on the two-way?' Paris had given her a small police-issue two-way radio. Rita nodded, tapped her purse.

Paris placed his two-way in his shirt pocket and opened the door to the Swing Set.

And although he didn't realize it – was simply not prepared to absorb the information – the first person he saw was Melissa.

Jack Paris worked within the Cleveland Police Department's vice unit a dozen years earlier. He had handled any number of cases ranging from prostitution stings to busting up child pornography distribution to going on shared duty and shutting down swingers' clubs in the Heights. He had heard about kiddie bars – after-hours, unlicensed establishments whose main attraction was their promise of girls and women who ranged in age from eighteen to their mid-twenties but could still pass for young teenagers. Although he'd never busted one, he knew enough to know that any night of the week, if you flipped the lights on in any of these clubs, you'd find a half-dozen girls under the age of eighteen, and always one or two that were as young as twelve or thirteen.

But when Jack Paris looked into his daughter's face for that brief, smoke-hazed instant – her hair piled high on her head, her lips painted a deep red, her eyes lost behind a pair of huge, heart-shaped sunglasses – he hadn't known her. He had seen her for a fleeting moment, then someone had stepped between them and blocked his view.

Weeks later he would realize that had he been a little bit better at his job, at his duty as a father, had he recognized *his own daughter* at that moment, the nightmare of what happened next might have been avoided.

*   *   *

The Swing Set was a large, square room, low-ceilinged. The smoke seemed to hang halfway to the floor like a thin blue parachute. The walls were covered with a cheap paneling that boasted decor that was supposed to resemble a teenaged girl's bedroom: hastily hung posters of teen idols and fuzzy, big-eyed kittens.

The handful of Swing Set waitresses were all dressed like little girls too. One, a petite, athletic-looking brunette, wore a very short plaid skirt, white cardigan and saddle shoes. Another was dressed like a junior-high-school cheerleader. Yet another like a Campfire Girl.

'I can't believe that they do exactly what I do for a living,' Rita said.

One of the Swing Set denizens – an obese, acne-scarred kid about twenty-five or so – asked Rita to dance. She pointed to Paris and Nick, and the kid decided, at least for the time being, not to give her a hard time. Paris was relieved. After Blue Flannel and his pal, he was ready to shoot the first asshole who looked at him wrong.

'I'm going to cruise,' Rita said.

'All right,' Paris said. 'Five minutes max, right here.'

'You got it. If something comes up, I'll buzz you.' She tapped her purse and Paris gave her a quick thumbs-up, in lieu of shouting at the top of his lungs.

Rita slid off her stool, took two steps and was immediately swallowed by the crowd.

'Can I get you something, Daddy?'

Nick and Paris turned and saw that it was a barmaid, the one in the white cardigan. This close, Paris could see that she was in her early twenties. Nick looked at Paris, then back at the waitress. 'Let me ask you something,' Nick said. 'Do your parents know that you—'

'We're fine for right now,' Paris said, clamping an iron hand on to Nick's shoulder. 'We'll give you a shout if we need anything.'

'There's a two-drink minimum, you know,' she said. 'Drinks are ten bucks each.'

Paris reached into his pocket and pulled out his dwindling roll. He dropped three twenties on to the barmaid's tray. 'That should cover the three of us, right?'

The girl looked at her tray, then back at Paris, with eyes like a lost fawn. It was easy to see how, in that outfit and with those baby browns, she'd clean up. Paris looked at the right side of her neck and saw that she had a small rose tattoo there.

He dropped another twenty on the tray and the barmaid smiled at him.

'Name's Gwen,' she said. 'Call me when you need me. Daddy.'

She turned and walked the length of the bar as the word 'daddy' dropped another rock into Paris's roiling stomach.

Saila had seen Jack Paris immediately. Melissa had not.

Saila knew that she couldn't take the chance of bringing Melissa into the Swing Set in any type of restraint – a girl Melissa's age was going to draw all the attention in the place anyway – so she had simply informed the young lady that her father would suffer a *most* horrible death if she didn't do *precisely* as she was told.

So far, she had.

The second she saw Paris, Saila grabbed Melissa by the wrist and said, 'We're going to the bathroom, little lady. Spruce you up some. Let's go.'

She stood Melissa up, took her by the arm and wove their way to the rest room.

The door was marked with a paper cut-out of Dorothy in *The Wizard of Oz.*

Rita, having been all but mobbed by every man in the bar, had walked quickly, purposefully, across the room, seeking some sort of refuge.

Within minutes, she found the ladies' room.

Dorothy in Oz, she thought with amusement as she pushed open the door. Yeah, *this* place is over the friggin' rainbow all right.

The bathroom was filthy and dank, scarred with graffiti, but it had three stalls and three large mirrors with lightbulbs arranged around them.

Surprisingly, the room was empty.

Rita – relieved to be alone, at least for the moment – ran her fingers through her hair, reached into her purse and retrieved what was, to her dismay, her last cigarette. She lit it and turned around, resting up against the sink, drawing deeply.

She thought she had seen it all in her day but this place definitely took it. She had absolutely no idea that there were clubs like this in Cleveland. Were some of the girls out there really as young as Jack's daughter? She decided that she would finish her cigarette, find the deejay booth, talk to Faustino. Then she would get back to the bar as fast as her five-foot-two, frame could carry her. She would—

She was not alone in the bathroom after all.

There was someone in the last stall on the right.

Someone whispering.

Someone *crying*?

Rita cocked her head to the sound, then quickly stepped into the middle stall and latched the door. She could tell that it was a woman talking in the next stall, but the voice was muffled. Rita glanced down and saw that whoever it was in the next stall was in a crouched position, one black high-heeled shoe curling under the partition that separated them. The woman also wore a thin ankle bracelet from which dangled a tiny pendant: a small silver cat with a solitary emerald eye.

Rita reached into her purse, fingered the edge of the two-way radio. Paris had shown her the basics of the two-way on the way into town, and having always been a quick study on virtually everything, she remembered to turn it off before walking into the ladies' room. The crackle of an incoming transmission would have been loud as hell in the confines of the bathroom.

She took a deep breath, opened the stall door and stepped up to the mirrors. Moments later, the door to the last stall opened. The woman who sidled up next to Rita Weisinger was absolutely stunning. Perfect skin, high cheekbones. A beauty mark. Rita would have killed for the woman's lower lip and half her lashes.

'Hi,' Rita said, looking at the woman in the mirror.

The woman met her gaze. 'Hi,' she said. 'You look very nice. Like a little girl.'

'Thanks.'

'How old are you really? If you don't mind my asking, that is.'

Rita Weisinger, already accustomed to creative accounting when it came to calculating her age, even at twenty-four, said: 'I'm nineteen.'

'You look even younger.'

Rita smiled, opened her purse, retrieved her brush, being careful not to reveal the black and chrome edge of the two-way radio. She glanced over her shoulder briefly, but the door to the stall from which the woman had emerged was closed. She could not see inside and there were no feet visible under the door.

'You're not here by yourself, certainly,' the woman said as she began to gloss her lips.

'Actually I am. I'm waiting for a friend.'

'Is that right? Sandy doesn't generally let in unescorted ladies.'

'Sandy and I go way back, though,' Rita said. '*Way* back.'

The woman turned to face Rita. 'Way back to where?' She stepped closer. 'And I mean *exactly* where.'

'Well I—'

'Don't lie to me. If you lie to me, I'll hurt you.'

Rita took a step backward, but remained silent.

'Because I *know* who you are,' the woman said. 'You're the little bitch from the Radisson. The barmaid with the big fucking mouth.'

Rita's heart sank. She could feel the moment slipping away. She reached quickly for her purse but, in her haste, knocked it over, spilling everything into the sink.

Paris barely heard the crackle of the two-way radio that signi-fied that someone was on the channel. He ducked into a hallway and put the speaker to his ear, but Faustino Nava's music was still deafening.

He signaled to Nick Raposo and the two of them bulled

their way to the front of the club and up the steps. Sandy, who was speaking to a petite Asian woman, didn't give them a second look. They stepped into the night. 'Rita,' Paris said, whispering into the radio.

Paris heard the channel open and close. Then, nothing. 'Rita.'

A short blast of static. Then: 'Jag.'

Paris looked at Nick. 'Say again?'

' . . . *yov goneer* . . .'

'Where are you?' Paris asked.

Another burst of static.

The radio went silent, save for a thin veneer of electronic noise.

Paris began to pace. Come *on*, come *on*, come *on*,' he said, tapping the abbreviated antenna against his thigh. Nick leaned against the building, his hands in his pockets, his eyes on the sidewalk, waiting.

Then it came. A loud whisper. Clear as a bell.

'Meet me out front. I have Melissa. I've got her. Everything's okay.'

Paris hit the button and positioned his mouth an inch from the radio. 'You've *got* her?'

'I've got her. She's fine.' The words were whispered now. 'Meet me out front of the Swing Set.'

Nick and Paris exchanged a quick high five, then walked over to the entrance. Paris put the radio into his pocket and stepped back into the vestibule, freezing Big Sandy to his stool with a flash of his eyes. He waited for Rita and Melissa to come around the corner at the bottom of the stairs.

Nick stood out front.

Minutes later, as Paris ran down St Clair Avenue at full speed, toward the alley next to the Good Egg, two thoughts came to him like a crystal bullet between the eyes.

One: There hadn't been any music in the background. Whoever had talked to him on the radio could not possibly have been *inside* the Swing Set.

Two: *Saila* was *Alias* backward. It had been there the whole time, taunting him, a rookie's ruse dressed up like a clue.

Saila. Only one type of person would be that fucking bold.

Nick Raposo, lagging well behind Paris, went left, up East Sixtieth Street. He turned the corner and cut across the vacant lot, where he found a dark alcove set into the building that overlooked the alley, a perfect vantage point from which he could see the parking-lot and the BMW. He caught his breath and hunkered down in the darkness.

Moments later, the darkness put the barrel of a 9-mm handgun to his head.

43

Rita Weisinger had always prided herself on her ability to adapt to any situation. You date a country boy, you wear your Levi's and chambray shirts. You date a doctor, it's Calvin Klein and pearls. Easy. Snow tires, reversible belts, wet-dry vacuum cleaners, she was good at it.

And she had a mouth. She could *talk*. Hers was one of the highest-grossing hotel bars in the city for one reason and one reason only. Rita Weisinger could schmooze the gilt off a gold card.

But when the woman in the ladies' room saw the cop-issue two-way radio lying in the sink, next to the Buck knife, all of Rita's systems shut down. She found herself trapped with a monster and there was nothing she could do or say.

With a force Rita thought reserved only for linebackers and dockworkers, the woman pushed her, head first, into the middle stall. She hit the door hard and it flew open with enough force to smash into the partition, shattering its lock. Rita tried to get up but the room was spinning out of control now, the floor was slick with filthy water. By the time she was able to right herself, the woman put her spiked heel gently up against Rita's chest and thudded her back down to the floor.

The last thing Rita saw, before she fell unconscious, was the upside-down face of Melissa Adelaide Paris, staring out from under the partition, surrounded by a cartoon universe of stars.

Saila had just gotten her key into the BMW's door. Her other hand held Melissa firmly by the wrist. They both heard Paris's footsteps in the alley before they saw him, but it was enough time for Saila to walk Melissa to the center of the parking-lot and put the barrel of the .25 semi-automatic pistol to the girl's temple.

Melissa closed her eyes and waited for the pain.

When Paris saw the two of them — perfectly posed, oddly familiar statuary under the lone street-lamp — he pulled up in his tracks and held his hands out to his sides.

He was twenty-five feet away.

'Hello, detective,' Cyndy Taggart said. 'Good work.'

'Cyndy, don't.'

'Pull it out, left hand, and place it on the ground,' Cyndy said. 'You know the drill.'

'Are you okay, Missy?' His daughter remained silent, but Paris could see in her eyes that she had not been harmed. If anything, at that moment, she looked simply exhausted. She wore a short black dress and earrings in the shape of red cherries.

'*Now*, detective.'

'Okay, Cyndy.' Paris slowly reached inside his jacket and extracted his weapon with two fingers. He placed the gun on the ground and kicked it along the asphalt.

'Talk to me, Cyndy.'

'What do you want me to say?'

'I want to know how we get out of this with no one getting hurt.'

Cyndy thought for a moment. 'What do you have for me?'

'What do you want, Cyndy? My hand to God, if I can get

it, I go get it right now, and I lay it at your feet. Tell me.'

'You know what I want. Everything you have on Pharaoh.'

'You've got it all. Think about it. Without those photo-graphs, they're never going to reopen the case.' Paris tried to remember something, anything, from his three hours of hostage-negotiation training. Of course, it was never supposed to be his daughter. 'The house on Tarleton Street is history. Everything *in* it is history. You get to keep the straight razor with my prints on it. You can set me up three years from now if you feel like it. What more do you want?'

Cyndy looked from Melissa to Paris, then back at the car, calculating the odds. '*She's* not going to shut up about this,' Cyndy said, fingering the trigger, nodding toward the trunk of the car. 'Neither is little Lois here.'

'Let me handle it,' Paris said, the motion not lost on him. His experience was that it meant that the shooter was getting ready to shoot. 'Diana will be pissed off, sure. But I'll take care of it. If you didn't hurt her, she won't press charges. I promise.'

Cyndy laughed. 'You don't know the first fucking thing about women, Jack.'

Then came a sound, a steel-on-steel sound, echoing from an alcove immediately to Paris's left. Although the alcove was engulfed in darkness, Paris figured it was Nick Raposo, trying, and failing, to arrive quietly at the scene. The sound instantly drew Cyndy's attention, causing her to relax her grip, her guard, for the briefest of moments.

But the moment was long enough.

Melissa, sensing the opportunity, shifted her weight, lifted her right foot high into the air and brought it down hard on the top of Cyndy's right foot.

'*Heee-yah!*' Melissa shouted.

'*No!*' Paris screamed.

Melissa ran toward her father as fast as she could.

In that moment, in that brief instant that Jack Paris saw his daughter running toward him – her long hair swirling fiercely about her face and neck and shoulders – he noticed, with curiosity, that she had Beth's face. Beth's wise, motherly, made-up, adult face on Melissa's gangling figure, the figure of a still-growing girl, a girl destined to become a tall, graceful woman.

But Paris also knew, in his shattering heart, that everything he had ever feared for his daughter was happening all at once: crib death, undertow, scarlet fever, cocaine, the pervert in the car parked near the school.

In that moment, Jack Paris knew that his daughter had lived her whole life.

And that he had killed her.

In that moment, in that brief instant, Cyndy Taggart hesitated, her right instep afire, her two lives colliding in a hurricane of procedure and pain and sexual disgrace. Her arms felt leaden and weak, her body seemed loath to respond to her immediate demands.

Then, just as quickly, she recoiled and sprang.

She raised her weapon into the air, took careful aim at the center of Melissa's back, and squeezed the trigger.

In that moment, in that brief instant that Jack Paris saw a mad-eyed woman fire a small handgun at his daughter, a much larger 9-mm bullet, fired from the alcove, tore into the left side of Cyndy Taggart's chest, then exited her shoulder blade in a furious gush of red tissue. The bullet clanked against the steel fender of a GMC truck halfway across the parking-lot, then skittered on to the asphalt.

Sergeant Cynthia Jean Taggart stood for a few moments, rusted in time, poised to make one final appeal, then followed the warm lead slug to the ground.

46

Melissa screamed once and stumbled forward the last few steps, slamming into her father's chest. Paris scooped her into his arms, turned on his heels and sprinted back down the alley, head down, not knowing for certain who had fired the other shot or where it had come from, not knowing if Missy had been hit.

They rounded the corner and burst into the fluorescent brightness of the Good Egg Restaurant. Paris ran the length of the black and white diner and lifted Melissa into the last booth, far away from the windows. He shielded her from the street.

'Are you okay, baby?' Paris dropped to his knees and frantically checked her back, her arms, her legs, her face, hoping, *praying*, that his fingers would not come back coated with red. *'Did she hurt you, baby?'*

'No, Daddy,' Melissa said, shivering now, nearing her ballast of tears.

'I'm so sorry, baby.' Paris held her tightly. 'I'm so sorry.'

He pulled back and took another long, careful inventory of Melissa's well-being. Cyndy had missed her completely, it appeared. Paris grabbed a napkin and began dabbing Melissa's face.

A minute later Paris arose and turned back to the diner.

The restaurant's five or six patrons were watching his every move in a state of near-catatonic silence, their sandwiches and eggs and Danish pastries poised halfway to their mouths. He asked of them all: 'Who's the owner?'

A pair of elderly rock-and-rollers in studded denim, sitting at the counter, pointed to a man restocking a potato chip rack near the front. Paris vaulted the counter and approached him.

'What's your name?' Paris asked.

'Akim,' the man said, his hands locked around five or six bags of chips each, his eyes nearly vibrating with alarm. He had heard the shots in the alley and now this man had run into his place of business with a little girl made up to look like a harlot. What was coming *next*?

'This is your place?'

The man nodded, his mouth too dry to speak.

'Akim,' Paris said. He put his hand on to the shoulder of the short, solid man in the greasy blue apron. 'I'm a police officer, and this is my daughter. This thing may not be over out here, I'm afraid. I have to leave for a while and I want her to stay right in that booth. I'm going to leave her in your care. Let *nothing* happen to her. Do you understand me?'

Akim had dealt with many police officers – first in Beirut, then in New York City, and now at the Good Egg in Cleveland – and he knew exactly what this particular brand of *Do you understand me?* meant. He dropped the chips.

'She will be safe,' Akim said. He looked into the back room, snapped his fingers twice and shouted something in Arabic. Almost immediately a stout, broad-shouldered woman of fifty appeared. She plopped down next to Melissa and thrust her big legs into the aisle.

Paris stopped at the front door and turned back to Akim. 'Call nine-one-one. Tell them shots were fired in this alley.

Tell them a woman has been badly injured. Tell them to send an ambulance.'

Akim picked up the phone behind the counter and punched in the numbers.

Paris left the restaurant and stepped, haltingly, weaponless, into the blackness of the alley.

The whole transaction had taken less than two minutes, yet Paris felt years older.

47

Cyndy had lost a lot of blood. Her body had the twisted, tangled look of someone just pulled from a hellacious high-speed crash. Her face bore a milk-blue pallor.

Paris had come around the corner and immediately found his weapon where he kicked it. It was still fully loaded. He called Nick's name a few times, but figured, after firing the shot that dropped Cyndy, Nick had probably come looking for *him*.

Paris followed the trail of blood around the green Buick parked next to Cyndy's car. When he skirted the trunk, and saw Cyndy's condition, his heart nearly went out to her.

Nearly.

Then he remembered Eleanor Burchfield's throat.

Cyndy was propped against the rear fender of the BMW. From the right side of her chest grew a short, purplish sprout of viscera. She was alive, and she had the barrel of her pistol pressed tightly against the car's gas tank.

'Don't come any closer Jack,' Cyndy said. 'Got your girlfriend in the trunk.' She tapped the back fender with the gun. 'Half a tank of gas, too.' She looked skyward for a moment, calculating something, then back at Paris. 'Five bullets.' She managed a crooked grin, then placed the barrel of the gun back up against the tank.

'Where's Rita?' Paris asked.

'Who?'

'Rita,' Paris said. 'The one you took the two-way radio from?'

'Oh *her*,' Cyndy said. 'Taking a nap on the ladies'-room floor. Probably having the time of her life, too, considering the way you dressed her for the evening.' Cyndy smiled, her teeth red and glistening in the light thrown from the nearby streetlamp. 'You sick *fuck*.'

Paris took another step, his weapon at his side. 'Cyndy.'

'So, what do you think, Jack? We're both pretty good shots, right? Which do you think will happen first? Me hitting the gas tank just right or you hitting a vital organ?'

'It's over.' Paris moved another step forward. He was five feet away now. 'You know there's no way out of this. EMS is already on the way. You've got to let me get you to a hospital.'

Paris attempted another small step, but the blast from Cyndy's weapon – the muzzle flash startling him more than the loud pop – shoved him back on his heels, his hands instinctively to his chest. Cyndy had aimed, without taking her eyes off him, and blown out the side light on the rear fender of the Buick.

Paris then heard Diana's muffled screams coming from inside the BMW's trunk.

'Four bullets now.' Cyndy struggled to sit upright. Paris could see the foamy pink saliva coming from the corners of her mouth. She put the gun back up to the gas tank. 'Let's deal.'

'Okay. Talk to me.'

'Let me ask you something first ,' she began. 'Why do you think women become cops?'

'Jesus, Cyndy. Is this what—'

'Answer . . . the fucking . . . *question*.'

Her tone was flat, commanding. In deference to Diana, Paris pushed the anger back for the moment. 'I don't know. Same reason as men, I suppose.'

'Only partially, Jack. With women, it's not just about control, you see, it's about control over *men*. The ability and the authority to tell men what to do, when to sit, where to stand. To handcuff them whenever we want. Fuck them up when we want. It's not just a job, Jack. It's an adventure.'

Paris tried to stop himself, but failed. 'Why the women, Cyndy? Why the innocent women?'

Another red smile. 'Don't be so quick to assume they were innocent. *Nobody's* innocent.'

It was a judgment call, but Paris decided to push it a little, to keep her talking. 'Why'd you kill Tommy?'

'Well, I was kind of hoping that that would be the end of things,' she said. 'See, I don't *have* to do what I do. It's not a drug, not really. And believe it or not, I didn't really have any plans to do it again. No Son of Saila conversations with my cat, I'm afraid.'

'Was Tommy Pharaoh?'

'What do *you* think? You're the detective.'

Paris took a deep breath and let it out slowly, knowing that the longer she kept talking, the more energy she would spend.

'I couldn't let you get to the Quality Inn, Jack,' Cyndy continued. 'Elliott would've surely reopened the case. You know that. The "Saila does Quality" photo you found was a mistake.'

'Please, Cyndy. Let's end this.'

'You've got nothing to tie me to Pharaoh. *Nothing* . . .'

'You're right,' Paris said. 'You're absolutely right. So let me have the gun, okay?'

It was then that Cyndy heard the first wail of a police siren in the distance. Black-and-whites were rolling. She closed her eyes and let the .25 semi-automatic pistol ring her finger. She dropped the gun to the ground. 'Just don't let that bitch in the trunk prosecute the case.'

Paris stepped forward and picked up Cyndy's gun.

'Three to five, max,' Cyndy said, drifting off. 'You'll see. Three to five.'

Paris thought about how easy it would be at that moment to just lean over and step on Cyndy's chest. To put all of his weight on her widening wound, grinding in the filth of a thousand infections. Or to simply wind up and stomp her heart right out through the carnage that was her back. Send her to hell in a red fucking dress.

But no, Paris thought. He had other plans. 'I don't think so, Cyndy,' he said.

Paris switched hands with his weapon and reached into his pocket. He held up the slender silver machine, the digital recorder Melissa had given him for his birthday.

'Listen to this,' Paris said. '*Kitty-cat.*'

He stuck the recorder near Cyndy's ear and pressed play.

'. . . *kill Tommy?*' Paris's voice asked from the tiny speaker. He raised the volume.

Then came Cyndy's soft, eerie alto: '*Well, I was kind of hoping that that would be the end of things, Jack. See, I don't have to do what I do. It's not a drug, not really. And believe it or not, I didn't really have any plans to do it again. No Son of Saila conversations with my cat, I'm afraid . . .*'

She looked at Paris with one hazel eye and one eye, unnervingly, the color of chlorinated water. Cyndy had lost a lens. 'Well played.' She closed her eyes.

Paris heard the EMS unit shriek to a halt at the other end of the alley and knew it was time to get down to business. He got very close.

'Where's the razor?'

Cyndy's head lolled on her shoulders. Her skin had taken on the color and texture of well-worn putty. '*Drazer.*'

'The *razor*, Cyndy.'

She opened her eyes briefly, then closed them again, the whites giving way to the green mucus gathering at her lower lids. She was beginning her death throes.

'*Where's the fucking razor?*'

Paris could hear the rattle of the aluminum gurney starting down the alley, a fifty feet away. The blue lights swirling on the dirty brick walls around him also told him that at least one black-and-white cruiser had already arrived at the scene. The call had gone out 'shots fired'. They would be coming down the alley with their weapons drawn.

'The recording for the razor, Cyndy. Where is it?'

Paris shook Cyndy Taggart once, violently, drawing thick bubbles of blood from her mouth and nose.

'Okay,' she said, fading now, near the extreme edge of consciousness.

'*Where is it?*'

Cyndy closed her eyes.

Paris began to rummage through her purse – Kleenex, Life Savers, Nivea, Tampax, Rolaids – but the razor was nowhere to be found. He was just about to search Cyndy's pockets when his hand closed around a plastic sandwich bag with a weighty, flat metal object inside. The feel of the scrolled tip and the small, smooth rivet told Paris it was the straight razor. He could also feel that the inside of the bag was still moist.

'*Police!*'

The shout came from the other side of the green Buick to his left. Ten feet away. Paris could hear the adrenaline streaking through that voice. The cop was young and pumped: inner-city call, shots fired, clear night, dark alley.

Paris worked open the zipped top of the plastic bag with one hand. He upended it, dumped the straight razor into the blackness of Cyndy's purse and began to move it furiously around with the back of his hand, the side of his hand, up against a leather glove, up against something that felt like an eelskin wallet, up against—

'*Drop it!*' came the voice from directly behind him.

Had he been seen with his hand in the purse?

'*Now, motherfucker!*'

Had he obscured his fingerprints?

Paris didn't know.

He dropped his weapon and held his hands high.

48

The nurse's aid couldn't have been more than twenty-two, but Paris managed to charm her into it.

'Okay, but you're not going to sneak him any food or liquor, are you?' she asked. 'He's been driving us nuts with that stuff.'

'Would a three-foot Genoa salami and a quart of fried peppers be considered food?'

The young woman smiled and wagged a finger at him. 'Don't be long. It's way after hours and I don't care if you *are* a cop.'

'Thanks . . .'

'Brenda,' she said, and turned on her squeaky white shoes.

'Brenda,' he echoed, and looked for 303.

He actually looked better than he had before he got shot. More robust, for some strange reason.

Because, although Paris learned a half-hour after the shooting that Nick had been knocked out cold in that alcove, and that it was not he, in fact, who fired the bullet that dropped Cyndy Taggart, he also found out that Nick Raposo had taken the bullet meant for Melissa. It had hit him in the upper left thigh and exited through his left buttock as he lay unconscious on the cement. Nick had missed everything that took place in the parking-lot, but Paris filled him in.

The identity of the person who fired the bullet that hit Cyndy was still unknown.

Nick had been in Cleveland Clinic for six days and he – like the staff, faculty, volunteers and support personnel around him – was more than ready for Nicholas Carmine Raposo to be discharged.

'What happened to the world when I wasn't looking?' Nick asked. 'A woman? A *woman*, Jack?'

Paris had no response. He remained silent.

Nick leaned forward, getting down to business. 'So, still no idea who bopped me? Or who shot Cyndy?'

'No,' Paris said. 'We have the slug but it's pretty common. Standard nine-millimeter.'

'Unbelievable,' Nick said. 'I mean, I'm standing there, I got a perfect view of the BMW, the next thing I know, I'm kissing the cement. *Man*, did that hurt. I haven't been hit that hard since I got jumped behind Leo's Casino when I was twenty-two years old.'

'And you didn't see anything.'

'Stars,' Nick answered. 'A whole shitload of stars.'

'And you think that—'

'And cologne. I remember that whoever sapped me was wearing cologne.'

Paris filed this morsel of information in its proper mental drawer. He'd add it to his final report.

Nick lowered his voice to a whisper. 'What's up with the case?'

'The prosecutor's office says that there's a good chance that the recording I made in the alley won't be admissible in court,' Paris said. 'Seems that because Cyndy didn't know I was taping—'

'Yeah, but *you* did. I thought the law was that only one party has to know.'

'That will probably be the argument.'

'Do you need the recording to nail her?'

'I'm afraid it's all there is to link her to the Pharaoh killings. Otherwise, she skates on those charges. The arson team hasn't come up with a damn thing from the house on Tarleton Street. Not a fiber, not a hair, not an unburned piece of paper. The place was sixty years old and the wood was dry as hell. It went up like kindling.'

Nick shook his head.

'The good news is that the coroner has ruled that Andrea Heller was already dead when her body was placed in the attic.'

Nick met Paris's eyes, knowing what a relief it must have been for Paris to find out that he hadn't help set the house on fire while the woman was still alive.

Nick looked out the window for a moment, then back. 'And to think Cyndy's in *this* building, right at this minute.'

'One floor up,' Paris said.

Nick poured himself some water, regarded Paris. 'How is your daughter? How's she taking all this?'

'My daughter,' Paris began, 'is amazing. I think she's going to be okay, Nick. She's seen a counsellor twice.'

Nick just nodded.

'But I don't think her mother is ever going to speak to me again.'

Nick smiled in understanding. 'And Rita?'

'She's okay, I think. She's tougher than all of us put together,' Paris said. 'The investigating team cleared her yesterday and she's going to visit her sister in Erie, Pennsylvania. I'm going to take her to the Greyhound station in a little while.' Paris looked at his watch. 'Actually, I'm due at her place in fifteen minutes.'

'I'm telling you, Jack. If I was thirty years younger.'

'Maybe that doesn't matter,' Paris said. 'I know for a fact that Rita likes older men.'

'Nobody's this old, though.'

Paris grabbed his coat from the hook near the door. 'Yeah, you're so old that you saved my sorry ass in a dark alley.'

'True,' Nick said. 'And what about that Diana? When am I gonna meet her?'

'Next time I see you. Hand to God.'

'Tomorrow,' Nick said, pointing a finger at him. 'When you bring the prosciutto.'

'Tomorrow,' Paris replied with a smile. 'I promise.'

Paris pulled up to the curb in front of the Greyhound bus terminal on Chester. A light drizzle began to fall as he put the car in park.

'Well, I have to tell you, you're a hell of a date, Jack Paris,' Rita said, opening the passenger door. 'What else could a girl ask for? Dressing-up, barhopping, assault and battery, handcuffs.'

'I can't tell you how much I appreciate what you did.'

'I'll let you make it up to me someday. Just get your VISA card paid up. You're not getting off cheap.' She leaned over and kissed Paris on the cheek, her face looking impossibly young and unlined in the gray light of the overcast day. 'Thanks for the ride.'

'Need help with the suitcase?'

Rita just glared at him. She stepped out of the car, grabbed her bag and shut the door.

'Sorry,' Paris said, hoping he hadn't trodden on any feminist doctrine.

Rita smiled and looked back in the half-open window. 'See you on the dance-floor, detective.'

'Sure thing.'

He watched her walk toward the tattered art deco building, a bright, capable young woman, and wondered if Melissa would one day be as resourceful and independent as Rita Weisinger.

He had a feeling she would.

49

She was still dressed for work. And she had cut her hair. Although Paris preferred long tresses on a woman, she actually looked better. Sexier, if that was possible, although he didn't see how.

'I can't say it's the way I wanted to get ahead in this town,' Diana said, pouring the last of the chardonnay into their glasses. They were in front of the fireplace at Diana's condominium in South Euclid. The flat was small, decorated in shades of peach, white and gray. 'I mean, the BMW-accessory jokes are already up and down the Justice Center.'

'Price of fame, I guess,' Paris said, stroking the back of Diana's newly cropped hair.

'Well, I would have preferred fame for some other reasons,' Diana said. 'Putting *away* people like Cyndy Taggart. I mean, I'm a lawyer, Jack, and a damn good one. I want to be known for something other than my ability to be victim of the week.'

'You will. Doesn't matter how people get to know about you, it's how you dazzle them once you've gotten their attention.' He leaned forward and kissed her, gently, at the corners of her mouth. 'And I *know* you'll dazzle them.'

They clinked glasses one more time, sipped, then fell into each other's arms for a few eager, impassioned moments.

Diana pulled back, smiling.

'What?' Paris asked.

'Got two questions for you,' she said, demurely now. 'Personal ones.'

'Okay.'

'Did you think I was unbelievably forward our first night together? I mean, me showing up with condoms and controlled substances?'

Paris *had* considered the fact that she was rather predatory that night. But compared to the other things he had suspected her of, being forward was well within the confines of accept-able adult behavior. 'Nah. I'm used to it. Women are always showing up in the middle of the night with rubbers and reefer. It's why I had to get such a killer dog.' Paris sipped from his glass. 'And what was question number two?'

'Have you ever done it in the trunk of a car?' Diana burst out laughing, snorting once, bringing her hand to her mouth.

'Criminally unhumorous, counselor.'

'Oh yeah?' She poked him with a stiff index finger. 'Then why'd you smile?'

'Because it was funny.'

Five minutes later, as Paris removed Diana's blouse – the two of them adrift in the thrall of their new and strange and genuine ardour – Paris looked over her shoulder and thought of the door to room 419 at Cleveland Clinic, the veiled visage of Cyndy Taggart lying still in her hospital bed, her once perfect body plugged into machines, connected to IV bags, guarded by one of Cleveland's finest.

An hour after that, as he and Diana lay near the chasm of dreams, Paris considered, as he sometimes would for years to come, the one photograph he had not taken with him to the Motel Riverview that night, the one that sat, at that moment, in a safe deposit box, in an envelope, in a twice-folded piece of bright white typing paper, all sealed up in an even bigger envelope.

A six-by-nine-inch envelope with a signature along the flap.

EPILOGUE

It had been eight months since the last of the Pharaoh killings. The Swing Set had moved three times and the people of Cleveland had since voted to retain Mayor Michael R. Brown.

It was the Friday before the Wednesday that would be Christmas Day.

Seven forty-five p.m.

The phone rang and I answered. 'Hello?'

'Danny, it's Jack Paris.'

Jack Paris was the cop who had killed Saila. Actually, he had lured her to a deserted parking-lot to do the job himself, but I had put the bullet in her. She did her actual dying in the hospital a week or so later – during my watch guarding her door, ironically, some sort of blockage in her respirator, I believe – but for all intents and purposes, Jack Paris had killed her.

I knew he'd call me, socially speaking. A lot of men hated me for my looks, my sense of style, my wardrobe, but, for the very same reasons, a lot of men wanted to be my friend, too.

The spillover and all.

'Jack,' I said, full of piss and vinegar and cop camaraderie. 'How are you?'

'Same shit, different diaper.'

'Merry Christmas.'

'Merry Christmas to you.'

'What's doin'?' I asked, as if I didn't know the answer. Once it gets under your skin, you see, you never really shake it. So I *knew*.

'I was wondering,' Paris said, 'if you weren't doing anything tonight, if you wanted to hit the Caprice. Or maybe go somewhere where the crowd has *active* DNA. Beachwood, maybe. You up for it?'

'Jack,' I said. 'You have to ask?'

'What do you mean?'

I laughed. 'It's *Friday*.'

The Echo Man

Richard Montanari

He's coming to get you . . .

It is fall in Philadelphia and the mutilated body of a man is found in one of the poorest neighbourhoods of the city. The victim has been viciously tortured to death. It's the work of a sadistic mind in free fall.

When homicide detectives Kevin Byrne and Jessica Balzano investigate, they soon realise that their crime scene is linked to the past. Eight years ago, another body was found in the same place, in the same position, killed in the same manner. That case was never closed. Apart from their killer's unusual calling cards, the crime scene photos – past and present – are identical.

As another brutalised body appears, then another, it becomes horrifyingly clear that someone is recreating unsolved murders from Philadelphia's past in the most sinister of ways. And the killer is closer than they think . . .

arrow books

Kiss of Evil

Richard Montanari

He's watching. He's waiting. He'll stop at nothing . . .

Christmas is just around the corner; the season of peace and goodwill. But this year, for Detective Jack Paris, the Christmas spirit is eclipsed by the hunt for a sadistic and twisted serial killer . . .

When an accused murderer is acquitted on a technicality then found dead of an apparent suicide, a spree of brutal murders terrorises the citizens of Cleveland. This vicious and vengeful killer tortures his seemingly unrelated victims in unimaginably violent ways, leaving them all with a strange symbol carved into their flesh.

When Detective Paris discovers that these murders are the grim handiwork of one maniac obsessed with the dark side of the ancient religion, *Santeria*, he's pulled into a web of danger and sexual deviance. Jack must catch the killer before he kills again. But on Christmas Eve, Jack finds himself right where the homicidal maniac wants him: questioning his loyalties, facing an impossible choice, with the barrel of a gun pointing at his temple and the whole world watching . . .

'Told at breakneck pace, with more than one truly frightening villain, and a protagonist whose tenacity in the face of evil makes him a hero for our times, you turn the pages as if your very life depends on it' *Daily Mail*

arrow books